To Matthew, thank you for everything.

Please return/renew this item by the last date shown. Books may also be renewed by phone or internet.

- 🖳 www.rbwm.gov.uk/home/leisure-and-culture/libraries
- ☎ 01628 796969 (library hours)
- ☎ 0303 123 0035 (24 hours)

Royal Borough
of Windsor &
Maidenhead

www.rbwm.gov.uk

Print ISBN 978-1-913942-02-1

PART I

1

Molly

Jacob is moving forward. He is stroking my face. I try and sit up, but he is stronger than me. He smiles at me, and then leans forward and kisses my neck. I ask him what he is doing; he doesn't reply. He is pressing his body down on me harder. His fingertips are gripping my shoulder. He is dry-humping me. My hips are hurting. He is too heavy. I want him to get off. I try to tell him. I cannot breathe: Jacob has his left hand over my mouth. I kick my legs. He releases his right hand from my shoulder suddenly and grunts; I kick again, but he is pulling my trousers and knickers off with his right hand. I can feel the panic rising inside me. What is he doing? I am trying to speak, I want him to stop, I want to say no, I try to scream but nothing comes out. The panic swells in my chest.

My body is frozen. I cannot move. I cannot believe this is happening. Jacob. I want Jacob to get off. He forces my legs open, and I can feel the burning sensation in my groin. I am too dry. It hurts. I close my eyes. I am not here. I am not here anymore. I turn my head to the side and look at the carpet; the tight weave of blue wool seems unrecognisable – I forgot to hoover.

Why, Jacob? You are meant to be my friend.

Jacob

He hadn't intended it to happen so soon. It was a surprise that the opportunity had arisen so early on in their relationship. He had expected that they'd spend more time together first, creating mutual memories and shared experiences before they reached this level of intimacy, but here they were snuggled up next to one another on her sofa.

He looked at her and realised she had fallen asleep. Molly looked beautiful when she was sleeping: her lips pursed emphasising her cupid's bow, her eyelashes fluttered. Jacob sat watching her for a while, he stroked her arms up and down with his hands trying to rouse her, she murmured something in her sleep and smiled, she seemed so relaxed. He leant forward and kissed her cheek gently. He had wanted to do that for so long.

Molly's eyes opened, she looked confused, he leant further towards her. Jacob wanted to calm her, he wanted her to know it was okay. He kissed her neck, she tried to push him away and sit up, but he knew she wanted it. She was just struggling to admit it. They had both wanted it for so many months now. He lay on her, and he ground his body into her groin. He could feel her enjoying it now: her legs were wriggling. He dug his hand into her shoulder; she went to say something, but he luckily kept her quiet; they didn't want her boyfriend, who was upstairs, to hear her moan. He ripped her knickers and trousers off and took her quickly. Jacob was surprised how submissive she was. He thought she'd be more theatrical when it came to sex but she just turned her head to the side as he fucked her until he came.

Stephanie

I cannot stand cases like this; I try to avoid them, and I hope a colleague is instructed to take them on before me. However, this time chambers have insisted I represent the client. Our clerk had received a request from a solicitors firm that uses our services regularly that I act on behalf of the defendant. It is a business first and foremost, and I know that it is paramount we keep the customers happy. I know why they have requested me of course. I am not proud of the reasoning but I find it easy to justify, for it is a job at the end of the day: a job I am very good at. Especially when it comes to getting the defendant off, especially in cases like this: cases where the victim knew the alleged perpetrator.

Criminal defence is not a glamorous job. In fact, I regularly wish I had listened to the barrister I shadowed many years ago during my first mini-pupillage, whenever he desperately tried to convince me otherwise as to this career choice. He would fix me with an intense gaze, and warn me of the dissatisfaction and frustrations I would encounter. With the unjaded hope that only the young carry I had ignored him. It is days like this I wish I hadn't.

This morning I have already had two client conferences. They both came to my office within an hour of one another: a minor case of affray; and a more serious charge of burglary. Both clients greeted me warmly. They would: I have known them both a long time. They are returning clients, those that keep criminal defence solicitors and barristers in business, proof that the system does not always work.

Adam Hook, the burglar, is a particularly gruesome character. I have represented him six times already and we're now awaiting the date of trial for lucky number seven. I first met Hook when he was seventeen years old, not long out of the young offenders institution. He was already too damaged, that much was clear, and on the path of no return that many a small-time criminal finds themselves treading.

I wonder often if I had known what I do now whether I would have taken this route. Were all those years studying really worth it? Did the long evenings of revision and coursework merit the end result? I am comfortable in the materialistic sense: I have a house – a four-bedroom Victorian townhouse. I can afford nice holidays, and I am able to buy nice clothes, organic food and expensive champagne should I choose. I drive the latest BMW, and I eat in boutique cafés at the weekend. I am wealthy in that sense of the word, but then there are many aspects of my life that are empty.

I do not sleep easily. I am aware I contribute to the safety of our streets and not in a good way. I know that every time I get people like Adam Hook off I am putting another innocent homeowner at risk. I, too, play my part in the future crimes he may commit because being successful at my job will enable him to commit them.

I am meeting Jacob Walker-Kent this afternoon. He has a good name, double-barrelled as well, which will subconsciously influence the jury's perception of his character. This is how I think when it comes to cases like Molly Smith's: how can I make my client more credible and Molly Smith more culpable? The fact his solicitor has requested I defend him indicates they already understand how the law plays out in this arena; women barristers are effective in sending a clear message to the jury that they should not be frightened by this man, he is no monster. I simply play on the collective view that jurors hold of rapists and confuse them. If another woman thinks he is safe, he must be.

Richard

Mornings like this were when Richard wished he'd planned his movements differently. He wished he'd stayed in his king-size bed, or settled in the corner of Starbucks over a cinnamon latte and refused to leave, or that he'd booked a holiday two months earlier, which meant he was not here when the case came in that day. Because, Richard knew – just knew – that the likelihood was he would lose. Richard struggled with cases where he knew justice would not be served.

Molly Smith's folder landed on his desk just after 10am and as he read the police statements taken from Molly and the defendant he knew he was in trouble. Cases like these sadly often rested on how deserving of blame the victim is perceived to be. If the jury believed she had brought the rape on herself, so to speak, she didn't stand a chance. Richard had discovered that the reality of rape and the stereotype of rape were considerably different, which made his job very difficult indeed.

Richard knew the classic rape situation that jurors favoured was a violent, sudden attack by a stranger in a deserted public place. Ideally the victim was sexually inexperienced, and led a respectable lifestyle. She would have done nothing to encourage the situation she found herself in. She would have fought the perpetrator, and she would have been physically injured. Afterwards she would have promptly contacted the police.

Sadly, this was not what had happened in Molly Smith's case, nor is it how the majority of rapes take place, nor how the previous rapes he'd prosecuted had played out. The problem was, the further away the cases were from the stereotype of rape the less likely it was that Richard would get a conviction.

He had browsed Molly's statement, and could already envisage the defence counsel tearing her to shreds. She was friends with her attacker; she had been drunk; she had invited him into her house; she had been wearing a short dress; she had fallen asleep in the same room as him.

It was a minefield for the Crown Prosecution Service, and he was surprised it hadn't dropped the case sooner. Most rape cases were thrown out early on, or the victim withdrew their statement for fear they wouldn't be believed. Richard thought Molly Smith was either exceptionally naïve or extremely brave to enter this legal gauntlet.

2

Molly

I had always felt safe with Jacob, since I first met him at a wedding. We had known all the same people, and I was surprised we had not encountered one another before. He had been polite, interested and fun. My boyfriend and I had argued earlier that day about the cost of the hotel room he had booked, and his sullen mood was yet to lift. We had avoided each other for the best part of the evening. I suppose that is how I got chatting to Jacob by the bar, as I stood waiting for yet another gin and tonic, what seemed like the tenth drink of the day.

He was attractive; not the kind of man I was attracted to, but attractive nonetheless. He was smarter than my boyfriend, and he had the air of a man of some importance. It was his personality that clinched it, though. It was as if he knew everything about me, and we had clicked instantly. It was not that I fancied him: I didn't. However, it was refreshing to meet someone new and different. It felt like one of life's unexpected gifts.

Our friendship had been intense. He had appeared, as some

people do, on my social radar rather immediately. It had not seemed peculiar as it had transpired he knew so many of my friends. At the time it had felt organic.

I hadn't realised that it was a little odd.

I questioned at one point whether I had feelings for him. Those months were so confusing: he had arrested me with attention; the flattery was so abundant that I was on a constant ego trip. It was silly, I can see that now. I was playing a very dangerous game. I had a boyfriend, and not that Jacob and I had done anything, but there was a closeness between us developing, an emotional bond forged through shared secrets and drunken ramblings. He remembered everything I said, sometimes bringing up comments I had long forgotten weeks later. He was very attentive like that.

We had been out together that evening, to a party. I had, as per usual, drunk too much white wine. White wine was my downfall, each glass holding the promise of another. He had walked me home. He had walked me home before. I didn't live far, but there was a dark secluded path involved that scared me. The wind was sharp and loud that night, which only added to the threat of the darkness. I had asked him to walk me home. I never felt safe taking that route alone. It was an innocent request. It was sort of on his way anyhow. It was not as if it was a detour.

I asked him in for a cup of tea because that is what I do: I ask friends into my home for tea or coffee whatever the time of the day. He had accepted the offer. I had sobered up a bit, although I had still swayed into the cupboards as I tried to manoeuvre my way around the kitchen to retrieve the sugar bowl.

My boyfriend was upstairs sleeping. He had left the party early: he could not bear me when I had drunk too much; he told me he found my confidence worryingly false. I had sniggered at him as he left, made a flippant comment about how he never let me have any fun these days. I'd found Jacob at the bar then. We'd downed a Jägerbomb together; I had retched then laughed. We'd ended up on the dance floor, where we had danced together to Beyoncé's 'Crazy in Love' among other songs before drinking more shots. By 2am I had tired, and we had decided to leave.

When we got back to the house, we had drunk three cups of warm strong tea each. I made two rounds of toast and buttered them generously. The melted Lurpak had dripped onto my dress. I had found this hilarious. Jacob had stared at me bemused. I do not know why a grease stain on a £200 dress had tickled me so much. I had risen from our basic IKEA pine table, which I had stained antique white the previous winter during my French interior chic period, and told him to wait there as I went and got changed. I had a habit of undressing after a night out as soon as I could and throwing a large pair of pyjamas on.

I had taken the stairs two at a time, and once I reached the landing, careful not to wake my boyfriend, I had tiptoed into our spare room where I had a spare drawer full of T-shirts and old ripped jeans, which I kept for jobs like touching up the gloss on the landing or painting a statement wall in our living room. I threw on a T-shirt that was far too small, a picture of snoopy in its centre, one half of a short sleep suit I had failed to throw out after university when I'd stopped going to the gym and gained weight. The only trousers I could find were a low-slung pair of Pineapple joggers that fell down a bit when I bent over.

When I returned downstairs Jacob was in the living room. He'd switched the TV on, and he was watching the film *500 days of Summer*. He was biting his nails. I slapped his hand and told him to stop. He pretended to look forlorn, and then smiled back up at me. He had the habit of looking like a lost little schoolboy when he wanted to. I could hear the slight high-pitched buzzing of our old Sony TV. He patted the seat beside him, and told me to sit. Then he asked me if I'd seen the film before. I indicated with my head that I hadn't.

I reached for a grey marl wool blanket that I kept in a wicker basket to the side of the sofa and I offered him half to cover his feet. I suggested popcorn and he chuckled, and said: "It's a bit late for popcorn, Molly." He fixed me with an intense stare, and I had felt momentarily uncomfortable, as if there were thoughts darting through his mind that he was trying to disperse before I managed to read them. He leant across then and with his thumb stroked a stray curl from my cheek and tucked it behind my ear. I smiled.

I shifted my body weight, just a little closer to the sofa arm away from Jacob. The air felt suddenly charged with a mix of sexual tension and danger. I thought about standing and making excuses, and retiring to my bedroom with my sleeping boyfriend; but then I did not want to be rude, and nothing had actually happened. The curl tucking was a friendly gesture; I smiled back. It was best left at that. I didn't think there was any need to cause a fuss.

I must have eventually dozed off halfway through the film. The last I remember is the bit where the guy has sunk into a deep depression because his girlfriend Summer had broken up with him. When I woke up the lights were off. It felt much later and Jacob was there still, right beside me, staring at me. He stroked my face, I yawned, and then I tried to sit up. He stopped me.

I felt him come inside of me. He was not wearing a condom. I shuddered, he laughed and kissed my cheek. I could not understand how he found it funny. I felt sick. I wanted him to get off me. My body was regaining feeling, and I found the strength to place my hands on his chest and push him away. I stood up, and moved away from the sofa.

"No cuddle?" he said.

I felt disconnected. I can't describe the feeling easily, but I didn't feel like I was in the room. It was as if I was watching myself in motion, but I was not there. Jacob was behaving as if he hadn't done anything wrong. I could not understand how he was acting so normal.

"You need to go," I heard myself say calmly. I wanted to scream at him to get out my house, but I found myself surprisingly polite.

He pulled his jeans up. I could not remember him undoing them and pulling them down. He stood up and yawned, and then smiled at me as if we had just shared a secret.

"Please leave," I heard myself say again.

He came forward and I felt my body stiffen. He kissed my cheek and stroked my right arm. I stepped backwards. I needed him to leave.

"Please."

He nodded and winked at me, and then he leant to pick up his wallet that was on the arm of the sofa. "Speak in the morning," he said nonchalantly, and he blew me one more kiss.

I heard the door click when he had left, and I felt myself breathe. I was acutely aware my boyfriend was upstairs, but I did not know what to do. I did not understand what had just happened: what he had just done to me.

I went and bolted the front door, then checked all the windows and the back door. I don't know what I was afraid of: I had already let evil into my house willingly. When I was sure everything was locked I took the stairs slowly. I did not know whether to wake my boyfriend and tell him... What if he did not believe me? What if he thought it was somehow my fault? Maybe it was my fault? Maybe I had encouraged Jacob?

I went to the bathroom first and mechanically turned the shower on, undressed and got into the cubicle. I knew in the deep recesses of my mind that I shouldn't shower, that this was destroying potential police evidence, but then I wasn't sure what had happened: I didn't know what to call it. It felt wrong, but he hadn't attacked me, he hadn't threatened me and I hadn't fought him off but I did not want it. I did not and had not wanted sex with him.

The water washed him away. I scrubbed my skin so hard with soap there were red welts from my vigour. I turned the temperature up as high as it could go, I wanted it to burn, to hurt, I wanted to see and feel the pain. I don't know how long I stayed in the shower for, but I know that the pain I emitted seemed to come from somewhere deep inside of me. My sobs rose from my stomach with such a force that they sometimes barely emitted any noise the pain was so great. I felt stripped, I don't know what he had stripped me of, but it felt like he had taken something and I knew whatever that was I would never get back.

It was only after I had wrapped myself in one of our large John Lewis cream towels, that smelt of the heavy scent of lavender, and I sat down on the floor of the bathroom paralysed by the evening's events, that the light on the landing came on.

My boyfriend, Luke, opened the door and still bleary eyed looked down at me slumped against the wall. "Molly, what are you doing?"

I went to tell him. I wanted to tell him, but when I went to speak I couldn't. I just couldn't find the words. I told him I had been tired so I had sat down to dry myself. He looked at me with a confused expression. For a moment, I thought he was going to question my response, ask me if I was all right. Maybe if he had I would have told him then, I would have said straight away, but he didn't ask. He walked over to the toilet and peed. I could hear the heavy trickle of fluid hitting the toilet basin.

"Well, come to bed then," he said as he shook himself dry.

"Okay." I took the hand he offered to lift myself up, and I let him lead me to the bedroom, where I lay awake in his arms feeling sick with dread.

Jacob

His company had done increasingly well over the previous five years. There had been substantial growth in the security sector, especially surveillance. Jacob always tested the services he provided. If a husband was concerned his wife was carrying out an affair, Jacob needed to ensure that their trackers, secret cameras and surveillance would guarantee he could prove it. If he was looking at going into business with someone it paid to find out about all aspects of their lives. He was thorough in all aspects of his life, even his personal life. He needed to know everything about potential girlfriends. He didn't invest his time easily, he checked their backgrounds first.

He hadn't spoken in person with Molly for years, she had been on his radar, she rented one of his properties, but it had been difficult to initiate a meeting. She was warmer than he expected. Trusting. It was endearing, if not slightly naïve. She was very friendly, too much so, but he was sure he could persuade her to be warier in the future, especially if they were to continue their relations.

It had begun slowly, their meetings together. He did not rush these things: he had scared too many girls off in the past. It was better to form strong friendships initially, to get to know Molly as well as possible. He played to his strengths: he was a good listener and always available. He knew girls liked a friend who was constant and took an interest in them. His mother had often told him so.

He thought back to a day at the beach together. Molly had a long weekend off work but was despondent with her free time, Luke was on a stag do for the weekend. He had suggested they go for lunch and she had agreed. She had pulled up an hour later outside his flat driving her Fiat 500. He liked her car, it suited her, the smooth lines and quirkiness seemed to embody her personality. As he sunk into the passenger seat the faint residue of her jasmine perfume wafted past; he had remembered this was what she wore: he had seen the bottle in her house. Her blonde wiry curls were kept out of her face by a blue floral headband with a bow on top, large black sunglasses masked her brown eyes but he knew they were under there, those deep dark pools. She was listening to Mumford and Sons – she listened to them every day on her way to work.

He wanted nothing more than to share endless days like this with Molly.

He was confused though. Molly had not been as affectionate as he had expected after they had sex. He knew she had enjoyed it because as he had come she had shuddered with joy underneath him, but then afterwards she had confused him. She was not as present with him as he had expected. She had pushed him away too quickly for his liking, and stepped back as he went to give her a kiss goodbye. It was probably the guilt she was feeling, what with her boyfriend asleep upstairs, but he did not welcome the feeling of rejection she had left him with.

Molly had asked him to leave. He did not question her request. He knew it was futile. She was obviously battling with what had just happened between them. He wished she would just own up to how she felt about him, but he decided not to push the matter. It was best if he just rung her in the morning when their minds were fresh and things were clearer.

He had walked home from Molly's, preferring not to catch the tube. He thought the fresh air would allow him to soak up what had occurred between them that evening. He wanted to relish the moment, to remember every little thing about her. It took him a fair while to reach his garden flat in Notting Hill. He lived just off Ladbroke Gardens in a property that had cost him a fair amount, and he enjoyed the status it yielded. The basement flat opened out to the private communal gardens in the back, and he always felt part of an exclusive, elite group of young people in London when he took his morning coffee on one of the benches on the weekends, as he was now.

Jacob did not have to work much these days. The majority of his money came from his company that sold discreet security cameras. His state of the art, hidden cameras were perfect for surveillance, under an inch in diameter they could easily be hidden anywhere. The width of the lens also meant his customers had a clear view of all of the rooms they were hidden in.

Over the years he had accumulated enough money to live very comfortably. He had invested the money wisely, mostly in properties in the south-east on the commuter band; and in stocks and shares. He used an agency to manage his properties, so he never met his tenants, he preferred to remain anonymous. He had found his security systems allowed him to monitor the properties, which gave him peace of mind. It was amazing what you could discover about people when they didn't realise they were being watched. His purchase in Notting Hill was not intentional: he had not favoured the area, but then London is extremely large, and there wasn't much point living four tube lines away from Molly.

He had fallen in love with her before he bought the property; it was absurd to risk 1.5 million pounds on a desire to be close to her. He would not have spent in the area on a whim that something may happen between them; but after a time he was convinced their connection was worth it. He had lived in north Islington previously: a lovely leafy area where the wealthy congregated. Notting Hill was trendier, and he got the impression that Molly, who was six years his junior, would approve of the opportunity to experience the quirkiness of Portobello Road Market, and the vegan eateries, and stylish wine bars.

He had employed her hand in flat hunting, and had seen the excitement she derived from money being no object. He had wanted to take her in one particular house he viewed and tell her afterwards, as they lay on the bare wooden floorboards, that all this could be hers, but he had resisted the urge. He had relished how her eyes widened when she first saw this apartment. He could tell she had fallen in love.

The previous owner had bought it decades ago, when the market in the area was far from desirable, and they had been shocked by the increase in its value over the years. When they had first visited the flat the rooms had been filled with relics of another life: ornaments from Africa and South America. Jacob had noted Molly's intrigue, and he liked the fact she expressed a desire to discover other cultures. He had planned for them to travel after they got together. Of course, it was a surprise he was going to spring on her, but her reaction to the décor here had confirmed his suspicions that she would appreciate the opportunity to explore.

He had decided to buy the place almost immediately. Obviously, Molly's reaction had influenced his decision. They had celebrated with a bottle of Veuve Clicquot champagne and calamari in a nearby bistro.

Molly had been buzzing as she chirped on about how they could decorate the rooms, and he had for a moment pictured their life together. She had caught him smiling and blushed, suddenly surprised and embarrassed at her enthusiasm. "Sorry, Jacob, I'm getting carried away, it's not even my place, it's not like I'll be living there..."

"But you could, Molly, you could live there if you wanted."

She had looked taken aback with his response, but she had then quickly thrown her head back and chuckled. "Yeah, of course I could." She had dismissed his comment as a joke, and carried on with her talk of scatter cushions, Laura Ashley visits and Farrow and Ball paint.

He had wanted to interrupt her and say, "No, I am not joking," but Jacob had let it slide. He knew their time would come.

Stephanie

I met Jacob Walker-Kent in the reception of chambers at 2pm He was strikingly handsome and very smartly dressed. He greeted me with a firm handshake and a nod of his head. He introduced himself and thanked me for my time in advance. A jury would love him: he was presentable and attractive. He did not look like a criminal, he looked like a brother, a son, a work colleague. He looked like an ordinary man.

As I led him through to the conference room I noted the expression he wore: he looked lost, like he couldn't quite comprehend why he was here. He looked at each door as if his presence in the building were a surprise. Again, I noted the favour this forlorn appearance would gain in a jury, especially if we were to get a couple of middle-aged women with sons the same age. He looked vulnerable, like a little boy out of his depth. This unwitting charm would have them onside almost immediately.

Jacob Walker-Kent followed me through the door and

waited until I took my seat before he pulled his chair out, an action that implied he came from class and money. I must admit he intrigued me. After we were both seated in the conference room, I gathered the papers and files of the case from my bag, and I presented them on the desk, he looked down at his lap. I was not sure whether he was nervous, or whether he was expecting me to scold him.

A lot of perpetrators of sexual offences are incredulous. They cannot quite believe that such charges are up against them. Others are mortified at the repercussions the accusations may have on their reputation. And then there are those like Jacob Walker-Kent. Those who seem to understand the severity of the charge and are quietly studious as to the matter.

I began as I often do in these cases: I asked him if he understood the charges against him, and if he knew that it was my job to represent him, that I was predominately to advise him and then follow his instruction. He nodded to all three questions and then finally looked up and met my gaze. His eyes were striking, piercing in their intensity. I do not like my clients to impact my professionalism, but I momentarily felt arrested by Jacob Walker-Kent.

"I want you to know one thing, Miss Clark."

"Call me Stephanie," I said, wary of any disclosure he was about to enter into.

"I love her. I love Molly."

I breathed a sigh of relief and nodded, thankful he hadn't just confessed to the alleged offence.

It is not unusual. In cases such as these there normally has been a previous relationship between the defendant and victim of the alleged offence. They may be ex-boyfriend and girlfriend, or workmates who once enjoyed an office flirtation or merely acquaintances.

It is more unexpected when the accused informs me he did

not know the woman bringing the charges against him. That's when I know we're really in trouble, because juries are certainly more likely to believe the victim who alleges rape where there is no connection, that is, where the alleged rapist is a stranger.

Richard

The thing Richard knew about cases of acquaintance rape was that they were nearly always at least partially planned – maybe not in the sense that the accused had premeditated the situation, but there was an element of opportunism. The idea may have previously floated through the perpetrator's mind. Maybe they had thought about their victim sexually, maybe even masturbated for months over such an encounter. Not that Richard was insinuating that these men were sexual deviants. Most of the time they were not. They were ordinary men who had sexual urges, and for some reason or another, had the mistaken belief they could exercise these urges, even if the victim was not necessarily a willing participant.

Richard had lost count of the number of times he had met men who did not believe that the event in question, or their actions, constituted actual rape. He knew first hand that the issue of consent was precariously difficult. Even the media of late had picked up on one buffoon who had floated the idea of "legitimate rape", as if to suggest there were different degrees of rape. Richard had laughed with disbelief at the notion that should the victim have fallen asleep and not outwardly said "no" to her rapist then it was a lesser offence than if the man had heard her objections and then ignored her requests to stop.

There was a level of confusion over what amounted to rape. There always had been historically, both in and out of the courts. He knew the situation in the UK was in dire straits when it came to the rape attrition rate, the attrition rate being the number of convictions in comparison to the number of rapes reported. The low number of convictions was alarming. He had read all the academic papers, studied all the legal changes, but when you were faced with the majority of society sharing a view about what amounted to, or did not amount to, the offence, then no amount of legal change stood a chance if the jury members were ultimately those who enforced justice in this area.

He thought back to the cases he had prosecuted and the responses they had elicited from the jury. The seventeen-year-old schoolgirl who had been pressurised by her older boyfriend into having sex: "she could have said no". The boss who abused his position of power: "she obviously wanted to get ahead in the workplace". The twenty-three-year-old student who had taken drugs, and was clearly intoxicated, before a man she thought was her friend had raped her: "she lived a hedonistic lifestyle; she probably couldn't remember saying yes; what did she expect?" The twenty-eight-year-old who had gone to bed with a man wearing her underwear and woken to find him having intercourse with her whilst she was asleep: "she went to bed in next to nothing with him, she was clearly asking for it."

Richard was all too aware that the jury's starting position was not to believe the victim; the unspoken truth was that the women were on trial more so than the accused. Her character and how her behaviour contributed to the situation she found herself in were central to the case. The appalling thing about these cases was that the defence counsel often ended up doing Richard's job: prosecuting. However, in these cases, they were prosecuting the wrong person, the victim instead of the perpetrator.

3
___

Molly

I did not sleep well that night. I woke every hour or so with cold sweats and a terrible realisation that the evening's events were real and not just some dreadful, horrible dream. Luke's arm cradled my stomach, and his snoring provided a repetitive background noise to the house.

I felt like I had cheated on him. I was terrified that is what he would think when I came to tell him, that he would think I had somehow led Jacob on and things had gone too far; and that now I regretted it, so I was fabricating a story to get out of it. Of course, that was what everyone would think. Maybe I had? Maybe I had led him on and caused all of it? I looked back at our relationship, our friendship and all the time we had spent together, and I couldn't quite believe how I hadn't gathered he'd always wanted something more. I had thought we were just friends. I felt so stupid. I couldn't understand how I had not seen it. How I had not gathered that he had feelings for me that extended beyond friendship?

I managed to drift off to sleep in the early hours, and I was awoken by a beautiful ray of sunshine that shone through our bay windows onto our bed. It was such a lovely morning outside; I could not understand how everything was as it always was. Luke slept late. I did not wake him. I flattened my side of the bed, so the duvet was neat, and I threw my dressing gown on. The house was cold this morning: late October was preparing to welcome the frost, and as I came to the bottom of the stairs and bent to collect the mail, I could see the faint residue of my breath in front of my face. I drew my dressing gown tighter.

In the kitchen I mechanically filled the kettle and stared at the scene before me – the plates strewn with toast crumbs, the two empty mugs. I loaded them into our dishwasher quickly, as if removing the evidence that Jacob had been here may make it easier to erase the memories of the previous evening. I made a large pot of coffee and kept it on the stove. I began to wipe the surfaces clean, slowly at first, but then a frantic need to clean everything came over me. Before long I had hoovered the downstairs of the house, polished, bleached and swept. I sat at the kitchen table in a slight sweat from exertion and poured myself a coffee.

I realised early on that expending energy helped me forget what had happened. Maybe I even realised that morning, as I had rapidly cleaned away our proof of living of that previous week.

By the time Luke finally rose at around one o'clock I had played and rewound the incident with Jacob repeatedly in my mind, trying to decipher when I had led him on, why I hadn't fought him off, why I hadn't been able to shout or scream. I felt a burning frustration and anger at myself for freezing, for not trying hard to resist. Maybe I had deserved it. It was possibly my fault. I should not have been so trusting, so naïve to think a girl and boy could just be friends. Had he thought that this was what I wanted all along?

Luke wanted to go out for breakfast. I wasn't hungry, but the idea of leaving the house was attractive, and I thought it would take my mind off things. He had day-old stubble, the kind he only allowed himself to have one day a week when he wasn't working on the construction site managing his team. I liked him when he looked a bit scruffy: it reminded me of holidays and our early twenties when we had first met. I had just turned twenty-three and was partying on Bondi Beach. He had walked past me and happened to know a mutual friend I was sharing a hostel dorm with. Over the other side of the world we had connected, even though we had grown up twenty miles apart in the UK.

That October morning we walked towards the river to a small café, which I often visited when the kids were on half term and I had a moment's break from the inner-city school where I worked as a teaching assistant. Luke ordered a breakfast panini whilst I opted for porridge with honey and raisins. My appetite was shot, but Luke did not seem to notice. We didn't discuss the previous night. He had asked me what time I got in, and I had murmured that it was sometime around two in the morning, and I had then tried to rapidly change the subject. I still did not know how to broach what had happened, and I tried to put it to the back of my mind.

Luke read the Sunday papers whilst I tried to concentrate on the magazine supplements, but I seemed to lose concentration too easily. I could feel my legs shaking underneath the table. I wanted to block everything out, but nothing seemed to distract me. I suggested a walk and then a glass of wine. Luke resisted initially but then agreed.

We ended up in Putney by the river in one of London's busy pubs. I ordered a bottle of red wine and some peanuts. I knew Luke was going to disapprove of the bottle; he had said he wanted to get back in time to watch the Grand Prix, but I would tell him I'd drink quickly. I could taste it before it reached my lips and knew that it would help. I could not yet confront the reality of my situation because to do so would mean I must confront my future, and right now the future after the events of last night was unthinkable.

Jacob

Jacob did not ring Molly on the Sunday: he preferred to let her clear the air with her boyfriend first; he also knew how well a cleverly crafted element of space worked when trying to win a woman's affections. No matter what they said he knew that most women desired the chase as much as men. He had of course wanted to contact her. Usually he did daily – it was often a little text or a quick phone call – but he knew that right now it was best to keep a little distance.

It was Monday when he tried to make contact. He had left it until the evening, as he knew she would be working. Molly worked Monday to Friday in a central London school with early years children. He had helped her with the school harvest production that September, and seen how popular she was with the children. They had all flocked to her. She had a gentle manner, and Jacob could not help but note what a good mother she would make.

He had tried to ring her three times and had texted her twice before he had any reply. She sometimes didn't hear her phone. London was loud and busy, and he had tried to reassure himself it was the hustle of rush hour that must have distracted her from her mobile, but then he received a text: just four words. Four words were enough though. She had managed to crush his feelings. All the hope he had felt for their future disintegrated when he read her message.

PLEASE LEAVE ME ALONE

He thought of the picture his mother had framed in her kitchen, the definition of *saudade*, the Portuguese word for a deep emotional state of nostalgic longing for a love that will never be returned. He had thought the picture a morbid reminder of his father, but now, faced with Molly's message, the phrase his mother had used to describe it was thrust into his mind: a love that remains even when you realise it is lost.

Stephanie

There is always a great deal of ambiguity in rape cases. For the prosecutor to prove beyond reasonable doubt that the accused is guilty they must convince twelve jurors that the victim categorically did not consent. If there is any inkling of doubt, or jurors question her credibility, I know I have done enough to win.

The truth is, society is not designed to sympathise with women who experience sexual abuse. We have grown up in a world that has accepted groping a women's arse or boobs as amusing. Where being whistled at as you walk down the road is just how it is. I am not alone: women everywhere lead their daily lives surrendering to sexual abuse.

During university, I had a male friend who after he'd had a few too many drinks would slip his hand between my legs from behind and grab my groin, I would bat him off, and he would laugh.

I have been propositioned for sex by way of forcefully grabbing my upper arm.

I have had a man in a club push his hard penis into my back.

I have been pinned down on a bench at the end of a party while a man I knew tried to seduce me.

I have been asked how much I cost.

One particular male tried to push an ecstasy tablet into my mouth whilst asking me if I wanted a threesome.

I was once at a wedding when the best man bent before me and asked me if he could go down on me, as if it was the most normal thing in the world.

I have had my neck licked, sucked and kissed when I was trying to order a glass of wine.

I have had a man try to get in bed with me whilst I was asleep; I have had a man who succeeded at this, but I woke up in time.

When I told people of these incidents they laughed. It became a funny anecdote, and I too would procrastinate about taking legal action. It never occurred to anyone that this was not merely a form of hilarity, that what was happening daily to women all over the world was wrong – well, it did, but then we did what most of us do, put it to the back of our mind and move on. Sex is power, and every time I let it slip so did millions of others, and slowly but surely, we all de-armed ourselves, because the biggest defence is often contempt, or a collective view that something is wrong. We need only look at the attitudinal changes towards smokers to see how effective it can be.

When we fail to respond with disgust to acts that deserve it, we normalise behaviour that should not be considered normal and we fail to protect countless victims.

Not once did I challenge these men beyond telling them I was not interested or forcefully pushing them away. I did not report what would clearly be considered a sexual offence in some of the cases. I accepted it as just what happens to women in our world.

I know perfectly well that in cases such as Molly Smith's the focus should be on the male, the choice to rape is entirely male-centric. Women never have the choice: rape for a woman is not a choice. Yet the onus of consent is not on the male. The courts target the female, I target the female, and we – we all – take her down. If rape cases were a sporting game you'd nearly always succeed on the defence team.

Richard

Molly entered Richard's office just after midday a week before the trial began. She was wearing a long berry chiffon dress that she had gathered at the waist with a cornflower blue belt and gold sandals. She had the style of Sienna Miller but with a little less thought. The mass of golden curls upon her head sprung in every direction. She was beautiful, he noted. The fact she did not look cheap, what would be considered a "slag" in court, pleased him: her appearance was demure, if not a little too attractive. He would have to find a way to tone down her beauty. Envious female jurors would not bode well for her case.

Richard knew that the appearance of the victim was central to the case. He frequently fought against the idea that what a woman wore affected the likelihood she would be raped. He hated the pretence she was somehow more deserving of sexual assault if she was wearing a short skirt and was drunk. However, Richard was not naïve enough to expect the jurors to share his opinion, and even if they did, he also knew how powerful the subconscious mind was. The flash of flesh before them may illicit the tiniest amount of doubt that could – and most probably would – grow until they reached a not guilty verdict.

He had seen the pictures of what Molly was wearing that night in the police exhibit file. He was the first to admit his heart had momentarily sunk – the defence would love it. The garment was a short dress, and for the purposes of evidence he had asked that the length of the skirt be measured; he needed to know what the defence would infer, and how much, literally, they had to play with. Looking at Molly now he was pleased to see she was fairly short. The dress, therefore, would have most probably come to just above her knee: no chance of knickers flashing or exposing her upper thighs, then.

Molly had taken a seat in front of his desk. She plaited and unplaited her hair as she spoke. Her fingers were shaking slightly.

He tried to calm her. He offered her a cup of tea and a biscuit both of which she refused politely. At times like this he wished he could pull out a bottle of brandy and they could both have a stiff drink. Richard moved over to the corner of his office nearer the window. An old filter coffee machine was on the windowsill. Despite the grimy watermark he poured himself one. As he turned he realised how dirty the room was, with papers and files clumsily piled all over the floor. Molly would have had to dodge numerous obstacles to get to the chair where she anxiously waited. He suddenly felt very embarrassed about the state of his workplace. He was hardly filling his clients with confidence as to his organisational skills.

The truth was Richard struggled daily to keep on top of his workload. The legal code of conduct provided that a barrister must not undertake any instruction that would cause him to be professionally embarrassed, such as "he does not have adequate time and opportunity to prepare for or perform", yet he regularly got thrown a case by the Crown Prosecution Service with little time to prepare or even to read the case notes before he was in front of a judge. He cringed at his lack of preparation for some of the cases he had received, only later realising he had missed out on vital facts that could have changed the outcome of the verdict.

He muddled through. He had to because most of the time he had no choice: everyone was fighting for time, fighting for the work. He had realised long ago it was the nature of his work: you win some; but more often than not when in Richard's position, you lose some.

He was always clear with his clients from the outset what he considered their realistic chances. As he prepared for Molly Smith's case today, there were a number of things he needed to clear up. He had wanted to prep her. He had wanted to be sure she was clear what the defence would do, how they would twist things. He had wanted to make sure she knew that it was basically her on trial rather than Jacob Walker-Kent.

However, Richard could not coach Molly Smith for what she was up against. He could not train her. He could not deduce the defence's case in order to advance his client's. He simply had to watch on as they tore her to pieces.

4

Molly

I didn't intend things to go as far as they did. It seemed that every day that passed the harder the words were to say, the more my throat constricted and my mouth dried up. I had lost weight, a considerable amount at this point, and my appetite had deserted me. I felt sick constantly; guilt forever rumbled in my tummy alongside a deep-seated dread that suddenly everything could come crashing down. My whole world could implode. Then without a moment's notice it did, it all did.

Luke and I had muddled on for weeks. I had managed to keep going to work for the first two weeks, but I couldn't manage it any longer. Since the evening it happened with Jacob, we had attended two friends' birthday parties, been out for three meals: a curry and two Pizza Expresses. We had watched the rugby in the pub three times and been food shopping five times; I had filled the car with diesel twice; Luke had been for eight runs; I'd been off work sick for nearly two weeks now; and we had made love once.

Since that evening, I saw my life in two distinct parts: before and after. I had taken to counting mundane daily events to get me through the days, as if by measuring life in small events I could somehow continue to wade through the drudge of living. Luke had noticed eventually. The excessive drinking had alerted him that something was wrong; not that we dealt with it in a way that a couple should or a self-help book would suggest. No, we shouted. I screamed. He slammed doors. We both grew more and more frustrated, and I continued to scream.

One night I screamed about the way he cut the onions for dinner; another night about the bra that he had washed on sixty degrees and so the lace had shrunk. I would lose my temper in an instant. I threw a whole plate of dinner at the wall one evening before sobbing into the tablecloth. Luke thought I was pregnant. This sent me off into another frenzied attack, which was followed by two bottles of red wine in the space of three hours. I slept on the sofa that night. Luke could barely look at me in the morning.

"I've left your cup of tea on the table."

"Thank you," I mumbled.

We were on the verge of that awful awakening when you discover that the relationship you once were a part of had disintegrated before you had time to realise. That was my ninth sick day off work, the last day before it all broke.

Jacob

He had checked Molly's Facebook excessively. At any given moment, he was on his iPhone refreshing her page, hoping for a glimpse of her activities. He had ignored her text message to leave her alone. He knew it was just the guilt talking. She had, of course, had second thoughts – most girls did when they had been with another guy. Sadly, he knew this from experience.

They'd tease you for months and months, and then the moment they took it that little bit too far and things went further than a flirt they panicked.

Jacob was not suggesting Molly was a cock-tease. He had always known that she would put out; but he just didn't expect her to seize up straight afterwards. He had rather hoped he could follow it up with a date: a movie, a meal, more time together. He liked Luke, but he could see that he would not satisfy her. They didn't laugh much together, he was far too sensible, always telling her to slow down, drink less. Molly was a good-time girl, she didn't need to be cocooned. She needed excitement, thrills and adventure.

He thought back to their last night together. She had been so excitable. They had danced to Beyoncé's 'Crazy in Love', her hips writhing, her skirt riding up as she pulsated to the rhythm. She had looked hot. She was wearing a little black dress, adorned with jewels, which revealed her pert cleavage, and he had seen the attention she received from all the men in the pub as she sauntered to the toilet.

He was the first to admit that when they were together he wished she would cover herself up a bit. He didn't like the attention she attracted: he was uncomfortable with other men looking, imagining what they couldn't have. Molly didn't even seem to notice it, she was oblivious to the eyes drawn to her. She bumped into the wall as she came back to the dance floor. She was so drunk. He grabbed her hand and took her to the bar. He loved Molly drunk, she knew how to let her hair down. She was fun, and he wasn't going to turn down an opportunity to have fun with her.

They ordered Jägerbombs and tequila shots; she insisted he get her a glass of wine. Jacob had laughed, surprised at her ferocity to drink, and he had tried to dissuade her. He didn't want to have to carry her home. It hadn't worked. She had downed a large glass of white wine in a matter of minutes before heading towards the dance floor. He saw her lunge forward but fortunately regain her balance at the last moment, and he had decided it was time they make their exit, either that or she'd be on the floor.

She didn't object to leaving; he thought she was glad of the suggestion. As soon as he led her outside the fresh air hit, taking her by surprise, and she suddenly leaned on him. He was grateful for this: he loved the feel of her body pressed against his. Jacob placed his arm around her waist and began walking. She was repeating herself. She kept asking if he would walk her home. He affirmed her request over and over again. She was in such a vulnerable state he wasn't about to leave her. He had to make sure she got home safely.

Stephanie

I am not advocating the notion of victim responsibility in cases of rape, but I must admit as a member of chambers you cannot help but recognise trends. You cannot help noticing the way certain girls do not help themselves in cases like this. I have seen the way jurors work. I have seen the way judges weigh up the cases presented before them. I cannot remember one instance where the alleged victim arriving in court wearing a see-through top and mini skirt worked in her favour. That is not to say I agree with this convention, but it is the convention nevertheless.

When I was much younger, new on the circuit, one prosecuting barrister took me aside and explained the difference between "technical rapes" and "rapes that you prosecute". I sat with him through a client conference. He had sighed before the lady had entered, and rolled his eyes as he slid the file quickly across the table to me.

I had read the outline of the statements: a lady in her early twenties had bumped into her ex-boyfriend. After a brief interlude both of them had decided to go back to his house for the evening. They drank a considerable amount of alcohol. They watched porn and kissed.

However, when he led her to the bedroom she suddenly changed her mind and wanted to leave. He didn't let her. Instead he pinned her down forcefully, and then he raped her.

She did not have any visible bruising or internal lacerations from forced sex; there were no witnesses; and she was found to have considerable amounts of alcohol in her system. She had, however, reported the crime straight away: "The first sensible thing she had done that day," the barrister whispered in my ear, as I repeated this fact to him. Before she entered he explained that this case was without merit, that the Crown Prosecution Service should have thrown it out. I asked him what he meant when he said "without merit".

"Well, it's technically rape, Stephanie. But come on, there was no evidence of force, no evidence of resistance; they had a prior relationship; she was drunk; they'd been watching porn; and that's all before we look at her adventurous sexual history and what she was wearing that night... On a scale of one to 'asking for it' I think I'd put it up there as a nine." He had laughed, and then as the lady had entered he had changed his expression, and he had looked sincere and concerned throughout the meeting. I had scribed during the client conference, all the while aware that the facts he had laid before me had nothing to do with consent.

Richard

Richard read the newspapers; he was on Twitter, he was aware of the general debates in this area, and he knew that it created considerable discussion. He had been for a walk that weekend and met up with some long-time friends. The kind of friends you have from way back, who remember you eating leftover pizza crusts out of your bin at 4am because it's suddenly all you have left in the house.

Bridget and Nathan had done rather well for themselves recently. They had slogged away for years, working non-stop on a variety of projects from landscaping, painting and decorating, interior design, to baking and copywriting. Finally, after years of below-minimum wage income they had a lucky break, and they had invested everything they had suddenly acquired into a company specialising in weddings in France.

They had both thrown themselves into French life. They had bought and renovated a barn near the Dordogne where they stayed from March to November before returning to London for the winter months, followed by a month on a Caribbean Island to rejuvenate. Bridget and Nathan were intelligent, they both had degrees. Bridget had graduated with a first in social policy. Yet, when Richard had begun to discuss work, namely Molly Smith's case, their response had astounded him.

Richard had forgotten that it was best not to discuss rape cases with Bridget and Nathan. Their stance had always been the same even when he was studying law in university. He could remember many late-night discussions after too many whiskies and ciders, with Bridget getting more and more infuriated about how silly and naïve these girls were, how they should think before getting so drunk and wearing next to nothing. Nathan had wholeheartedly agreed, whilst Richard had tried to point out the emphasis of their argument always found fault with the female, attributing blame to the girl rather than the male who committed the act.

"These poor men, these girls destroy their lives and reputations, don't they?" Bridget had looked at Richard with a surety that he would reaffirm her opinion. "I mean, do they not realise what a big thing that is to say about someone? They could lose their jobs, their families..."

"Well really, was it really rape?" had been Bridget's response, as if this answered the whole conundrum. If Richard's anger had slightly flared they had both retreated into what they considered their fair and reasonable argument: "Obviously if it is rape, I would never want a sexual predator running around. The poor girl, I mean she must have been badly beaten. God, yes, he deserves to go down then. I totally believe rapists should be punished."

Richard had felt like he was banging his head against a brick wall. If even his educated friends didn't believe it was rape unless it was a violent attack, what hope did he have with a jury? Bridget had tried to pry into his current caseload further, but he felt himself shut down. The last thing he needed was a lecture on how Molly Smith had brought the rape on herself.

The rest of the afternoon was perfectly pleasant. As soon as the subject had veered away from legal matters it had been refreshing to get out of the city and retreat to the country. They had stopped in a local pub with a roaring fire, its features quintessential English, and they had feasted on a pint of prawns with a rich yolky mayonnaise dip and soda bread, whilst they shared a bottle of crisp New Zealand Marlborough Sauvignon Blanc.

For a little while there Richard had managed to switch off and enjoy himself, but then the thought of Monday and work came hurtling towards him. With only an hour's drive back to London and a lonely chicken pie to look forward to, he had bid Bridget and Nathan farewell and set off.

Richard had returned home and nipped to the shop to grab

some essentials. He had taken a detour to a bar for a quick pint: the earlier bottle of wine had primed his taste buds for alcohol, and he was thirsty for more. He had meant it be just the one, but Richard had bumped into an old friend he hadn't seen for months, and they had got carried away. He stumbled out of the pub three hours later, twenty pounds lighter and full of beer before he finally made it home, his dread for the week ahead now diluted.

5

Molly

Every time my phone rung or my screen lit up I felt so anxious. His phone calls and messages had begun two nights after the incident. I did not understand why Jacob kept trying to speak to me. I could not understand how he thought everything was okay. I thought he'd leave me alone, but he was doing the opposite. I thought he may regret what he did. I'd tried to ignore his voice messages and text messages. I was trying desperately to block him from my mind, but they'd become relentless. I tried to delete them before I could read what he had to say, but I had seen the most recent message before I had the chance:

"We need to talk about what is happening between us."

I didn't understand. He thought there was an "us". I kept thinking back to the night. I went over and over how I had behaved. Had I encouraged him? Had I led him on? Did I make him feel like I had wanted that: that I had wanted him? Maybe I was too friendly. I did not realise he thought we were anything else but friends though. I felt betrayed. I hadn't seen it coming. I hadn't realised that he even liked me like that.

I thought it might help. It may make him stop if I messaged him back at first. I didn't answer his questions or agree to meet up with him, as he kept asking me. I just asked him to leave me alone. I thought he may listen. He didn't. It made it worse, his messages became more and more frequent. I worry Luke may read them. I keep my phone on silent now.

I was terrified Jacob was going to destroy everything for me. Deep down I knew that he already had, but I hoped that if only I could forget, if only he would go away I might be okay. There was still an element of hope that the past would simply evaporate from my memory.

Jacob

Molly had begun to test Jacob's patience. He had rung her repeatedly and he had left answerphone messages. He had sent texts, too, but, apart from the message she had sent asking him to leave her alone, he had not heard anything. She was playing games, and Jacob hated games. He had considered visiting her, just turning up casually, but there was something niggling at him that suggested that method of attack might backfire on him. He just wanted to see her, to talk about it. They had spent so much time together that he couldn't bear that she had just cut him out of her life without a second thought.

That afternoon Jacob meandered down Bond Street mindlessly looking in shop windows, occasionally popping in and purchasing an item of clothing to kill time before he met his mother that afternoon. She had come up to the city for the weekend. He had not seen her since August, and although it had only been a mere eight weeks, as he was an only child and his mother a widow, he knew to her it would seem much longer.

His late father had been a surgeon. Unlike some of those in

the medical profession he did not live for the medical world. He had too much fun outside it to make his job his sole priority. Jacob's childhood memories were filled with lavish parties: loud laughter and plenty of his parents' friends, copious amounts of wine and platters of food passed from crowd to crowd throughout the downstairs of their house. It seemed like there was a party every weekend when Jacob looked back, but he realised now that the time and reality of childhood gets blurred in a way unlike any other stage of life.

His parents were happy; they worshipped each other. He had often felt like he was intruding on their lives, so consumed were they with each other. He often questioned whether this was why they had only had a sole child – because there simply wasn't enough room for anyone else when it came to their story.

His father had left them both very suddenly: there had been no warning, no sense, or fear, or feeling that it was all about to go wrong. It had been a cold December's morning just a week before Christmas. Jacob was nineteen years old, and he was home for the holidays from Bath University, where he was studying business. His mother had risen particularly early to head to their local farm shop; his father had requested scrambled quails' eggs for breakfast the previous night.

Jacob was sitting at the breakfast bar still bleary eyed when his mother arrived home, laden with Gloucestershire's finest local produce. He had just poured himself a black coffee, and the scent of roasted coffee beans filled the air.

"Your father not awake yet, my darling?"

"Nope." He had been uninterested as his mother had left the room and taken the large spiral stairs to rouse him for breakfast. He had ignored her first call of his name, he had pretended not to hear. It was only as the panic rose in her voice and swam down the staircase that he suddenly paid attention.

"Jacob, Jacob, call an ambulance. We need an ambulance,

quickly, call an ambulance now. Your father– he– your father–
There is something wrong."

The remainder of that day was segments, fractions of time.
There was no flow to the proceedings from there on in: just a
series of events that all linked up to change their lives forever.

Stephanie

The week had taken on an urgency that always increased my
anxiety levels and no amount of nightly yoga or swimming
could relax my mind. It was at times like this I took to cooking. I
had spent a week the previous summer in Provence improving
my culinary skills; holidays for one were easier when they
involved an activity, a purpose, rather than a lonesome seven
days dwelling on my singledom. Since I had arrived back from
that week of blissful Mediterranean living, the act of cooking
had become my favourite pastime.

The slicing of aubergine, squash, sun-ripened tomatoes and
green beans, onions, leeks and garlic, followed by the dousing of
olive oil, rosemary and thyme, transported me back to days
when I felt the sun beat down on my eyelids. I'm reminded of
the evenings I spent sipping on wine before enjoying our daily
delights from the kitchen; eaten on the lawn with my fellow
cookery class companions. The sun setting over the lavender
meadow.

Tonight, I am attempting to make leeks in white wine with
Parmesan. Jacob Walker-Kent is on my mind as I heat the olive
oil in the pan before braising the leeks. I have been reading
through the case notes again, and I am confident we will
succeed, but there is something niggling at me about him. I can't
put my finger on it, but he has got under my skin. It could be the
blatant charm offensive he pulls every time he comes into my

office, the gentleman he presents himself as. However, even I am dubious as to whether this is the case as I do not suffer fools easily, nor do I succumb to subtle flattery. But there is something about him: something I cannot place.

I discovered Richard Clarke is opposing council today. I know him well enough, that is, in a vaguely professional sense. We came to the bar within a few years of each other, and we would both be considered young in this profession. He is good, if not obviously jaded, and it is quite apparent he is beaten down by the workload from the Crown Prosecution Service. I have no outward concerns as to my chances. His job is far more difficult than mine.

The leeks take about thirty minutes. While I bring the wine to the boil I ring my friend Sally. Sally is thirty-five years old, only slightly older than me, but she lives a very different life: one laden with children, school runs and an acutely lazy husband. She is monumentally busy and often highly strung, and as much as I do not envy her juggling act I do envy the company she yields. Whenever I ring there are voices around her. There may be shouting, but there is also laughter and life. She is flustered when she answers the phone, and we have a disjointed conversation interspersed with her telling the children to *be quiet, stop fighting and put your pyjamas on.* I find myself growing increasingly frustrated at her inability to concentrate on one thing at a time, so I make my excuses and say goodbye.

The wine and water had evaporated nicely by the time I get off the phone, so I transfer the leeks to the baking dish, where I scatter them with Parmesan and season with salt and pepper, before returning them to bake for a further twenty minutes.

I pour myself another cold glass of white wine, and I sit on the stool next to my kitchen workbench. I idly flick through an *Ideal Home* magazine that I bought because an old-school friend's house apparently features as a four-page spread. My mind cannot settle, and I find my reaction to the beautiful Georgian house my friend now lives in is lacklustre.

I check on the leeks every few minutes, but they take longer than I expected to crisp up. I am starving by the time I finally sit down to eat. I flick the TV on and angle myself so I can see it from my kitchen table.

I have three episodes of *EastEnders* on my Sky planner, so I settle in for an evening of depression and excessive cockney shouting.

Richard

Richard woke up around 6am with a groggy head. His mouth was parched, and he spent around ten minutes frantically brushing his teeth to get rid of the dreadful furry coat on his tongue. He regretted the decision to allow himself another pint in the pub last night – especially since he had already found his speech lazy, and his friend seated opposite him had begun to appear blurry.

Richard found the lure of alcohol seductive, the promise that he would truly be able to switch his mind off from the avalanche of thoughts he experienced daily had always been far too compelling. He had failed to avoid excessive booze plenty of times in the past and things didn't seem to be progressing in that area.

Richard walked to work. His weary jaunt that damp Monday morning meant he appeared old and slightly haggard: his physique did not reflect his age. The spring in his step had withered, although he still had the taut chest of a thirty-five-year-old in his prime, his shoulders were stooped. He grabbed a cinnamon latte from the nearby café, and he began the stroll to the office. He planned to spend the day scouring through Molly

Smith's case notes. He didn't want to leave any stone unturned: he desperately wanted to avoid missing anything the prosecution could pounce on.

He passed the entrance to Islington and Highbury tube station in a daze, focusing only on not spilling his hot coffee, whilst trying not to swing his leather satchel into oncoming commuters.

She passed him in a blur, but he was certain it had been her. He was momentarily frozen to the spot, images of Suzie whirling through his mind, pulling him deeper into the past. He knew it was not her, of course it wasn't. It couldn't be: she was the other side of the world. Wherever she now lived it was the evening and she would have been settling down for the night. He wondered if she was enjoying her nightly one glass of Malbec red wine, or whether she had continued her Monday tradition of a chocolate bar at breakfast, something she insisted always lightened the beginning of the week.

Richard spent the majority of his days trying to forget her. His weekends were a haze of mindless activities, which he hoped would eradicate Suzie from his thoughts. It had been seven months since she had left, and it had not got any easier.

Initially he had refused to believe that she was serious. He had thought her departure from their flat a threat, a lesson she was trying to teach him. Two weeks later though, after numerous begging phone calls, two meals in expensive restaurants, flowers, and an attempt to book a romantic weekend away, he had become concerned she was serious.

When Richard had met Suzie, she was so laid back. She was unlike the other girls in his profession. She was not impressed by the law or his knowledge of it. She did not believe it gave them an automatic higher standing in society. Instead, she found it rather pompous and removed from the reality of the actual situations they were dealing with. When Richard said he practised law after she asked him what he did, instead of her eyes lighting up at the thought of a plump wallet she had laughed, and then said: "I didn't ask what you do for a job. I asked you what do you do? What do you like to do?"

Richard was fascinated by this woman in a city bar, who despite looking like a typical twenties female power dresser was like an alien to the surroundings. She enchanted him with her outlook on life and he was stumped by her question. So, in the end she answered for him.

"For example..." She held her hand out so he could introduce himself.

"Richard," he had replied, bemused.

"For example, Rich, if you were to ask me what I do, I would say the following..." She paused and looked at him wide-eyed. "Ask me then." It was an instruction, rather than a question.

"What do you do?"

"Well, I do a lot, Richard. I like running. I'm in a climbing group. I love to surf when I can get to the Cornish coast, where I grew up. I cook – mainly bread and cakes. I have a large family and loads of friends, so I spend a lot of time visiting them. I love going on holidays, three times a year if I can. I like nothing better than to sit in a pub on a Sunday afternoon and stuff my face. On a Wednesday I have a bath, but every other night I have a shower. I swim on Thursday nights for an hour, and I walk every morning, before I go to a place where I can earn money so I can do all those things."

Richard couldn't help it, she made him laugh so much. It was as if she opened a door to a different world for him: a world where everything he thought was important wasn't. A world he had immediately wanted to be a part of.

6

Molly

Alison had arrived at the house just before midday on Sunday. She had managed to finish her planning for the following day in school early, and she had wanted to check in on me. I had worked with Alison for four years. She was only a year older than me, and she was an excellent early years teacher. She was patient and kind. The children adored her.

Since I had begun working in Bradley Primary School I had only ever taken two days off through illness, at which point I'd ended up in hospital with mild pneumonia. I never took time off because I enjoyed my job. I loved the children. I knew how important it was that the whole team were there. I knew that a staff member down affected how hard the children were to manage, and I didn't want to be the teaching assistant that let the others down. I had always tried to please.

The strange thing is that right now I just don't care. I am not bothered about anything, I cannot bring myself to even rise off the sofa to put a wash on or eat. I feel despondent and pointless.

All I want to do is to be left alone. I just don't want to be around anyone anymore. I would rather be on my own, isolated from the world beyond this room – it is easier.

I know I should clean. I have always taken pride in our house, but I do not have the energy. I know Luke will be disappointed I haven't hoovered again or done the dishes, but I do not have the motivation to do any housework. It all seems so pointless. Everything seems so hard.

Alison is soaked when I answer the door. She is attempting to shield her head under a wool coat with a cowl neck collar: it is not working. I can see the stream of water running off her nose, I did not know it was raining today, but now as I stand frozen at the door, on the edge of the outside, I realise it is torrential. As I step back to let her in I notice how she almost recoils at the sight of me, I am not wearing any make-up, and I have just thrown some old clothes on and they are hanging off my increasingly slight frame.

"Moll," she sighs, "how are you?" Alison comes towards me, and she wraps her arms around my bony shoulders.

"I'm good, yeah good..." I mumble although I know my appearance suggests the total opposite.

"How are you feeling?"

"Better, a bit better, yeah I'm okay. Would you like a cup of tea or something? A drink? Coffee? Squash?" I say this secretly hoping she answers "no".

"No, no I'm okay. I just wanted to check in on you."

I am momentarily relieved she said no, but my relief is short-lived. "Oh, I'm fine." I try and plaster a bright smile on my face, but it is too difficult, I look forced and strained.

"Why don't we go out for a bit, Moll? A little walk, some food. We can have a proper chat." Alison stands firmly in the doorway to my living room, and I realise that this is not really a question, she is informing me this is what we will be doing, whether I am comfortable or not: "I'll wait here whilst you shower and change. I'm in no rush."

I nod. I do not have the energy to fight anymore, I do not have anything in me other than submission right now. I climb the stairs slowly, and I enter the bathroom where I turn the shower on mechanically. As I stand underneath the hot fountain of water I begin to cry, because I think I know that enough is enough, I can't continue to keep it a secret anymore.

Jacob

Jacob's mother had brought a gentleman friend to dinner. Jacob was perturbed by this development. She had never introduced him to any male friends before, and he sensed a deeper relevance in this meeting than she initially let on. As he entered the expensive eatery, his mother had risen from the table and dramatically flung her arms wide. "Oh, darling! He is here, here's my Jacob. Come here, oh it's so lovely to see you."

Jacob had approached his mother, a little self-conscious of the overt display of affection. She had always been forcefully proud of her only son, telling anyone who would listen about her "darling Jacob"; from shop assistants to waitresses. His mother spoke of him as if he were a well-known celebrity.

He had become accustomed to her propensity to put him on a pedestal, but he now saw their relationship through the eyes of the gentleman who stood shyly next to his mother waiting to be introduced to "Darling Jacob" himself.

Jacob shook the hand of the man who his mother introduced as Brian, and he eyed him warily. His mother was a very wealthy woman, acutely enhanced by his father's passing, and he wanted to make sure that Brian's intentions were honourable.

They ordered Chablis, his mother's favourite, and they each decided upon a simple crab linguine dish with chilli and lemon. Jacob's appetite wasn't particularly in overdrive, but should he suggest this to his mother she would panic and turn into a whirling mass of protectiveness. Since the incident between Molly he had been off his food. He was lovesick, but he was not about to disclose this over dinner.

He had previously introduced two girls to his mother; it had been a disaster on both occasions. No female was ever going to fulfil his mother's expectations for him. The poor girls had to sit through a meal where they were stared at with disdain and disgust, before his mother had eventually pretended that it was only Jacob at the table, and she had shot them both a look should they dare enter the conversation. In all honesty neither of them were to Jacob's taste. Both girls had succumbed to his charms far too quickly: the chase had lasted a few hours before he had bedded them. There was no challenge. He had merely chosen to introduce them to his mother as he was bored, and he had found the whole affair rather amusing.

Today was no different. His mother fussed over Jacob for the entirety of the meal. Jacob barely had a chance to respond to her questions, before she began another flurry of misplaced interest in his life. Brian looked shell-shocked throughout, as if he was meeting the father of his girlfriend and desperately hoping he would gain approval. He clearly wanted to leave their meeting without the worry that Jacob would quash their relationship.

Jacob had no particular problem with Brian: he was courteous, polite and obviously enjoyed his mother's company. But – and there was always going to be a *but* – he was not his father. And, for that reason, Jacob could not and would not approve. And, if Darling Jacob didn't approve nor would his mother.

Stephanie

I fling my keys onto the front desk as I enter chambers. I have been driving around for fifteen minutes trying to park. The spaces seem to have been allotted to small-time criminals this morning, whose convenience I do not much care for. The receptionist looks up at me desperate for instructions, and I snap back at her to park my car anywhere she can as I am already late.

I do not admire the trait I sometimes chose to exercise: using my position of authority rudely to order those around who are considered lesser in the workplace. However, on days like these I cannot help my impatience. I have a conference with my client in ten minutes, and I am yet to organise myself in the office. There is nothing I cannot stand more than starting a meeting on the back foot, especially with this client.

As I frantically organise my paperwork, case notes and arrange the line of questioning, reception rings through to inform me that Jacob Walker-Kent is early. I sigh. Of course he is early, because that is the kind of person he is: punctual, courteous, focused. Yet I cannot determine whether this is his true character, or whether he is particularly good at this façade; whether he too has been trained like myself, to imitate what we know others need and want to see.

As he enters my office he leans over the desk to shake my hand and his eyes fix on mine. I stutter his name, and I tell him to sit, but he remains standing until I pull my chair back, and convey that I am ready for the meeting. He has manners that are from another decade, from the years of my grandfather when men opened doors, pulled chairs out and held umbrellas for their ladies; behaviour that is now considered peculiar in this day and age where equal treatment has scraped away the very notion of traditional romance. It unnerves me.

Jacob Walker-Kent tries to entice me into pleasantries. He asks me how my weekend was; he talks of a meal he shared with his friend and casually slips in that he is hoping to book a holiday this week before asking me where I like to holiday. I gracefully ignore the latter inquisition. I do not allow any snippets of my personal life to fall into the hands of my clients, no matter how upstanding, moral and charming they appear to be.

I begin by reading Molly Smith's statement to Jacob. I try to piece together his reaction. I am unable to read his body language. Apart from a slight widening of his eyes, he is guarded and appears unshocked. This is not a bad thing, sometimes overt emotion on the alleged perpetrator's behalf can alarm a jury. A grown man weeping can easily be interpreted as regret or guilt.

I move on to read Jacob's account of events. They are both extremely similar: neither statement rejects the factual events of the evening. The only difference really is that Molly Smith states she did not consent, and Jacob Walker-Kent says he is of the belief she did.

We discuss the case at length. I talk of the implications of their friendship, how this will not bode well for Miss Smith. I ask him if she gave him the impression she was indeed keen on a romantic relationship with him. He is affirmative that she did, he says he was of the belief that they would become a couple until the police turned up on his doorstep. I run through the evening of the alleged rape. I ask him to remember all the minute details. I need to know everything that will help our case. I need to paint Molly as a willing participant in the events that unfolded that evening. If she touched his arm, if she danced too close, if she said anything suggestive, if she texted him or rang him in the lead-up to the evening. I need to know every last bit of information about their encounters so that when it comes to court I can tear her testimony to pieces, and prove that my client did have sex with her. That she was not just a consensual adult in the act but also a more than willing, enthusiastic participant.

Richard

When Richard finally arrived at the office after a lengthy detour, where he had aimlessly walked around Hyde Park trying to dispel the urge to contact Suzie, the sun was high in the sky which suggested it was almost time for lunch. He cursed his lack of focus due to a woman, and he continued to his desk where he was determined to make the remainder of the day productive.

No matter how many times he read Molly's case notes the evidence that she had failed to report immediately would be considered damning. The fact was that it was totally normal for rape victims to be in a state of shock, to try and continue as if nothing had happened.

Many women hope that it will all go away, and never report the case. All the evidence suggested that Molly's reaction was entirely normal: in most cases the incident will not be reported immediately. Why then, Richard wondered, was the most plausible response considered the most damaging to such cases?

Richard ran through Molly's character profile in his head. Her strengths were plentiful in terms of her job, her living circumstances and her lifestyle. She did not veer too far away from the stereotypical role prescribed to women who do not want to be raped. This was beneficial: the further away a woman was from this prescribed role, the less worthy of justice and sympathy she was perceived to be.

Richard found it frustrating that it appeared that in order to be deserving of the right to defend your body you needed to be an upstanding citizen: a near perfect one at that.

He was thankful she was not what they in the business considered a bad victim; a bad victim meaning the type of woman a man could rape with impunity. However, it was still not going to be easy to convince a jury of Jacob Walker-Kent's guilt. Richard himself did not realise quite how hard that would be until the evidence admitted by the defence fell on his desk later that afternoon.

He shifted the TV on his desk and made sure the DVD player was connected. He wondered what damaging material Stephanie Beaumont had managed to get her hands on. He knew she was ruthless; he had often been surprised she was a defence barrister because her line of attack was so scathing, so forceful. She took no prisoners in the courtroom, including the judge, should she happen to lack respect for who was sitting. Richard was as surprised as the other barristers that she had not received significant warnings for her conduct in court.

As the blurred image filled the screen Richard grappled with the large remote to adjust the volume before he pressed play. But as soon as he did he regretted the decision because what he saw potentially lost them the entire case.

Molly was in the centre of the frame. She was wearing the black dress from the night of the incident, her hair loose and flowing. She was standing close to a man – a man he was sure was going to be identified as Jacob Walker-Kent.

The video was a collection of footage taken from the CCTV that night, CCTV Richard had hoped would not have been running as many pubs just use the threat of cameras as a deterrent. Regretfully he was wrong: it had been running, and it seemed to have caught everything that had happened in the pub that night between the pair. Their voices were difficult to detect as the music was so loud, but the body language was there: the signals, the flirting, the encouragement. Molly didn't stand a chance.

7

Molly

Alison wanted us to go for lunch. I was not hungry, but I did not have the energy to argue with her. She had a car, so suggested we go out to the country. The last time I left London I'd been with Jacob. He'd driven us to the beach. I hated that memory now. The rain eased the further away from the city we got. I stared out of the car window as the world rushed passed in a blur. We pulled into a car park of a country pub called "The Kings Head". There were picnic benches on a lawn. It wasn't raining here. I wished I'd brought an extra jumper.

"Shall I order for us?" Alison said as I sat down.

"Yes, yeah fine," I mumbled my reply.

"I'll be back now." I watched her walk towards the door. I could feel my anxiety rising. I had nothing to talk about. The car had been stilted. I was usually so chatty, I knew Alison had noticed. I tried to think of all the things I could speak about, but my mind drew a blank.

She returned to the table, and presented me with a knife, fork and an ice-cold bottle of Coca Cola. She ripped open a packet of peanuts and laid them before me. "So how have you been?" Alison just sat quietly opposite me, waiting for me to talk, to tell her what was happening to me. I had managed to return to work for a few weeks after the incident with Jacob, but I had been distracted, impatient, vague giving directions to the children. I had called in sick, because I knew my work was suffering, but I didn't know how to mend things.

We sat until the food arrived, I tried to skirt around the issue, and Alison kindly allowed me to for a brief amount of time. I didn't know where to begin, how to start to say, how to even move forward and wade through all the thoughts swirling around in my head. I didn't know how to say it.

I didn't know what to say, how it had happened. Why it had happened. But, I wanted to now. I wanted to unburden myself of the mental torture, of the blame, of the "what ifs". I wanted and desperately needed someone to tell me it would be okay... that I would be okay. I could not cope with the guilt I felt any longer.

Jacob

His mother had insisted on meeting one last time before she returned home and left London. She assured Jacob that it would just be the two of them today. Sunday lunch would be a measly afternoon tea, he discovered after she rung his mobile to inform him of the location. Small, perfectly neat triangular sandwiches and fussy cakes combined with overdressed women who believed they were posh was not what Jacob had in mind; he was hankering after a roast lamb dinner with all the trimmings. However, his mother's idea of dining revolved around how she would be perceived, so it was apt she had chosen this destination.

He left Notting Hill early, and he had stopped in one of the pubs for a pint. He had found a spot in the beer garden that just about allowed the sun to shine upon him. He pulled his phone out and did the usual routine of checking Molly's Facebook. She had not updated anything on her profile for weeks. He was mildly annoyed by this: it allowed him no insight into her existence. Next, he re-read their text messages. He rarely went back to the start, but he had a few favourite messages from her that suggested to him that she was hoping for more than friendship.

He studied the last message she had sent him, wondering if in fact it was a test. Maybe she wanted him to chase her, to show her how far he would go for her. He decided that he would text her again, just to touch base, just so she knew he was thinking of her. As he tapped the message into his phone he felt a bit brighter, the possibility of contact spurring on his energy.

He didn't want it to be too casual; he needed her to respond; he needed to open with questions. He hadn't mentioned what had happened between them yet but maybe it was time he did. He realised that she could do with some gentle persuasion to meet with him, just enough that she understood that he was not playing her game anymore – that she couldn't just stop now that they had taken things further. He did not want to scare her, but he needed her to know that he must see her. The suggestion of the consequence if she didn't was enough. He needn't overtly state what he might do, he just had to leave the doubt hanging in the air, and he knew she would come around, she'd have to.

Molls, where have you been? We need to see each other. Talk about what happened between us. I saw Luke earlier. I was thinking of asking him out for a drink, but maybe it would be better if it were YOU I met with? J X

Stephanie

I had been surprised when the CCTV film arrived on my desk at how quickly it had been processed. I had only rung the pub just after Jacob Walker-Kent had left my office on Monday. It must have barely been 11am but by 2pm I had the footage I was sure would guarantee his freedom, all in an easily presentable montage of clips of him and Molly. It had almost been too easy, the game over before it had begun.

I surveyed the evidence as I ate my lunch. The first clip was grainy, as the camera must have been quite a distance from Jacob and Molly. It showed them by the bar, drinking shots together and laughing, followed by Jacob buying Molly a large glass of wine. This concerned me somewhat because at this point he was not buying himself a drink, and I did not want this to be interpreted as an intentional act to get Molly inebriated. The fact they had both been drinking shots together previous to this was reassuring, but it may be a hurdle to overcome if the prosecution picked up on it.

The next clip was of the dance floor. The quality was surprisingly good, and their facial expressions could easily be made out. Molly Smith is smiling widely, her head tossed back and her body loose to the music. She is dancing closely to Jacob and swaying her hips seductively. Jacob is smiling and so is Molly Smith.

Richard

By the time the weekend arrived Richard was overjoyed at the prospect of some time off. His week had felt endless, filled with hefty cases and client calls. He had collapsed into his bed nightly, and the long, deep sleeps had done nothing to energise or refresh his spirit. He had dreamt of Suzie. The dreams were obscure and confusing, and they had added to the avalanche of emotions he still felt towards her.

He had become lost in memories of her this week. He replayed days or evenings spent together hoping he would gain some new insight: that he could understand at what point she had started to feel discontent. He could not remember when she had started to pull back. He could pinpoint a few instances when she was distant, thoughtful, but he didn't think anything stood out. He had not expected her departure. He knew his work had been frenetic, that he had spent too many nights in the office having to forgo dinner and plans with her, but he had thought she had understood, that she had realised that this was what he had to do: it was the nature of the job.

He had assumed it was just Suzie's wanderlust fuelling her discontentment, but the longer she refuted his attempts to solve the issues that blighted their relationship the more he panicked as she grew further and further away. Even after she had left him, he was blinded by hope that they would once again be a couple. It had taken her getting on a plane to the other side of the world for him to realise that she was not actually coming back.

The weekends were the only snippets of happiness he now clung to, but since Suzie had gone they had become increasingly empty and hollow. Fuelled by alcohol and sex with strangers, he failed to gather any contentment from his experiences come Monday morning; the females becoming more faceless as the weeks passed.

Weekends with Suzie felt like an entirely different lifetime: trips to Cornwall straight from work on a Friday followed by long, lazy walks, fat pub lunches and fresh salty air, coupled with copious amounts of laughter. A slower pace and a feeling that there was another option outside the city had been the perfect therapy for Richard. A chance to escape what otherwise became so consuming: his job.

Suzie had taught him to surf, albeit not well, but he had thrown himself into the ocean early on Saturday and Sunday mornings, relishing the invigoration and sense of peace it ignited in him. She had ridden waves elegantly, her body effortlessly swaying as she carved the sea wall. In those moments, he had loved her more than he thought possible, this beautiful, carefree Cornish girl who represented so much more to him. He had not been to Cornwall since, until this weekend that is. He was taking what he considered a pilgrimage to Suzie, in the hope that he could put her and the place that haunted him with happy memories to rest.

8

Molly

My phone beeped. Every time I heard that noise my stomach flipped, and I could feel myself shaking. I knew it might be him, it made me physically sick, and I had to sit on my hands so Alison couldn't see they were shaking.

"Are you going to look at that?"

I feigned confusion.

"Your phone, Molls, you've had a text."

"Oh, have I? I'll look after."

"It's not a problem: you can look now."

"No, no it's fine." I needed Alison to drop it, but it was as if the phone beeping had given her a way in, and she wasn't about to leave it there.

"You look shaken. Is it the text, Moll? Is someone harassing you? You can tell me what is going on."

"I'd rather leave it please. Can we just talk about something else?"

"No."

Alison's response took me aback. "What?"

"I said no, Molly. We cannot talk about something else. I came here today to find out what exactly has happened – is happening – to you. Because you've gone from Mrs Carefree to an anxious wreck. You've dropped too much weight. You were always distracted in work, and now you've just stopped coming in. You never go out anymore, and when your phone as much as lights up, or vibrates, you look like you're about to have a nervous breakdown. So, no, I won't talk about anything else, until you tell me what is going on."

"It's nothing, I'm fine." I wasn't. My lip was trembling, my voice was cracking, and I was on the verge of losing it. My phone beeped again.

"Who is it? Who is sending you text messages? Is it Luke?"

"No, no it's not Luke," I murmured. "It's fine, please, Alison."

"Read it then, if it is so fine, read the message. Tell me what it says, and I'll believe you."

I had no option. As I reached for my phone I hoped it was not him this time. Jacob hadn't texted for a few days. If it wasn't him I wouldn't have to explain who this male was. I brought the screen up to my face and opened the message. I could see Alison watching me trying to decipher every little reaction.

I read the text message.

It was from him.

I tried my hardest to remain calm. I did not want to expose myself in front of Alison, but the words he'd written made me feel so trapped. There was nothing I could do as the frustrated and scared sob left my body.

Jacob

When Jacob arrived to meet his mother, he had already drunk three pints in very quick succession. He had intended to just have a swift one, but after he sent the text he became agitated awaiting Molly's response. He was late for his mother. As he entered the five-star hotel in search of the dining area he spotted her in the reception looking anxious, with a hint of annoyance in her brow. Her face relaxed when she spotted Jacob. She launched towards him and flung her arms around his waist. He was too tall these days for her to reach his shoulders.

"Oh, Jacob, where have you been? Mummy's been worried."

He could not bear the pretentious reference to her parental role. "Tube closures." He was stand-offish and did not offer any further details. His mother, picking up on the atmosphere, backed away from the subject.

They entered the dining area and were seated in plush velvet seats. The room was opulent, the lights over-the-top and the detailing in the furniture incredibly ornate. His mother was frantic in relaying her weekend to him. She leapt from subject to subject as if time with Jacob were about to run out. She barely had a moment to take a breath before she started up again with another fact he simply must know.

Jacob smiled and nodded in all the right places, and he tactically remained silent when she mentioned Brian; he only had to look slightly brooding, and he knew his mother would panic about upsetting him so end the affair. She did not want to upset precious Jacob. They ordered the afternoon tea. The sandwiches were uninspiring in their aspirations to be typically British, and the cakes were slightly dry, the sponge sticking to the roof of his mouth. He thought of the word "cloying". His mother merely nibbled on the spread, the quality of the food irrelevant in comparison to the appearance. He quaffed the champagne, and they finished one bottle in no time at all. His mother raised her hand and requested another with a nod of the head.

"Jacob, may I ask, darling, is there something bothering you?"

He shook his head, but he was unable to make eye contact so she pressed him further. "Come on, Jacob Bear, you can tell Mummy. Is it money? Do you need money? You know you only must ask me, my darling? It is money, isn't it? Oh, goodness why didn't you say? How much do you need? Jacob, it's not a problem. Money is not a problem, you know that, my angel."

"It's not money. Money is not a problem." He had snapped back at her a little too quickly, and she looked wounded. He had not meant to upset her. He tried to soften his voice: "It's just some things are going on, but I'm fine. It's all fine."

She stared back at him: "Oh, Jacob, how did I not guess? It's a girl. It's to do with a girl." She smiled. "Tell me everything, darling boy. What is this girl like? Are you in love?" His mother looked excited and expectant.

He did not want to disappoint her, and they would be together soon enough. Jacob told his mother of Molly, of all the things she wanted to hear, and all the things he was certain he could and would make happen between them. He spoke of a future he so desperately wanted to happen.

Stephanie

I throw my coat onto the leather sofa, as I walk into my open-plan kitchen, living room and diner. I am laden down by shopping for tonight's meal. Matthew is coming over at seven this evening for dinner. I could not decide what was appropriate to cook, so I spent way over the allotted time I had given myself staring aimlessly at the food in the aisles of Waitrose.

I seemed to have created a menu clearly dominated by chicken. For starters, I am making cognac and chicken liver parfait alongside some homemade sourdough, followed by a chicken, bacon and leek dish in white wine with creamy mashed potato. I have not seen Matthew for a month, and I have been looking forward to the evening immensely this past week. Friday night could not have come quick enough, the idea of a lie-in and a bath tomorrow morning seems divinely heavenly; albeit I must read over some cases for the majority of the day, but I do not need to get up as the sun rises, and I can afford a couple of hours in bed dozing and reading the morning papers.

I first met Matthew when I was in university studying for my finals. We had been studying together for the past three years, but never crossed paths in our seminars. The lecture halls housed at least 300 people, so it was not unusual that we hadn't spoken. During my final exams, I saw people on my course I had never seen in the whole duration of my university life. I found the library strangely comforting during those last few months. It was not somewhere I dreaded going; I rather enjoyed the quiet lull that could be found there. I liked the old library lamps and the smell of books. I spent most of my revision time there, stopping for a black coffee every now and again.

I had noticed Matthew on my course during fresher's week; it was hard not to, he was alarmingly good-looking in an effortless "just got out of bed" way. I had never had any reason to talk to him though, his friends and mine did not intertwine, and he forever seemed to have a blonde beauty hanging off his arm, looking equally chic. We struck up conversation by pure chance really. It was a coincidence that I was ordering coffee at the same time as him. It was also by chance that it was at the unfortunate moment a girl fainted by our feet.

As I struggled to put her in the recovery position, Matthew knelt beside me and called for help. She came around rather quickly, and it was apparent her faint may have had something to do with her looking like she was barely consuming 500 calories a day. But, in those moments Matthew and I began to speak, and we haven't really stopped since.

He paid for my coffee after the girl's friends arrived, and we sat at a table together. We both knew we were studying law, and we also knew that we were both practically living in the library, and this mutual daily slog seemed enough for us to bond. From then on, he would approach me if he was having a break, and I would do the same: following him outside where we both smoked Marlboro Lights, and we laughed about how we would implode if the pressure of the exams increased any further.

The strange thing was that despite his looks and easy-going nature I did not fancy him. I developed feelings for him but they were those of friendship and trust. We have never kissed; we have never been romantically involved. We really were, and are, just friends of the opposite sex. I am grateful for our lasting friendship, and although our meetings are sporadic and sparse, we still make an effort to keep in contact: to call each other and check in, just sometimes only to say hello.

Annalise, his fiancée was unable to join him tonight, but I was secretly pleased when Matthew told me. I find her infuriatingly superficial. I cannot escape the feeling that she pounced on Matthew at the first given chance purely for his money and looks but not so much for his personality. She spends money on the most absurd of items. Her wardrobe is filled with expensive handbags, the cost of which could have fed a school of children for over a month. Matthew is utterly besotted though, so I dare not mention her lack of intelligence or substance.

Not only was it a relief to be spending time with Matthew without Annalise, it meant I would be able to broach the subject of Jacob Walker-Kent without appearing to be deliberately excluding his princess. I had showered and prepared all the food by the time Matthew arrived, and I was in the middle of opening a bottle of ice-cold Sauvignon Blanc, when he shouted through the letterbox. Even though my doorbell worked he had always insisted on signalling his arrival in this manner.

As I opened the door we embraced casually. I had poured him a glass of wine and taken it with me to the door so handed it over. "Now, this is service, Stephanie. I'm not even in the building, and you're plying me with expensive alcohol."

I laughed and batted his upper arm. "I'll take it back if you're complaining... Come in. Go on, it is freezing outside."

Richard

The drive to Cornwall was long and painstaking. Shortly after Richard passed through Devon the road was consumed by fog, and he was forced to drive at a speed more suited to riding a bike. He was staying in Porthleven, a tidy fishing village at the very southern tip near Penzance. He had not stayed in the pub he had booked before, but Suzie had loved it there and insisted they pass through every time they had made a trip back to her home, parking up on the quayside.

His eyes were drooping, and he had developed a headache by the time he arrived at the pub. He practically downed a pint in the bar before taking his bag to the double en suite room he had booked. It was nearly nine o'clock – he'd luckily finished work at three o'clock, and managed to make the journey in the five-hour time frame, so he was still in time for dinner.

He had been to this pub once before with Suzie. It had been after a long day in the sea being battered by the waves. Her hair had been windswept and tousled, her skin glowing with the promise of summer and days filled with freedom. They had shared cod and chips, followed by more chips. They had expended so much energy surfing that avoiding high calorie

69

food was not a consideration. Richard had loved that about Suzie: she had an appetite for everything, and because of this she could consume everything in excess, because somehow it all balanced out.

They had drunk cider and slept in Suzie's dad's camper van overlooking the harbour. In the morning, she had risen early and woken him with steaming black coffee, they had sat on the stone harbour wall and delighted in the chorus of seagulls. She had thrown on Richard's oversized white shirt and a pair of Uggs; he had never seen her look so beautiful. When he replays Suzie in his mind she is always here, throwing her head back, her morning hair swept back, her mouth wide open, her laughter filling the salty sea air.

He sits in the bar all night reminiscing, wondering why he has driven himself to this place of all places, why he is allowing himself to endure such torture. Richard had thought Suzie would last forever. He had not questioned that she would not be a constant, that someday he would not be enough for her, because she was all encompassing for him. Life with Suzie had felt like he was spinning around in a fairground, the bright lights, adventure and excitement coming from all angles, he hadn't expected to have to get off – to end the ride there. Suzie was meant to keep taking him places, reminding him of how to live.

As Richard drunk his sixth pint of the evening he became increasingly maudlin. He could not help but stare at the young woman sitting by the bar with her friend. She looked Cornish, honey coloured taut limbs and tousled hair brushing her shoulders. She was wearing a strappy dress that kept falling off her left shoulder. She smiled as she spoke to her companion, and she stroked her neck when she tilted her head to the side. Richard had promised himself he would not do this. But he was lonely. He would not look to other females to fill the void of another evening without Suzie, but he longed for company. He thought that maybe a night with the distraction of strangers may exorcise his ex. Offering them a drink would be harmless.

He meandered over to the woman. Her friend smiled up at him first. He felt a bit of a fool, but alcohol had given him the confidence to approach them. He began by asking them for recommendations for lunch the following day.

"Hi, sorry to interrupt, but would either of you know the best place to eat lunch around here?" They were happy to help, and Richard was thankful for their advice. He kept the conversation flowing longer than he expected. They had grown up in the area, so were more than happy to share with him all the best places to visit. It seemed organic to offer them a drink in exchange.

"Can I buy you ladies a drink?" They asked for white wine, so he bought them a bottle: middle of the range. They told him he was welcome to pull up a seat, he politely declined once as not to appear desperate, but when they asked again he had obliged. He was grateful for the human interaction.

They were chatty, sweet girls, and Richard knew that young girls were what they were, because they must have been no older than twenty-four. At over ten-years their senior he suddenly felt slightly seedy, but it was easy company and the conversation meant he was not thinking of Suzie.

They flushed when he said he was a prosecuting barrister in London. He often got this response in Cornwall. His career seemed far more thrilling and impressive here than it was in reality. They stayed at the bar all night. Richard bought drink after drink, and they all got less inhibited. After last orders were called he invited them to bring take-outs to his room.

He realised his mistake immediately as the girls withdrew from him. He had not meant it like that, he had just wanted to continue drinking and chatting. He wanted to forget himself for a moment, to forget Suzie.

Richard had tried having sex with total strangers before, he thought it may have helped to block out images of Suzie; he had initially found it was therapeutic even if it only lasted briefly. The fact that Suzie was in his head straight afterwards, and it made him miss her more, he denied. He had just wanted to feel the arms of another woman, to feel another body pressed on his. He just didn't want to feel lonely.

He told the girls to forget he had asked and retrieved himself quickly. He feigned tiredness. He retired to his bedroom, where he feasted on a family-sized bar of Galaxy chocolate he had purchased earlier, and he drunk the bottle of red wine he had brought in his bag. He stayed awake until just before dawn, when he passed out on the bed with the TV still booming in the background.

9

Molly

I did not eat my lunch. The barman had approached with a Ploughman's for each of us but mine remained untouched in the centre of the table. Food turned my stomach, even the smell of it made me feel sick. Alison tried to consume her food as we talked, but I could see she was distracted. I had shown Alison the text in the end. She had looked at me confused. I told her to scroll back over the past few weeks, her eyes widened as she took in the extent of his one-sided communication.

"Who is he, Molls? It's like he's stalking you."

I explained our friendship, how we met, how much time we had spent together. Alison remembered him then, how he had come into school once and helped with the harvest concert.

"But he seemed so nice. What happened? What does he mean: *we need to talk about what happened*?"

It came out in a muddle of words, of mixed chronological times, of irrelevant facts, of pointless interludes. I interspersed it with stories of me and Luke arguing. None of it made sense, I didn't make sense. I could see Alison looking at me perturbed.

She looked utterly confused. I started to panic. This is what I had been worried would happen, this is what I had been so afraid of. I knew people would blame me. I was terrified of what people would say, how they would interpret the facts. Alison continued to stare at me, a look of shock masking her emotions.

"Sorry, I shouldn't have said. I knew people wouldn't understand."

"No, no, God no, you should have said, Molls. I'm just trying to get my head around it, start again. Start from the beginning, tell me everything that happened that night but slowly."

It was a relief. I had not realised how much tension I had been carrying around. It was as if I was breathing for the first time in weeks, as I replayed the evening, and I told Alison every little detail I felt lighter with each sentence. She nodded and sympathised in all the right places. And, when I had finished telling her what had happened for the second time, she said what I had hoped for, yet what I had not hoped for all at the same time. It had been in the back of my mind, but I hadn't vocalised it myself. I didn't want to sound over-the-top, dramatic, or make something out to be something it was not, part of me just wanted to forget and move forward, but the other part of me knew I couldn't and I wouldn't be able to do that. I knew it was wrong, but I didn't know quite how wrong it would be perceived to be. Alison reassured me that all those niggling doubts, all those fears were unfounded.

It was Jacob's fault. He was in the wrong. It was not my fault.

"Molly, you should have gone to the police. You should have told someone what he did. He can't get away with that. He raped you."

That was all Alison said when I finished telling my story, but to be able to put a label on what he had done, what I had been so confused about, helped. It did help. Jacob was in the wrong. He had taken something from me that I had not been prepared to give. There was still that niggling doubt it was my fault because although I hadn't said yes, nor had I said no.

Jacob

He had learned to live with grief. It had become his strange companion since his father's passing. Jacob had always thought that when someone died there was a period of sadness, and then everything returned to normal. Since losing his father he had discovered that his childhood ideas surrounding death were entirely uninformed. His grief was something he usually kept hidden away. In the moments when he was truly on his own he would let a tiny bit of his pain slip to the surface, but he had to be clever about when to allow this, because the magnitude of his sorrow would be too much to manage in one sitting. Jacob let grief into his home a little at a time, he could control it in this manner; that way he could still carry on.

Shortly after his father had died he had gone to bed and been unable to rise for days. His tiredness was so profound he had become bedridden. He was awake for a matter of hours before needing to sleep again. It was only in this unconscious state that he still managed to find any comfort. His mother had been the same; their house became shrouded in slumber.

Jacob's feelings of injustice had been substantial. His overriding anger at his father's death was intense. He could not fathom that he had actually left. His father had not meant to die, yet he could not help but hate him for doing so: for leaving him alone with his mother who had now become an irritant. Her dependency on Jacob's life to fulfil her happiness was a burden he had not been prepared to bear.

He knew his father would be proud. He had made an impressive amount of money since finishing university. He had property in London. He travelled. He had been a forceful man, and he had instilled the same notion of living in Jacob: if you want something then you go and get it, no matter what. He wondered, as he walked arm in arm down the street with his mother back to Notting Hill, whether his father would have liked Molly. Jacob thought he would have found her pleasing to the eye. His father had always had a way with the ladies: he remembered holidays abroad where he would slap the waitresses' backsides and pull them in for a fondle. His mother had looked on and laughed. He was sure he would have seized the opportunity, like Jacob had, to become intimate with Molly.

Jacob's mother was rambling on, but all he could think of was what advice his father would give now. He considered the question momentarily before they entered his street. It was only then he saw the flashing lights, the police car and the two officers standing outside his front door.

Stephanie

My head hurt. I could hear Matthew plodding around the kitchen below me, and I knew I needed to get up: to tear myself away from what was a divinely comfortable bed this morning. We had got rip-roaringly drunk in the end, so much so the room had circled when I had finally made it to bed. After three bottles of expensive wine, Matthew had decided it was time for champagne. A fatal move as I always managed to get somewhat carried away after champagne, cue further gin, elderflower, strawberry and cucumber tonics (my new favourite drink). I am sure Matthew's presence escorts my behaviour back to the years of my early twenties.

He must have been awake awhile. I had not woken when he left the bedroom. We had shared a bed together last night which is not unusual: we have always slept in the same bed together. It is usually because we can't stop talking, so it is easier to fall asleep while we are still in mid-conversation. We had discussed Annalise at length during the meal and her need for him to propose. I had found it profoundly hard not to present all the reasons why he shouldn't, namely the fact the idea hadn't organically presented itself to him.

I was glad for the distraction of food, every time the moment arose where I desperately wanted to object I would stick another forkful in my mouth and chew, until my anger had subsided. I did not believe that Matthew loved Annalise. I knew that he idolised her, that she was seen as precious by him; elevated almost to evangelical status where she was unable to disappoint him, but I did not see any love there, only the image and the idea of what a couple should be. Annalise would give him beautiful children, fit in her size eight jeans at the age of fifty, smell of expensive perfume and smile in all the right places throughout their lives, but she wouldn't bring him fun or intellectual stimulation. She was a trophy bride if you like, but Matthew despite his astuteness hadn't seemed to see her, or them, for what they were, and I sure as hell wasn't in a position to lecture him on his love life.

We rambled on for hours about all aspects of our lives, the conversation flowing from one subject to the next. It was late before I broached the subject of Jacob Walker-Kent. In retrospect, the entirely wrong time as I knew Matthew's opinion on my position to defend such men in cases of rape was negative, namely because he knew my tactics. It is not that Matthew does not believe that every man deserves legal representation, because he does, but it is rather that he wholly disagrees with the manner in which rape cases are treated in court, namely by people like me.

Richard

Richard spent the day musing along the harbour wall, stopping occasionally to perch on a bench and reflect upon the scene before him.

He was tired today. For once he was allowing his body to feel so; he was letting himself stop. It was only now he'd left the city that he had the chance to look back on the preceding few weeks.

He found himself thinking of Molly Smith. He could picture her across from him in his office, her bottom lip sticking out and quivering ever so slightly indicating her anxiety. He had noticed she jiggled her right leg with nerves, and he felt so responsible for her in that instant. She had no idea how brave she was being but also how naïve at the same time. Richard hated to admit it, but he felt cases such as hers were a waste of time, not because this Walker-Kent didn't deserve to pay for what he had done. No that was not why, but because ultimately Richard knew the way the system worked or rather didn't: it simply provided no justice to victims like Molly. They had it all wrong; everyone knew it. It was always front-page news: *Rapists only prosecuted in four per cent of cases* etc., etc. Yet nothing was being done to change that.

The issue of intoxication and consent was a minefield. Molly's drunkenness on the evening in question equated to her being less credible. Consent is defined under Section 74 of the Sexual Offences Act 2003 as: "where a person agrees by choice and has the freedom and capacity to make that choice". Drunken consent is still consent, and the drunken intention to commit rape is still rape.

It is impossible to have a set of questions relating to capacity and consent. You cannot determine the issues on a case-by-case basis, using some prescribed set of standards regarding alcohol consumption. Alcohol consumption and capacity differs from individual to individual. "Richard, some areas of human behaviour are unsuitable for detailed legislative structure," a piece of wisdom that Richard always heard in the bellowing voice of his sociology of the law lecturer.

The fact was at least a third of all rape cases involved women who had been drinking alcohol before the alleged attack. There was a high risk that Molly's evidence would be thrown out by the judge. Richard could almost hear the dismissal of the evidence: "The accuser was intoxicated at the time in question therefore her evidence is unreliable."

The problem when it came to capacity and consent was that if drunken consent is ruled invalid, there is the possibility that whenever sex takes place with a drunk woman, a man could be considered a rapist by definition. If this follows then surely drunkenness in a man could mean that he was as incapable of seeking consent as the drunken woman was incapable of giving it. Richard knew that ultimately the consequence of being drunk should be a hangover, not rape.

And then there was binge drinking. That just added complications to an already grey area of law. Intoxication just muddied the waters further. The reality of the law in action does not compare to the law in statute. The reality of the law on rape was that it was not delivering what it was intended to for the victims.

Richard believed that there was a need for expert evidence concerning rape myths. He thought that good character evidence should be allowed with regard to Molly, as well as third-party disclosure, that being any earlier admission a victim made concerning the rape before contacting the police. It would all contribute to strengthening the victim's case. He wished that Molly's colleague... what was her name... Alison could testify about Molly's earlier admission. That would help the jurors understand the case as a woman's lived experience, rather than just a courtroom drama.

But juries are strongly influenced by myths not grounded in fact. They have been influenced by media makers. Richard found his teeth gritting and his fists clenching every time he saw a narrative of mischievous accusation in a drama or in a news story.

The police, too, maintained the momentum of the myths. Officers were meant to be specially trained to understand sexual abuse, but Richard knew all too well that there were still old police attitudes and practices running through the force, and adherence to correct procedures was inconsistent to say the least. The police, too, played their part.

It was ludicrous the idea that a victim of rape was responsible for being raped. No other crime carries such connotations of blame. But ludicrous or not, that was the reality.

Jacob fitted the profile of an acquaintance rapist. Richard had read all the research papers by the leading scholar in law and policy in relation to rape and sexual violence published in *The International Journal of Law, Crime and Justice*. He knew there was a certain type of man who committed these acts. It was typical to ply the female with alcohol to incapacitate them and to push their boundaries to make them vulnerable. Often they harnessed a certain amount of anger towards women.

Richard also knew the usual defence to acquaintance rape: the rapist was receiving mixed signals so the communication was confused; she had played upon her sexuality and had been flirting for weeks.

Jacob fits the profile of an acquaintance rapist, and their typical defence, thought Richard, kicking beach debris washed on shore out of his way. The understanding that there was nothing he could do about it hit him so hard that tears sprang to his eyes.

10

_____

Molly

Girls like me don't get raped. Girls like me are too sensible. Girls like me try and keep safe. I have been to self-defence lessons; I've done countless exercise classes where I have been taught boxing. I know where to punch an attacker, I know how to fight back; I have specifically learnt how to for the moment when something bad happens to me. I know that if you are attacked you should shout "fire" instead of "help". Girls like me can protect themselves. Girls like me don't get raped.

When I first moved to London, a fresher in university, new to the city, I carried a rape alarm with me. I have never walked home on my own late at night, I have always made sure someone knew where I was. I would ring or text my close friends, or Luke, and inform them. I even asked them to walk me home so I was safe. Girls like me don't get raped.

Yes, I like to get a little bit drunk, who doesn't? But I always try to stay safe: I would not walk down a dark, isolated street alone at night. I would not get into an unregistered taxi. I have never led a man on knowingly. I am not easy. I am not promiscuous. I do not dress provocatively. I have only ever slept with six men. Girls like me don't get raped.

I work with children. I studied sociology. I like to bake at weekends. I am in a relationship. I am in my late twenties. I am happy. I am not an easy target. Girls like me don't get raped.

I am a girl who knew better, who was too busy watching out for the man in the bushes, who forgot instead to watch out for the one walking beside her. Girls like me don't get raped.

And I know that girls who are raped should not shower, that they should report the incident straight away, that they should seek help. I knew all of this yet I did none of the above. I showered. I did not tell. I did not find help. I thought girls like me don't get raped.

Jacob

Jacob cannot believe Molly has accused him of this, of all things, of rape. He has spent the morning scouring the internet searching for similar cases, something that will provide him with some insight into this position he has found himself in. He comes across an article published in the online magazine *Lads United* detailing signs that the alleged victim is making a false allegation. He has jotted the signals down in his Filofax, so he can present them to his barrister Stephanie.

Molly fits the profile the author talks of perfectly. The main three points, he concludes, are typical to his and Molly's case. Firstly, there were no signs of a struggle; it seems an entirely reasonable assumption that in cases of rape there would and should be. In Jacob's opinion if a girl doesn't want sex with someone she should at least put up a bit of a fight, shout or scream. How are men meant to know they are doing anything wrong if the woman just lies there passively: if she didn't even say "no".

Secondly, the alleged victim invited the man into her house. It was so blatant what she was after at this point. He couldn't believe there was an article on it suggesting this could be interpreted any other way. It is a well-known fact that inviting someone in for a "coffee" isn't actually for a "coffee".

Lastly, the article cited failure to report to the authorities or police for a prolonged period of time. He couldn't believe how similar to his case this was. Molly had, like many others in a similar situation, made this false allegation to avoid admitting she had slept with him.

What a callous, manipulative bitch she was being! When he looked back at the evening, he may have taken things too quickly, but she had been asking for it for weeks, months even, and it's not as if she was a virgin. She knew exactly what she was doing.

Jacob was a nice guy. He wasn't a rapist, he couldn't be. He didn't feel like a rapist. He didn't beat Molly up, he didn't ever intend to rape Molly. He'd maybe been a bit more domineering than usual but that wasn't rape. She hadn't shouted no; or screamed at him to stop; she hadn't fought back. She hadn't told him she didn't want it. She had done absolutely nothing to show him she didn't want sex.

So many of his friends had boasted about their sexual behaviour in the past, incidents that were far worse than what had happened between him and Molly. Only the year before he'd been at a party where there was a drinking contest. His friend Arthur had been winning. A pretty brunette had been sitting on his lap, touching his arm. Jacob had, like the others, thought they were obviously going to get it on. When his friend had been declared the winner they had all cheered. Arthur had stood and lifted the girl up and kissed her. Then he had pushed her up against the wall, pulled her knickers down from underneath her dress and started having sex with her. They had all cheered again.

Looking back Jacob thought his friend had been quite forceful, and the girl had tried to push him off – but he had agreed that it was only rough sex not rape. Everyone had been drunk, it had just felt like part of the party. The girl had run out the house crying afterwards, but it was only a bit of fun. They all expected it, that's just what happened. He couldn't believe Molly would suggest what he did was rape. He wasn't a rapist. He was one of the good guys, and he sure as hell wouldn't let her get away with this.

Stephanie

When I finally managed to drag myself out from under the duvet, I was hit by the autumnal chill in the air. My body shivered, and I quickly retrieved a jumper of Matthew's off the back of a chair and threw it over my head. It smelt of him, a deep masculinity laced with hints of spicy vanilla. I padded my way down the stairs to see him topless making eggs Benedict in the kitchen. Matthew had always been a brilliant cook, yet he rarely found himself in the kitchen these days. I smiled at him and went over to fill the kettle.

"I could get used to this, Matthew... breakfast, a half-naked man in my kitchen, it's just a shame it's you." I laughed to myself, and he pretended to hit me with the tea towel. This was what I liked about both of us, that we were so comfortable, that there was no awkwardness. I know many of my female friends had misinterpreted our relationship over the years: they could not understand how we shared the same bed, wore each other's clothes, cooked for one another, had no problem with public displays of affections, and talked on the telephone all the time, and all the while there was nothing romantic between us.

I had questioned myself many a time. It would have been so much easier to fall for Matthew. He would make the perfect husband, father, provider. We loved each other's company, nobody knew me quite like him, but there was no chemistry, and everyone knows chemistry is one of the main ingredients in longevity when it comes to relationships. If it doesn't exist in the first place you won't be able to create it. That is not to say that Matthew and I did not have chemistry of some kind – we have a chemistry based on companionship, comfort and familiarity, but I want the passionate kind of chemistry. The kind of reaction that occurs between two people that means you cannot stop thinking about them: your body tingles every time you see them, that makes their touch electric. I want the kind of chemistry that begins, and ends, with lust.

Our chemistry was lived in, it was a known quantity. There would never be any sparks, a monumental lightning bolt that meant we could not keep our hands to ourselves. We would be the kind of couple that quite happily visited IKEA on the weekends, carried out chores around the house, planned our finances, washed the tea towels with bleach, and remembered that one of us disliked parsnips whilst the other particularly liked cabbage. We would have lovely, relaxing holidays where we'd read books and be attentive to one another, but there would be no sex, no moments of pure passion when we simply must have one another. We would not have blazing arguments that reignited our fire or meant we did not speak for a week. We would never forget a birthday, or an anniversary, but it would be boring, we would know what was around every corner. And, no matter how beautiful the horizon is, if it is always the same it inevitably becomes tiresome, and you cannot help seeking out new views, new places to visit. The allure of change and excitement too tempting.

A hearty breakfast of eggs was just what I needed. I washed it down with an ice-cold can of Sprite. I could taste my dehydration I was that thirsty. We slobbed on the sofa and watched re-runs of *The X Factor* auditions.

We did not discuss Monday, or work, or Annalise. We sunk back into our old selves: the people we were when we used to spend the weekends wrecked from excessive consumption, lying on sofas in pubs whingeing about the non-existent pupillage we were chasing, wondering how we would pay the bills. When we were together we became young again, the mildly carefree students who had the rest of their lives ahead of them, and what difference would a day of gluttony make? I missed that age.

At the time I had hated it, fraught with what-if's and financial stresses. I felt like we were practising at being adults. It was only when I was that bit older, nearer my thirties, that I suddenly realised the responsibilities that now presented themselves. Well, it was only then that I had been able to comprehend how free I had actually been. My career was not yet in motion. There was no bricks-and-mortar that I had signed my soul to. I did not dream of case files suffocating me or wake in the middle of the night panicked I had missed a detail, forgotten a crucial part of my client's case. No, instead I worried about where I should go and how I would get there and, more than anything, how quickly I could. I was so focused on the destination I hadn't stopped to look at what I was missing out on during the journey.

Richard

The rest of Richard's weekend was spent travelling from coastal town to town. He made his way around the quaint shops in Mousehole; and he ate scones with Cornish clotted cream. He headed to St Michael's Mount, where he had fought against the wind to walk the length of the beach. In the evening, he went back to Porthleven, and he ate in the sixteenth century pub across the harbour, rather than the one he was staying in. He ate more battered cod and chips before absorbing himself in the newspapers.

After an hour of reading about the day's events across the globe he felt restless, he finished his pint and walked outside into the fresh night's sky. Summer was drawing to a close, the temperature had dropped significantly. Daylight had ended at seven o'clock this evening, and he could feel winter drawing in. He didn't mind so much: he preferred his workload when the rest of the world didn't appear to be on holiday or in a beer garden of an evening. He often looked forward to the hibernation that November yielded, albeit this year he was not looking forward to the lonesome evenings in his flat that last year was still occupied by Suzie during the cold, dreary days leading to Christmas.

He checked his emails again. Since Blackberry and iPhones had appeared in the workplace he could no longer go an hour without checking his account. He wondered if others, like him, had been naïve to the impact that such technological advances would have on their lifestyles. No matter what time of the day, or day of the week, Richard never really felt like he could switch off from the world. Even when he was on holiday he panicked that people wouldn't understand that he wasn't instantly contactable. His stomach cramped every time he allowed himself just one day off checking his emails. He never felt an *"out of office"* reply was adequate. It seemed that now it was possible to work from anywhere, there was no actual reason or excuse not to.

His messages were mainly generic sales but seated in between emails from Virgin Atlantic and Vodafone was a message from Suzie. His heart leapt: she had only replied to one of his many emails since she had left. The anticipation of this second reply lifted him, it gave him hope that maybe he had not lost everything, that in the deep recesses of her mind she may still be willing to give him another chance.

11

Molly

The police station was a haze of questions, of rooms, of polite smiles and reassuring nods to begin with and uncertain eyebrows later on. I had approached the front desk and suddenly lost my words. Luckily Alison had found them for me: "We want to report a crime of a delicate nature," she told the desk sergeant.

I was led into a back room where a mumsy female officer and young man seated me before taking a statement. I could tell they didn't believe me – well he certainly didn't. The more I spoke the less plausible it all seemed. I knew how it sounded, how I would be viewed. I was so angry at myself for allowing this to happen to me, so angry, yet somewhere, deep down, there was a little voice telling me to go on: to carry on talking, that Jacob should not get away with what he did, that he had to pay for what he had taken from me, that what he did was not fair.

I wanted to ring my mum. I wanted her to know what had happened, what would now happen, but I knew that was impossible. What would I say?

I had not spoken to her in six months: she lived abroad with her boyfriend. It had been weeks since her last email, which was typical of my mother. We had never had the closest relationship, not that we didn't get on, but we were different. My mum had always been much more glamorous than me and I always felt like she was disappointed in me.

I stayed in the police station three hours in total. They offered me a solicitor, but I refused. I had not done anything wrong, so I could not understand why I would need legal advice. Alison waited with me.

I felt an element of resolution initially. I had hoped for this moment where I would feel absolution, the weight of it all finally lifted. I was wrong. It was intimidating. The police were dismissive, and as we left the building I knew how ridiculous I had sounded, how silly I had been to assume otherwise. I just felt exhausted and sick.

Jacob

Jacob knew the policy of automatically believing victims was redundant in reality. The police were mistrusted by rape accusers, maybe because they were all too aware how quickly their lies would be exposed.

Jacob found the whole process inherently surreal. It was clinical and dismissive and the police treated him with indifference. The case quite clearly a waste of their time as much as it was of his.

Molly's lies had probably gathered pace before she'd had a chance to thwart them; he could imagine how she'd become trapped in her own web of words. Jacob was aware what he needed to do. Molly's account would ultimately be inconsistent and he could expose the irregularities in her story quickly.

Molly's anger was all too apparent to Jacob. She could not handle her feelings towards him so had twisted the whole situation until she appeared to be the innocent party. He was aware of the growing social injustices of our time, of the abhorrent manner in which men were treated by such women, their lives a pawn in their constructed versions of events. What disgusted Jacob the most was Molly's willingness to discredit what real rape victims would have experienced; her malicious act remaining anonymous whilst she undermined rape victims everywhere.

The procedures in these cases seemed illogical to Jacob. The stigma associated with such a charge could not be eradicated once a case was dropped. And it would not even be erased if he was found innocent, as, ultimately, he would be. He could not understand why anonymity did not apply to both parties.

Stephanie

Jacob Walker-Kent's mother was at reception. I had no idea why she had come to see me, but Audrey had telephoned to indicate her presence. I cannot discuss a case with anyone other than my client unless instructed or they are present. I would let her in to my office and tell her this, then I would ask her to leave politely so I could focus on the case in question. That usually did the job with overbearing relatives. Plus, I had court shortly and many emails and letters to process before I left chambers. I did not have time for this.

I headed to reception to greet her. The lady standing waiting was very striking. She had the face of someone who had been stunningly beautiful in her day. She was tall, and extremely slim and immaculately dressed in a white suit which I had seen in Reiss the week before. I had avoided the temptation as the price tag was too extravagant. I introduced myself, and I told her to follow me through to my office.

Mrs Walker-Kent, or Ms as she had quickly corrected me, took a seat eagerly. I had hoped I could tell her my predicament regarding her son whilst she was still standing and she'd be on her way, but it was apparent she was forceful when it came to Jacob.

"Miss Beaumont." She addressed me with the assumption I was single. "I am here to ascertain what you intend to do for my son in this frightful situation. Jacob has informed me you are more than capable, but I insisted I need to confirm your credentials myself, from the horse's mouth shall we say." She paused and stared at me intensely. I had not realised she had come here to interview me.

I was briefly taken aback by her stance, I had never in all my years been interrogated by a grown man's mother as to my expertise when it came to defending a client.

"Well, Ms Walker-Kent, I can understand your concern, but I can also reassure you that I am more than qualified to represent your son. If you would like I could print you a copy of my CV that you could take away to peruse." I could not disguise the hint of sarcasm in my reply.

"I would prefer you to tell me whether you have represented such cases as my son's before and if so the outcome you achieved. I would also prefer if you told me how exactly you intend to prove that this whole business is a pile of nonsense. That despicable girl doing this to poor Jacob, it is just not right, and I would like to know how you intend to stop her. That is my sole concern here, not some documentation of your university results."

I bit down on my tongue, and I tried to remain composed. I had met many people like *Ms* Walker-Kent during my time on the bar.

She was the type of woman who had gone through the years believing that her standing and importance hold some weight with people like me. She was misplaced in her snobbery and arrogance; the type of lady who would talk down to a waitress; and assume that because she wore Louboutin shoes and Versace scarves that people should look up to her: envy her. She was full of materialistic swagger, but I could guarantee beneath all the fashion and money there was little to her. I imagined a vacant life filled with shopping and lunches involving copious amounts of wine.

I had no doubt she loved her son, and I admired her overt protectiveness of him; however I wanted to outwardly sneer at her ignorance. For she had managed to create a man who saw himself above the law; a man who she believed was beyond justice whether he was guilty or not. Her precious Jacob could do no wrong, and I knew from the start that I could do no right, so I did not pander to her. I did not succumb to flattery. I was rude back, and, though I did not know it at the time, I think this won me her respect.

"Ms Walker-Kent, I think you will find my university results reflect my capabilities. The fact I received the highest grades in law school when I graduated is not irrelevant: it is a reflection of my competence. I am not a successful defence criminal barrister because I am not very good at my job, and I do not appreciate the manner in which you have approached me and questioned my ability today. If you care that much for your son rather than waste both our time by assuming I need to prove myself to you, you would think to leave my office, and let me get on with the job in hand: proving Jacob's innocence. Now if that is all, I will ask Audrey to show you the door."

At that I buzzed through to reception, and I asked Audrey to escort Ms Walker-Kent out of the building. The woman looked dumbfounded as if no one had challenged her in years, I however felt like I had won a small victory, without even knowing I had been going into battle.

Richard

Richard returned to his accommodation to read the email. He headed to his room overlooking the harbour and ordered room service: bread and butter pudding and a pint of real ale. He had requested that the log fire be lit in his room, he pulled the large leather armchair in front of the wood burner, and he placed the burgundy woollen blanket over his lap. He placed his feet in the sheepskin slippers he brought with him from London and leant his head back breathing in the smells mingling together in the room; the nutmeg and cinnamon from the pudding coupled with the wood smoke. He was reminded of his childhood spent in his father's small bungalow an hour's drive from London.

Richard had grown up in a small suburb of Swindon: a soulless place full of people hoping to make enough money to get out. Green land was sparse, as was outdoor activity, which was limited to a rundown park rusted around the edges, the swings creaking eerily of memories of childhoods gone by. His friends and he spent hours kicking balls up against the neighbour's side wall, dreaming of places they could escape to and hoping that the day would come sooner than they had all imagined.

His father worked at Aldermaston, the nuclear weapons plant. They survived comfortably, and their house was full of quiet, studious study in the evening. His father had loved to cook dishes from his northern English heritage, and Richard had lived off pies, toad in the hole, faggots and thick stodgy puddings for the majority of his childhood. It was only when he was fourteen years old, a gangly teen, that his future stepmother had come to live with them, and his diet and lifestyle changed overnight.

Suddenly Mediterranean, Indian and far eastern dishes were served at the dinner table, as were talks of holidays to places where the waiters smashed plates, or the women wore clothes over their faces. Places where the children didn't go to school, where the shops closed for two hours in the middle of the day for people to sleep; places entirely foreign to him floated through their conversations.

Cathy, as he had always called his stepmother, opened the world to him. It was the most unexpected gift, and Richard had not since stopped unpacking it. However, work had taken over more and more recently, and slowly those trips to other cultures, or the meals to restaurants to taste new flavour combinations, had dwindled, until he realised he was living in a box: just like the one he was born in. Yet, this time he was the one who had put himself there, and he was the only one who could escape the cage he had created.

12

Molly

I had finally gathered the courage to tell Luke about Jacob when I returned from the police station. I no longer had a choice as to whether it remained a secret. I knew he would find out eventually, and I wanted it to come from me. I had expected Luke to be angry, incredulous even. I had anticipated a fallout, a lack of belief, horrid words and an explosive row. Alison had warned me on the way home that Luke's reaction may not be pretty, but given time he would calm down; he would understand why I had not told him. I was worried that he would lash out, I did not want him to get into any trouble by beating Jacob up or something stupid like that.

What I had not considered was silence. A distinct absence of reaction. I had not expected him to tell me he was leaving, to stay somewhere else whilst he got his head together. I had not imagined that I would have to miss him, that he would leave me. I had hoped he would believe me. I had just wanted him to fold me into his arms and tell me it would all be all right.

Instead he put a distance between us instantly. His body

recoiled towards the doorway, and it was as if he couldn't get to the exit soon enough. I knew in that moment that all he felt was disgust at me, at Jacob, at what had happened. He was simply disgusted by me.

The last thing he said as he closed the front door haunts me as I lie awake weeks later in our empty house. The noise of the first cars are beginning this morning. It is 5.43am, and the work brigade are starting their daily journeys. The hazy light of dawn begins to illuminate our curtains, and I am glad the day will begin soon. It means I no longer must lie here: awake, alone and scared of all the noises in the house. I can rise soon and dress. I can wash. I can pretend I have some purpose. I can put up my barriers and face another day. I can play make believe and wish I was anywhere else but here, when internally I crumble all the time replaying that last cutting sentence Luke delivered:

"And to think, Molly, you let me inside of you after you'd fucked him."

The memory still makes my stomach heave, my heart lurch. My mouth fills with bile again. The one man I thought I could trust disintegrating in my memory. I rush to the bathroom and vomit over the basin.

Jacob

Jacob had just sat down for what felt like the first time today with a cup of tea when his mother appeared at his elbow. "You really should use a coaster, darling."

Since the arrival of the police on his doorstep he could not get a moment's peace – or as Molly used to say, "a piece of quiet". She had refused to leave London after that day. She had assumed responsibility for Jacob's well-being even though he had not needed, or wanted, her help.

He had tried to raise the issue, he had looked at train times, and told her she could leave on numerous occasions, adding, "Would you like me to buy you a ticket?"

But she had stood tall, and said, "I am not leaving my little boy, not when he needs me. Mummy is here for you, darling."

He had wanted to push her physically out the door at that moment. The role she created as his mother was nauseating. She had always mollycoddled him, but at any sign of danger her protectiveness increased to immeasurable levels. She had spent the previous weeks endlessly scanning the internet for evidence, or research, into false rape allegations that would help prove his innocence and increase his chances of acquittal.

She had been to see Stephanie once to discuss the matter. She had told him beforehand, but when she returned home she refused to talk about their conversation or what had occurred between them. Now, whenever he mentioned his barrister's name his mother lifted her chin, and went quiet.

This pleased him somewhat. He liked the fact that Stephanie offended her in some way, and he thought more of her than he had before, he liked her fiercely defensive manner and intense professionalism.

He wondered what it would be like to get under her skin, to know the real Stephanie, the woman behind the suit. He wanted to know where she lived, what she ate for dinner, what she did of a weekend. He wanted to see her stripped bare: no make-up, no guard, just her, rather than the barrister, the lawyer, the career-driven woman. He wanted to know what book was on her bedside table, whether she wore pyjamas or knickers to bed, if she moisturised, what music she listened to, where she holidayed.

He had thought Molly was his type, his ideal wife, but now he saw the error of his ways. Molly was incapable of owning up to her convictions: to how she felt, to making love. Molly he had thought of as sweet and reliable, but now he realised that Stephanie was much more his type, a woman who was not afraid of herself, who would not backtrack when it came to her actions. She was the type of woman who could take control of a situation, and Jacob wondered what it would feel like for Stephanie to take control of him.

He had found himself emailing her an awful lot. Of course the content concerned his case, and any further developments, but he got a thrill if her reply was even slightly casual; it meant he was managing to break down her barriers.

He was on strict instructions not to contact Molly as this may damage his case, but he had not been told that contacting her friends was not allowed, so he sent the odd text, left answerphone messages with some of them. He did not contact any of them more than twice, as knowing Molly and her twisted mind she would claim he was harassing them. He had spent time with these people, he had socialised with them, eaten meals with them, drunk in bars with them and now it was like he had never existed. They had pooled around Molly, and her story, without giving him even the chance to explain what had happened.

It hurt him deeply that they would not hear him out. His mother had told him that he should not bother with their type anyway. She had given him an ear-bashing as to how they were not of his standing, and told him he could do a lot better than wasting his time with them: "For one, Jacob, isn't that Hannah, her friend from school you told me about, isn't she unemployed?" She had raised an eyebrow then as if that excused any further explanation.

To a certain extent Jacob agreed with his mother. It was true a lot of Molly's friends had little prospects. They whinged about the government, refusing to take responsibility for their unemployment or situations, living a bohemian lifestyle whilst not contributing to the state they wished to feed off. He hadn't ever really liked them, but it was the principle that they thought they could just wash their hands of him without a thought as to how Molly may have wrecked his life and his reputation. They did not care for the stress she had created for him or what really happened that night.

It is typical of women, he thought, *to collude with one another, to reinforce each other's unreasonable behaviour. They play the vulnerable card, and the victim, when in fact most of the time it is the other way around.*

Stephanie

I had not intentionally wanted to start running again. It was as if my body suddenly had the urge to take up the hobby I thought I had put behind me years previously. Running for me had always represented an escape from the reality of the pressures in my job, the endless caseload. When I put my trainers on there were moments when I would almost reach a meditative state, I would forget about life around me, what I had left to do that evening, I would concentrate on the rhythm of my body moving, one foot in front of other.

In my late twenties I had run many half marathons. I even tried my hand at the London Marathon one year, only to be blighted by injury for a year afterwards, which stopped my running routine in its tracks. At the time, the training had quickly become part of my lifestyle: the eighteen to twenty-mile runs on Saturday mornings. It was only after I completed the challenge that I realised the gravity of such a feat. I had not been able to remember the majority of the course as soon as I had crossed the finish line, as if my conscious mind had erased the pain I had experienced and the determination I had conjured up throughout it. I vividly remember the deafening noise of the crowds, the overwhelming feeling of having so many people scream my name for four hours at a time. I had snapshots of different points throughout the race, Tower Bridge being one, the noise had almost knocked me over as I had turned the corner to cross the famous structure. It was intensely loud, so different to the quiet training runs I had undertaken for five months, where I was anonymous as I paced the pavements.

I had only run one more event after the marathon, and it had not held the same thrill. It was as if I had completed the best in the world, and the crowds, the course, the feeling of achievement when running could never compare to London itself. Now I ran for fun, I did not push my breathing so it became laboured. I ran so, if I wished, I could talk, I could sing. I ran to relax, to forget and most of the time it worked, but not today.

Jacob Walker-Kent's case is endlessly travelling through my thoughts. His statement and Molly's replay in my mind. There is something niggling at me about the case, yet I cannot pinpoint it. I cannot decipher what does not add up.

To all intents and purposes, it is clear-cut, a classic case of a girl who cheated on her boyfriend and then tried to backtrack. Jacob presents himself well: he is polite, respectful, from a privileged background and well educated. He has all the hallmarks of a perfect client who will get off. Yet, there is a minute doubt in the back of my mind concerning him. I cannot help but question whether his privileged upbringing has made him think he is entitled. Entitled to Molly Smith for instance.

Legally speaking, to secure a rape conviction the prosecution needs to prove two things, plain and simple: firstly, that the complainant, Molly in this case, did not consent. And secondly, the defendant, Jacob, did not reasonably believe that the complainant, Molly, was consenting. I cannot see how Richard

Clarke intends to play this case in court. Whatever his tack, he is going to have a job on his hands. He may be able to convince the jury that Molly did not actively consent, but I cannot see how given the evidence – the videos, Jacob's statement, the text messages sent after where she does not mention "rape" – he can convince them that Jacob reasonably believed Molly wasn't consenting.

S1 (2) of the Sexual Offences Act 2003 clearly states that whether a belief is reasonable is to be determined having regard to all the circumstances. Cue my opportunity to involve Jacob's interpretation of Molly's "sexual signals"; her intoxication on the evening; and her behaviour in the lead-up to the event. All I need to do is put a tiny doubt in the jury's minds and they cannot convict. If they have any reasonable doubt as to his guilt, they must acquit him. It is almost too easy to play the system, to win the game, and that is all it is in court: a game, where someone wins, and the other one loses. Most of the time it is nothing to do with truth or justice at all.

Richard

He read Suzie's email slowly and repeatedly. He re-scanned her words trying to find some suggestion that what she was saying was a cruel joke just to hurt him. He hoped desperately that her news was a hoax. He could not fathom how she had moved on so quickly, how she could do this to him.

Suzie had started with the usual pleasantries, outlining her surroundings, the climate, how her work was going before launching into an account of her new life. She wrote about how happy she was, how she had made the best decision moving out of the UK, and now she was reaping the rewards. She wanted to make sure there was no bad feeling between them, and to reassure Richard that the choice to separate had not been a mistake, or an easy decision at that. Suzie wrote how sure she was that Richard would be pleased to know she was well, and how she had received an unexpected gift from her new partner... a baby developing inside her.

Richard had retched when he read this last bit, and he had been overcome with anger, resentment, sadness and shame all in one.

It took him a while to absorb the news, he just sat in his chair blankly staring at the wall. He did not read on past that point. He did not need to. It was so final. The moment he read that she was pregnant, all the hope he had been clinging to disintegrated. He had fooled himself for months that she may come back to him, that she may change her mind, she may realise that it had been a terrible mistake.

He had felt numb initially to her leaving, as if he was caught up in a scenario that didn't particularly involve him. He had been surprised as to how worried his family and friends had been about him. He had felt fine, though, as if he just had to hold on until it all went back to normal.

Suzie had been such a constant. She was always there, and he had assumed she always would be. He now realised that this was his downfall. He had taken for granted the most precious thing in his life. Suzie had just become part of the daily surroundings, the background noise of normality. He hadn't realised she had minded. He had thought her so laid back: for instance, she had looked mildly disappointed when he had forgotten to get her a card on her birthday, but he had bought her one, two days later, so assumed she had moved past his error.

He had been working too much, and maybe neglected the fact that she too had a job. He had looked forward to their weekends when he could let his hair down and forget his troubles; but she had become irate by his urge to drink copious amounts of booze and his hangovers. He had not understood. In their twenties, they had both enjoyed a hedonistic lifestyle, but Suzie was suddenly growing up, and he couldn't seem to catch up with the change in her. He had battled it, he supposed, resented the fact that she wanted to leave the carefree party days behind. He suddenly remembered ranting at her: "I'm not changing for anyone. You've got no right to stop my fun."

He had thought she would listen, she would back down. He certainly was not going to allow her to control him, but in retrospect he realised that what she was saying was, "I want to get off. I'm not enjoying the ride." He hadn't realised she wasn't prepared to stay on for his sake. He hadn't realised that one day she too would value her happiness as much as his, and even put hers before his.

When she had left, she had not really said much. It was as if she was quietly resigned. She was normally so feisty with so much to say, but after she packed her bags she refused to see him for a week. When she finally did she sat there blankly as if she'd heard it all before.

"I'll change," he'd said. "I didn't realise how far things had gone. I'll do anything to have you back."

But it was as if a switch had flicked in her brain. All the guilt and responsibility she had harboured for his happiness had vanished. She no longer had the capacity to care so deeply for him because he had abused it so thoroughly in the past.

He wished now, he could have stopped things getting so far. It was only months later that he really understood the pattern of behaviour that had irreversibly damaged their relationship. It was only when it was all too late that he finally realised what he had to lose.

13

Molly

When I think back to the evening it happened I must reassure myself that just because he did not follow me down a dark alley, and he did not threaten me with violence or death, it does not mean what he did to me was okay. He was not a stranger. He is not tall and powerful. He did not leave me beaten and bloodied – but I must remember that this does not matter. It was still wrong – what he did was wrong.

I try to continue as best as I know possible. I attempt to drown in London and all its busy trappings. The case is a few weeks away, and I am living in a constant state of anxiety. I have forgotten what resembles normality. It all seems so alien to me now: a place I used to occupy that no longer exists. On the weekends, I jump from tube to tube. I search the streets for a purpose to get me through the days. I am blindly wandering, hoping that if I look like I have a direction I may in fact find one.

I tend to go where deep pools of people congregate. Today Oxford Street is swarming. The crowds surge forward into shops and back out again; Hamleys has already adopted their one-way system, and it is only November. I enter the store aware how busy it will be, but I cannot resist the temptation of children's toys, the larger-than-life playroom that makes me imagine a film set. It will also kill time for half an hour or so. I wish I had come here as a child, that I had seen the delights piled high through the eyes of a little one. Even now as an adult the shop feels magical in its entirety. I do not know why I spend so much time browsing. I do not want to buy any of the toys, but the shop is comforting. I think I feel safe here with all the noise and lights. Everywhere I look there are families looking forward to festive celebrations.

I think of Christmas and realise that the court case will be in full swing by then, and I suddenly feel sick, claustrophobic. I need to get out of the shop. Sweat beads on my forehead; the anxiety begins to rise in my chest, I battle the sea of bodies and break into the fresh air just in time. It is raining. I let myself get soaked. It will give me something to do when I arrive home. I will need to undress, bath, warm up, re-dress and wash my clothes. It will take up at least another hour of my day, that once was filled with Luke and friends and is now just an empty abyss, the light long extinguished at the end of the tunnel.

It takes me over an hour to get back to my front door, and my skin has begun to wrinkle I am so soggy and cold. I rush inside, and flick the lights on in the hallway. It is already dark outside. The lights in the living room and kitchen are already on, I do not switch them off anymore. I methodically turn on every other light in the house, and I search the rooms for any evidence of a break-in. I do not trust this house any longer. It tricked me once with its pretence of safety.

After I wash and dry myself and load the washing machine, I layer myself in two vests, a jumper, leggings, pyjama bottoms, slippers and a thick dressing gown. I am always cold.

It is still only 7pm, and I have the whole evening ahead of

me, I decide to make food. I busy myself with chocolate chip cookies to begin, then I make creamy mash potato and sausages soaked in gravy; I manage five forkfuls of mash potato and a bite of one of the dozen cookies, then throw it all in the bin. I do not eat dinner. It is the process I enjoy rather than the result of cooking these days, that alongside the fact I am never hungry – eating seems pointless to me, but cooking fills my time. The thought of food makes me queasy. My body seems to be rejecting anything that may replenish it: everything tastes off.

After I have cleaned my mess I settle in front of the TV to watch *The X Factor*. It is the usual candidates: the pretty office worker, the handyman who has a hidden talent, a band that have been trying for years, and one that has been put together last week. I allow myself to get sucked into the commercialism, the world of vacuous entertainment. At 8.36 I receive a text. It is from Alison. She asks if I would like to join her and one of the fellow teachers for a drink at 9.30. I hurriedly text back:

Sorry plans tonight. I have friends over. Thanks tho, see you soon x

I sink back into the sofa and the thought of my own endless company tomorrow. It is easier this way.

Jacob

He spent the last of the autumn nights and the beginning of winter alone and drunk. Jacob had soon realised that he had many fair-weather friends, and it was increasingly difficult to meet up with them as news had spread of the charges Molly had brought against him. He was angry and lonely, and he sunk into a depression that revolved around sleep, alcohol, the internet and the TV. He had managed to banish his mother from his house briefly. She had suffocated him for weeks, and he wanted nothing more than to wallow in his own pity and determine how he spent his days.

His neighbour, a divorcee in her fifties with expensively coloured hair and the tendency to wear too much perfume, had tried to help, and she had taken to dropping over Tupperwares of soup. She knew he was having some personal trouble, and he was certain if she were to discover its nature the well-meaning gifts of food would soon halt. As his father used to say, "shit sticks". He was innocent, but that was not to say the allegations would not give rise to questions from even his closest friends.

He has stopped trying to contact Molly: it is against his bail application for a start, but he really has nothing to say to her. He still cannot believe the level of betrayal on her part. He does not know what he has done to deserve this treatment.

When he is not drunk, Jacob trawls the internet looking for anything that will support his case, he searches through endless amounts of press on false allegations, and he stalks Molly on Facebook and Twitter for evidence of their relationship and how she behaved towards him. He prints out reams and reams of paper documenting their communication; he takes photos of his texts and prints those too; he collects evidence of their relationship from beginning to end; he prints endless selfies of both of them posing for the camera, their heads touching, smiles plastered on their faces. To the outsider they appeared very much the happy couple in these snippets of time; the fragments that are now left of their relationship.

Jacob has been out on a few nights with some of his male friends, but their bravado and surety that he will get off irritates him. They dismiss what Molly is doing to him as just "another difficult girlfriend episode". They do not seem to understand how much she is ruining his life, destroying his reputation and everything he has created for himself. She has turned him into an "accused rapist" for Christ's sake, and they just slap him on the back, and tell him not to worry about it as they order another pint at the bar.

He feels alone. There is no one he can talk or turn to – his mother is his biggest supporter, but she gets angry at Molly, and she tries to control him. His female friends seemed to have evaporated within a matter of weeks, and everywhere he turns there are whispers and rumours surrounding his life. He feels the need to get away, but then he does not want to look as if he is running because it has all become too much to handle. He knows he must stick it out. He must maintain his presence because, ultimately, he has nothing to hide. It is Molly who should be ashamed. She is the one who led him on, slept with him and then lied. She should be the one on the stand here but instead it is him.

Stephanie

It is a minefield when it comes to burden of proof issues in cases such as Jacob's: where there is no witness involvement, no forensic or medical evidence. If a man can equivocally prove that there was consent it would make the process a whole lot easier, less grey shall I say? There wouldn't be so many shadows lurking over the defence.

I believe the onus should be on men, that rather than concentrate campaigns on women and their personal safety we should target men, increase their awareness of their responsibilities so they can ensure that sex is always mutually agreed. I don't advocate victim-blaming, however I use the notion of it to win.

A friend I used to know had the following analogy to explain how the thought process occurs: "If someone is walking in the middle of the road and they are struck by a car, there is an element of responsibility on the victim who was involved in the road accident. We can easily say that they should have been on the pavement; they weren't being road aware, there were steps they could have taken to assure they stayed safe; there were steps they could have taken to prevent the accident occurring. It is the same with rape cases: a girl who goes out and gets drunk, puts herself in a vulnerable position, is more likely to get raped – just like someone who stands in the middle of the road is more likely to get hit by a vehicle."

We skate around this idea of responsibility of one's safety as if it is an unthinkable principle to mention when it comes to rape. Feminists scream out in all the newspapers, "Rape victims aren't to blame." I am not saying they are to blame, I am rather advocating that taking responsibility for one's safety is necessary in all walks of life. Of course, if the unthinkable happens, and you are a victim of rape, it is awful; nobody deserves it, but I am also an advocate for, where you can, prevention rather than cure. This does not mean you can prevent all cases of rape, but taking responsibility for your safety is certainly a useful tool when we are discussing stranger-rape. If you can avoid putting yourself in a vulnerable position then I say do so.

I am not an anti-feminist because I argue this, I am not shunning rape victims everywhere I am merely talking about common sense. Do not walk home on your own late at night, make sure your friends know where you are, carry an alarm, get into a registered taxi, do not get so intoxicated someone can take advantage of you. Of course they shouldn't, no matter what kind of a state a girl is in, but have more self-respect for your body; look after it so someone else doesn't have to, or worse still, someone else doesn't have the opportunity to do what they want with it.

But Jacob Walker-Kent and Molly Smith's case is different. I do not believe that, if Jacob is guilty of rape, Molly for a minute believed herself to be at risk. I do not think she was looking out for the man walking beside her, the man who said he'd make sure she got home okay. No, I think Molly was probably looking for the stranger in the shadows, the monster hiding behind the hedges. But regardless of this, can Molly honestly say she didn't lead him on? She didn't make him believe that she too wanted sex? I have seen the video. It is quite clear she is teasing him, toying with his emotions. She may have merely wanted a thrill whilst her boyfriend wasn't looking, but was that fair on Jacob? And could her behaviour be misconstrued to the point that he honestly did believe she wanted sex, that she consented to sex?

The questions that keep on bubbling to the surface when I think of Jacob and Molly repeat themselves over and over. Is it reasonable that Jacob thought Molly fancied him? My logic says yes, she got drunk with him, she danced provocatively, she asked him to take her home, she asked him in for coffee, she snuggled up with him under a blanket on the sofa. Now, in this sequence of events if I were to say: "and then things got more passionate, they kissed and this led to sex", there is nothing shocking here? That could reasonably be the outcome of the facts I have laid before me, but I must remember that this is not to say that is how it happened.

I must keep a clear mind, because when I believe the case in hand is a certainty, that there is no ambiguity, I miss things. I miss details. I forget to clarify facts, and that is when I'm in danger, because that is when I put myself at risk of losing, and no one wants to lose no matter where the truth lies.

Richard

Richard pulls his dressing gown tighter. He had underestimated the cold, the temperature has dropped by around eight degree Celsius, it is making moving harder than it need be. Cornwall seems like a distant memory as he plods around his flat on Tuesday morning. He glances over at his unpacked suitcase still discarded by the front door.

He flicks on the television, as he waits for his Nespresso coffee machine to work its magic. The Steubenville rape case is the topic of conversation again: the young football stars involved in raping a classmate whilst she was so intoxicated at a party she was unable to consent. The accused were in the news again following the Stanford rape case, which had reignited the issue of sexual assaults on university campuses.

He sat on the sofa with his coffee and listened to the news anchors take on the case. What fascinated Richard most about the case was the way in which the perpetrators of the crime were treated: how they were perceived in the media. He held the coffee mug firmly in his hands, his knuckles clenched so tight they turned white. He hated this "culture of rape". Richard knew that Steubenville was not particularly unusual. Across America there were countless cases of rapes that occurred in similar circumstances. Richard wondered how you shifted society's discourse.

The accused come into view on screen, they are confident, assured. It is no wonder. The perpetrators were worshipped in Steubenville. He placed his empty coffee mug down and sighed as he walked towards his window to check the weather. The wind whipped against his window, the tree opposite had shed all its leaves, he had not noticed. He sighed as the television continued with the report in the background, the anchor was discussing the prevalence of these incidents and attitudes towards them, but they were not limited to America: it was a worldwide problem. The case was transcendent: unlimited to one geographical area in its narrative.

He went to the bedroom where he changed into his suit. He despised the fact he must wear a suit every day. He was going to be late. Given it is inevitable, he decides to walk to work – he is in no rush to get back to his caseload. He finds his brown brogues, as he bends to lace them the lady on screen begins to discuss the fallen careers of the football players, she is emphasising the fault of the victim and her level of intoxication. He paused in exacerbation at the sympathy towards the perpetrators. The star quarterbacks were assumed to not have known what they did was wrong, apparently they did not understand their behaviour at the time. His head in his hands now, he wondered what they were teaching in schools these days, if these kids could not even safeguard one another from making terrible mistakes, which they would all later pay for.

He switched the television off, he could not bear reporting of this context any longer. He scanned the fridge quickly before he left, there was nothing worthy of a meal so he'd have to stop off on his way home to pick up dinner. He left the flat and was hit by the crowded streets, even though he hadn't stayed long in Cornwall, it always hit him how busy London was on his return.

He put his headphones in and tried to distract himself with music, but he could not help replay the Steubenville case in his mind. The case at a basic level was the story of superior male athletes who sexually assaulted a girl, filmed the assault, laughed about the assault, and then assumed they were entitled to protection due to some misplaced elitist belief. Following this they still received sympathy from the world's press. *Unbelievable.*

He is waiting for the traffic lights to change so he can cross the road, when the woman in front of him turns her head, "Pardon. Have you got a problem?"

He hadn't realised he was speaking out loud. "Sorry, that

wasn't aimed at you, I was just thinking aloud. She turns away, clearly disinterested in his response.

The longer he walked the more he turned over the idea in his head. Richard could only conclude that the current climate had a value system where women were sexual currency, and men were enabled to get, or take sex, from them. But then this did not shock Richard, after all America was the country where in a number of states if rape results in a baby the rapist could end up with visitation rights to the given child. The UK was not far behind with its elitist misogynist legal system, with laws against marital rape only being created in 1991.

Richard knew that people just did not think rape was awful enough to ruin someone's life for: it simply wasn't considered that bad a crime. He knew that to change societal attitudes about rape people had to understand different viewpoints, even the viewpoints of those boys in the Steubenville case. If people were not willing to attempt to understand the attitudes, motives, starting points and values of those who rape, and instead just disagree and disregard their views as invalid, then how could anyone change them? Richard believed you had to infiltrate to instigate change. He thought if he, or society as a whole, could get into the minds of these men; the minds of the judgemental and prejudiced jurors; of one-sided sensational media commentators, the problem of this deep-rooted rape culture could be tackled.

Richard knew the facts, he knew that worldwide women between fifteen and forty-years-old were more likely to die or be injured at the hands of male violence than from cancer, war, malaria or traffic accidents combined. But, he also knew this fight, this statistic, could not be changed with feminism, with accusations of misogyny. The transformation required needed a far deeper understanding.

Only yesterday morning he had read facts and figures

concerning sexual assaults across the world. He was disgusted to discover in South Africa a woman was raped every four minutes, and women there were three times more likely to be raped than receive an education. In Sudan, an eighteen-year-old woman who had been gang-raped by several men was facing a possible death sentence as she was charged with adultery. Richard was strangely unperturbed: he was not shocked by these cases. The coverage ignited his fury, but it was not a new or even a recent awakening for Richard. He had known about these injustices for years, and more often than he cared to remember he had witnessed them on his own doorstep.

Maybe it was the casual use of the word "rape", the way it was used in jokes – a term so easily laughed at and dismissed as trivial. Richard had heard his friends using it to describe a losing team after a rugby game, "they so got raped, man". He wondered when this shift in language had occurred, when rape and sexual assault had entered the language of humour, downgraded in its seriousness.

As he reached his office, he wondered whether this too had affected the boys' perceptions of their behaviour in the Steubenville case. Had they grown up in a world where rape or sexual assault was something to joke about, a laugh with friends, something that happened to girls who secretly wanted it?

Maybe along the way the idea of rape got blurred? Maybe the boys did not even realise that their behaviour that night would be considered rape. Maybe they had truly believed the taunts of "it's not rape if…" Maybe they honestly thought that if a girl is too inebriated, or asleep, or was flirting earlier on in the night that it was okay. That they had a free pass to do what they wished with her.

He waved at his colleagues as he entered chambers, he had no interest in conversing with anyone today unless it was absolutely necessary for work. As he sat down at his desk, a pain shot up his back, his sciatica always flared up when he was stressed with work. He opened Molly Smith's file and wondered if society had a part to play in this world we have grown up in, a world where we allowed rape to be used as a form of humour, a world where forms of sexual assaults were accepted and normalised as part of our existence. *And if this is the case*, he thought, *we should all be morally responsible for the actions of the teenagers and their learnt behaviour.*

14

Molly

I do not sleep these days. Sometimes I seem to doze, but I never drift off properly; my evenings are filled with cold sweats and night terrors. I lie awake listening for any unknown noise – my heart thumping in my chest. I am always on high alert. I run over my behaviour in my head: the woman I am or have been. I terrorise myself with memories of my inappropriate flirting and body language when I was with Luke.

I question who I am, all the decisions I have made, I cannot help but beat myself up. It is as if the personality I have been given, have grown into, is suddenly not right, I feel like it has hijacked me, led me to a place where men whom I thought were friends could take something from me: men who I allowed into my house, who I flirted with, who I danced with, whose laps I sat on, whose drinks I accepted. My world is now a place where men I trusted betray me. Maybe I had led Jacob on. Had he thought I fancied him all along? I'd spent lots of time with him, maybe I had flirted. When I look back I wonder why it came as such a shock, because when I look at it all objectively there is only one conclusion I can come to that this – whatever it is – is all my fault.

Why hadn't I just gone home early that night. If I'd just stuck with Luke. Why had I not just left with him, taken myself home quietly. I could never leave with him on a night out, never take myself home quietly. I think back to how much wine I had drunk, how I was dancing. Maybe I had wanted him to want me. Maybe I liked knowing that I could have Jacob... if I wanted. I liked being in control. I didn't realise I had no control at all until it was all too late.

I wish I could go back six years and start all over again. I desperately wish I was in Australia again. Luke and I had just met, and it was the heady light exhilarating first weeks of our relationship. I had felt so young then, younger than my early twenties. I had felt like I was sixteen years old again when I had first met Luke. He was so spontaneous and I found myself wanting to keep up, everything I thought I had feared in the past I became fearless of when I was with him. We had stayed in Australia until our visas ran out, until the reality of Britain called us home, and we gave up fighting "settling down" and "starting our careers".

If I had known what I do now I would have not rushed to start it all so quickly. I wanted to be secure with Luke, and for some reason I assumed that "security" was rent, mortgages, nine to five, but I had never felt as secure as when we were both having fun, living in the moment with one another. Literally, taking things day by day with only adventure on our side. Everything I thought I needed had ended up being not what I had wanted at all.

Jacob

Looking back, he could not understand how he hadn't seen it. How hadn't he realised what kind of girl she was. She had presented herself all sweetness and light, the Miss Honey persona from *Matilda* had fooled him, but there was no denying the reality of Molly now. She was a cock-tease. The kind of girl who needed men around her to flatter her; to make her feel like she was something special. He had met girls like her many a time before, but Jacob had thought Molly was different.

He could clearly see the web she had woven now, though. Her twisted game of reeling him in, getting him to love her, until he wanted more. She could not cope with her emotions, so instead of being honest she had cried wolf; tried to get out of what she had created. Jacob was disgusted by her. What kind of woman spends that much time in a male's company, is so affectionate with them, and when they finally deliver what she has been wanting all along, then twists the whole affair, turns it into some sordid sexual assault, because she couldn't cope with what she'd done.

His barrister Stephanie had questioned him thoroughly. She had wanted to know what Molly did to suggest she had wanted a relationship; how physical Molly was with him, and the more and more he talked about it the more he realised how much Molly had enticed him, how much she had teased him.

"Stephanie, what kind of girl sits on another man's lap when she has a boyfriend?" He had questioned in her office just yesterday.

Stephanie had rolled her eyes in agreement. She was not the kind of woman to offer herself up so freely, to put her body out there so openly. She seemed like a lady: honourable. Ladies, like Stephanie, would never offer themselves up like Molly had done.

Jacob always seemed to choose the wrong girl. The loose women, as his mother would refer to them, the kind that he needed to remind to cover up. His previous ex-girlfriends had all been too explicit in their language or their dress. He had found them difficult to maintain, to control. He had found their behaviour infuriating. It was at times even offensive. He had been astounded at how they had behaved, all he wanted was a woman with a bit of class, a woman who did not get so blind drunk she was anyone's.

He had seen Maria, his last girlfriend, flirting with another man in front of him. She had had her hand on his chest and was laughing in his ear. It was not unusual of Maria though. They'd attended a Christmas Eve party once, and he had found her leant against a man, too drunk to hold her weight, whilst he clutched her waist. Jacob had been disgusted: not only was she embarrassing herself, but she was embarrassing him. Maria had been flightier than the other girls. She had refused to listen to his feelings; she had ignored his protests; she had not respected him or his wishes at all. She was a product of today's society, where women behave and act like men. He had eventually ended the relationship. He had told her what he thought, maybe in not the kindest of ways, but she needed to hear it. She was in Jacob's eyes a slut in disguise – and it wasn't even a very good disguise.

But, he was surprised with Molly. She was less jaded, she had this purity about her that had seemed so genuine, yet she had betrayed him in the worst possible way. His judgement of her had been mistaken, he had observed her for so long that he had really thought he had the measure of her. He was angry with himself that he had got it so, so wrong.

Stephanie

I throw myself into cooking dinner when I get home from court tonight. I want to punctuate the end of the working day. More and more I use cooking to do so, a type of therapy, slowly sedating my usual pace of life. More often than not cooking is accompanied by a glass of wine. I crave the relaxation, my state of mind altered so my daily stress is stilled.

I try to limit myself to three glasses of red wine a night – too much some would say – but I am finding it harder not to finish the bottle off. As I laze in front of the TV, it is all too easy not to pay attention as the burgundy tonic slips away. I do not drink excessively on the weekend. I am not the kind of woman that would spend the evening trawling bars desperately seeking men, necking shots and champagne. I left that behind in my twenties where it should be. There is nothing worse than seeing a woman approaching her forties, or in her thirties, still of the belief she is of the same allure of the young girls surrounding her: those spritely girls just out of university and starting internships in the city. No, I am the generation of women wine drinkers that use alcohol to switch off from their high-powered jobs, the women who lean forward so much in work they need something at home to make them feel laid back.

Tonight, I am making a stew, nothing fancy, but it is the kind of evening that demands I have something warming. I like to add an array of ingredients to my stews. I am not content with following the recipe book word for word. Alongside the chicken stock and plum tomatoes, I add a can of ale and a glug of red wine, I throw in a handful of cocoa powder, a spoonful of whole-grain mustard and five bay leaves.

Matthew despairs at my experimental style of cooking. He is more rigid when it comes to creativity in the kitchen, only following the combinations that have been tried and tested by other chefs. Matthew does not like to take risks.

I had texted him earlier, casually inviting him for dinner. He declined politely as he had already booked a table for him and Annalise at an up-and-coming exclusive eatery in North London. I had felt rather deflated at the rejection, it is not often I have the urge for company, but for some unexplained reason I rather hoped I would have someone to converse with over dinner tonight.

As I put the stew on to simmer I text Sally, in the vain hope that she may be free and not up to her eyeballs in domesticity. I take myself to the bathroom, and I run a hot bath. It is steaming when I enter and my skin feels scorched. It is strangely comforting. I can hear my phone vibrating as I lie back, and I try to switch off my brain. I have often thought I should learn meditation. I have read all the celebrities are doing it, but it just seems too self-indulgent to me; the thought of looking at my inner being, or whatever they encourage, makes me want to either laugh, or fall asleep, so I rely on other methods instead: on baths, on running, on wine, on cooking.

Come to think of it, I don't rely on anything that really slows me down apart from soaking in water, and I rarely allow myself more than ten minutes to do that. Most of what I do to relax involves moving, doing, drinking and chatting. I cannot remember the last time I properly stopped. I mean I do on holiday, when I am out of the country I allow myself to read, to sunbathe, but I suppose I also try to do an awful lot. I always sign up to activities, courses, days out. I wonder if this is because I like being busy. It is simply who I am: a doer. Or, whether I can't face the thought of stopping, of slowing down, because then I would have to reflect on my life, on where I am, who I am and why. And just maybe if I look long enough I won't like what I see.

Richard

"Richard, you don't want to be wasting your time on any of those subjects. You need a proper degree, one that means something. Law – a good, solid foundation, none of these arts degrees." He vividly remembered the conversation with his family during his youth about what direction his career should follow.

"I beg to differ, I've always thought of my son as a science man, takes after his father, don't you, Richard?"

He had barely got a word in edgeways, as they sat eating one of Cathy's Greek dishes that Sunday afternoon.

"Knowledge is power, Richard." His uncle was an activist, and thought Richard could promote positive change in the law from within.

"This is delicious, Cathy." Richard always enjoyed her cooking.

"Thank you, Richard. And don't listen to these two, follow your heart – study ancient history, art – anything you want. Just think you could spend your summers exploring Greek islands." Cathy's idea did appeal to Richard, but ultimately he had ended up in the legal profession. His father, a physicist at heart, had been mildly disappointed when it came to his university applications.

He thought back to the day when his future had lay before him and he could have travelled in any direction he wished. Winter had arrived sooner than expected, and Richard was finding it harder to stay motivated and focused on his career. He felt despondent with the criminal system. He did not even believe it worked. Justice was redundant in his eyes.

Richard now realised what an idealist his uncle had been. He had always said, "It only takes one person to change the world, son," and Richard knew that history had proved this remark true, but he did not hold such rapture, charisma. He was not so passionate he could inspire others to join his cause. He wanted the law to advance, he wanted fairness, and justice and transparency. He wanted the profession not to be dominated by the wealthy elite, white males, but what you want and the reality of what you are faced with are often different.

So, Richard dealt with his disappointment by knuckling down and avoiding the challenge. He stuck to the book. He caused no fuss. He was unnoticeable. Hard-working and competent, but forgettable nevertheless. He was the kind of barrister that people would need a minute to recall. The type who quietly moved around chambers, who changed into his robes in court without discussing the ins and outs of his case with the other barristers, and laughing at the unfortunate clients they were lumbered with: clients who, quite frankly, they did not care about.

Of course, Richard knew they weren't all bad, but he had just found it harder and harder to see the good in any of them. As the years progressed he became more and more cynical. He supposed he had begun in law with the idealism of a socialist; he saw so many cases that were creations of poverty, class, standing and lack of education. He realised quite early on that the law was not the instigator of change, only shifts in societal attitudes and increased opportunities would alter the course of many children's lives. We are not born criminals. It was not the courts' responsibility to change the world. Law was just the enforcer of our failings in society.

15

Stephanie

It is a rarity that my friend Sally is free these days. I open my phone and notice she has replied affirmatively to an invitation for tonight I sent earlier. I am pleased as I get out of the bath to see tonight is one of those times she is available. It is also rare that I crave company so much over dinner. Granted she has asked if her friend Melanie can join us, which I am struggling with, but it is company all the same. I have just enough time to get out of the bath and dress before they will arrive. I already have copious amounts of wine in the cupboard so that isn't a problem, and dinner will easily stretch to three. I am certain there are some expensive chocolates I have previously hidden from myself in the cupboard that I can use as a dessert too.

I threw on a black cocoon dress, and I pulled my hair into a chignon. I did not look glamorous as such, but presentable for an evening with friends.

Sally arrived twenty minutes later, three bottles of wine in hand, and a smile on her face that said she was more than just relieved to escape her children. "Melanie's parking," she said. "She's just behind me."

Melanie was the kind of woman you did not want at your wedding: she was self-involved, insensitive and materialistic. She compared the cost of everything and highly valued the wealth of everyone. Melanie sucked all conversation out of any dinner gatherings, mainly because all she was capable of talking about was either herself or money. Melanie did not talk with you, she talked at you. I had forgotten this until I spent five minutes in her company, and it quickly became starkly apparent why I choose not to spend time with her.

Melanie had married young. By the time she was twenty-three years old she already had the house overlooking the sea in the south-west, the flat in central London and a bank balance to substantiate her wealth. Not that it was her making. Her husband Cliff bore the brunt of her lifestyle. Not that he complained either, he had singled out Melanie as soon as she had begun drinking in the bars he frequented. She quite clearly had a game plan; thirty-five years his junior she had set about becoming a kept woman from a young age. I was astounded by how superficial her world was. A world based on money and image. As far as I could see she had no real purpose except looking good for her ageing husband, who would soon be approaching seventy.

I had never comprehended how Sally could maintain a friendship with Melanie, but then shared history is a powerful thing, and I had seen enough unequal, inadequate and unexplained friendships, to realise that human relationships were not always based upon liking one another. I suspected that Sally felt a sense of loyalty towards Melanie because a bond formed in their early years, which she seemed incapable of breaking later when their paths veered so wildly from one another.

The evening went quickly. Melanie talked incessantly, but I numbed her conversation with at least a bottle and a half of wine, which helped make her a lot less offensive. Sally was lively and insisted on opening bottle after bottle. She had not been out for weeks, and a night away from just being a mother was quite clearly long overdue for her.

Later in the evening after we had forced dinner down, our appetites stunted by alcohol, the conversation turned to Matthew. Sally had long ago stopped quizzing me on our *platonic* relationship, as she liked to call it. I think she realised early on that even if I had stronger feelings for him, I would not discuss it with anyone. After all he was with Annalise, and I was not that kind of woman.

Melanie, however, seemed to be socially inept when it came to judging when to leave a conversation alone. She went on and on about how handsome Matthew was and how much time we spent together, before beginning a long-winded rant about how she had always assumed Matthew fancied her until she had seen us together. I found it difficult to listen to. Her misplaced confidence and arrogance when it came to attached men only further made me want to ask her to leave.

Melanie did not view marriage or cohabiting with a partner as something she should be respectful of, but rather a challenge. I was sure Cliff must know of her extra-marital flings, and turn a blind eye to his young wife's dalliances. But it frustrated me no end that Melanie was so self-absorbed and involved that she could not consider the female on the receiving end of her philandering behaviour. Whether I liked Annalise or not, the thought of Melanie and Matthew made me inexplicably angry.

Sally sensed my change in mood and quickly changed the subject, but by then I had crossed a line and didn't feel like I could reverse the feel of the evening. I scared myself with the feelings Melanie ignited in me, and if I hadn't known better I may have put it down as jealously.

Richard

In Richard's eyes rape was a unique case that required a unique system to deal with it. He believed that an inquisitorial system should be adopted, rather than an adversarial, when it came to sexual assault cases.

Richard particularly hated the aggressive and confrontational manner in which he, and other barristers, behaved in cases of rape under an adversarial system. He knew it was common practice, because it had the desired effect, but just because he had partaken in such tactics it did not mean he supported the legal stance in court when it came to cases of rape.

In an inquisitorial system, the judge would oversee the case once the charges had been laid. Richard believed that the fact the judge would be able to decipher which witnesses to call, and what path the investigation took, would mean the proceedings would be more balanced and neutral. Something, Richard thought, would be more effective than the win or lose attitude currently employed. Not only this, but Richard truly believed that the process would enable defendants, and victims alike, to be more actively involved in the case as participants in their own destiny.

16

Molly

Luke called. I have not seen him since he heard what happened, since that day I said what Jacob did to me.

I knew he blamed me, but he hadn't given me the chance to explain. He'd jumped to all the wrong conclusions. I'd felt guilty, even though what happened wasn't a choice, I still felt responsible. I wished he wasn't so angry. I am intrigued as to why he wanted to talk. I ignored the call: he could leave an answerphone message for all I cared. I was not ready to face him straight away, to hear his excuses, the reasoning behind his lack of support, his disappearing act. It still hurt too much.

I waited a whole day before I listened to his message. I was nervous. I didn't know what he was going to say. I hoped he'd want to meet up. I hoped he'd calmed down. I couldn't bear the anger and resentment. I wanted to see him, but every time I tried to imagine us back together – I couldn't.

I had envisaged Luke and me together many times. I had tried to find ways that might mean we could work again, that all was not lost between us, but I always hit a brick wall.

When I finally had the courage to play the message I had already become despondent. It was as if I had created a protective shield under which I seemed void of emotion. I put the phone on loudspeaker, rather than hold it to my ear: for some reason his voice so close felt too intimate after this length of time.

I listened mechanically as his voice filled my surroundings.

His message was monotone, devoid of compassion, he spoke with manners and misplaced politeness as he told me his forwarding address.

All he had wanted was his mail.

Jacob

Jacob hated the word "feminism". He hated what it represented, and how misused it was. Women threw it around as a defence for all types of behaviour. If you criticised a woman for being drunk, loud or easy you were an anti-feminist, or worse still, you were encouraging a culture of misogyny. If you questioned the behaviour of a certain set of females you were hunted down and abused on social networks. Yet, Jacob had witnessed women behave in ways that men were supposedly not meant to. He had heard the phrase "everyday sexism" coined recently, highlighting how women were treated on a daily occurrence, and how their sexuality was exploited, jeered at or used against them. He had observed the uprising against the misogynist, casual rape culture. Yet why was the responsibility always placed on the men, not the women of this type? It seemed to Jacob that women used the word "feminism" to excuse themselves; as a mask to hide behind, and validate whatever behaviour they wished.

Jacob knew that he saw women as objects. He knew most of

his friends did. He was not the first or the last who enjoyed a one-night stand, and wished to leave it at that: an exchange of sex with no returns. He never offered anything else, so was not misleading the girl in question. He found they were often more than willing to partake in sexual acts that he could later relay to his friends, alongside photos of them naked. They often protested before posing for these images, and they all believed him when he said he wouldn't show anyone. Of course, the girls knew these photos would be shared, that was the thrill of it. Why else let a complete stranger take such pictures? It was all part of the experience.

Jacob only needed to have left his WhatsApp group conversation open on his phone for them to see that their bodies were immediately shared with his friends, who, similarly, reposted photos for his perusal. It was a bit of fun. Everyone was doing it. It was part of your twenties and early-thirties. If women wanted to be sexually adventurous they needed to own the consequences of their behaviour, rather than spinning the "feminist" line and expecting to be respected.

He wondered why these women thought that it was then okay for them to ogle men. How were they allowed to perv over the male form and talk about their bodies as if they were objects? He had seen women pinch men's bums in bars. He had seen them flirt provocatively, just enough lip service to take a free drink then leave them alone again. They used their sexuality to exploit men for their money. He had witnessed hen dos with male strippers and "butlers in the buff". He wondered why this wasn't openly discussed: this culture of "misandry". A society that saw men as objects: wallets, abs and sperm donors.

It began with *Sex and the City*. The uprising of the loose female. Those who wanted to walk and talk like a man, but be treated like a lady. The programme openly saw females talking about the size of their sexual partner's penises, their performance in bed, their appearance, their wealth, yet it was deemed liberating for females, rather than derogatory for men? *When will the gender argument be equal?* he wondered. *When both sides accept their part, rather than females constantly laying the blame.*

17

Molly

I have been on edge for weeks now. I am anxious and agitated, any slight noise in the house and I panic. My senses are constantly on high alert. I lock all the doors and windows obsessively. I cannot concentrate on anything, and when I do get around to doing anything I feel detached as if I am witnessing myself trying to socialise, or attempting to carry out a task. I am not really there. I am failing.

My nights are filled with terror, and sweats, and dark dreams that I cannot escape, even in the hours when I lie awake. I blame myself. I lie in the depths of the night, and think of everything I could have done that evening to prevent Jacob doing what he did. I list all the possible consequences and outcomes had I hit him, had I screamed, had I told Luke straight away. I think of all that could now be different if only I had not invited him in.

After two weeks of sleepless nights my skin is turning grey, my eyes are sunken and hollow, and I no longer fit in any of my jeans, they hang off my limbs. I am always exhausted. I am desperate to switch off, to regain some control. I have lost my relationship, my ability to work, and myself. I drag myself to the doctors in the hope that they will prescribe me powerful sleeping pills that will numb the pain, and ease the nights. As I sit in the waiting room I notice I have developed a twitch: my right leg uncontrollably bounces up and down as I tap my right hand with my left index finger. It is as if I am physically trying to maintain a rhythm in all the chaos. I try to sit on my hands, but notice that the twitch in my right leg becomes more pronounced when I do so. I hope no one is watching, as I become increasingly embarrassed at my behaviour. I feel nauseous, but then I always do these days.

The twitching becomes worse when I enter Dr Ericson's office, and I am acutely aware I must look like I am after a methadone fix; I would not blame him for thinking me a junkie. He brings my notes up on screen, and I momentarily panic. I do not know what is on record, and I had not prepared myself for talking. I do not want to speak with him about what happened to me.

I ask Dr Ericson for sleeping tablets. I explain my predicament, I relay my nightly routine. I tell him the strategies I have tried. He listens and nods, and I am certain he is on the verge of prescribing the tablets when my leg begins to twitch violently again.

"Is there anything happening at the moment, Molly, that may be the cause of your sleeplessness?"

"Like what?" My hands start to shake. I see Dr Ericson acknowledge my physical response to his questions; I just want to hide away at that moment. I am done talking already.

"I'm not sure. I mean is there something going on in your personal life that may have caused you to drop weight, lose sleep, appear anxious...?"

"Something is happening, but I don't really want to talk

about it." I look down. I desperately try to stop the conversation. I do not want analysing.

"Okay, okay. We don't have to talk about it, but maybe you could explain how you're feeling, what has been happening with you. Am I right? Have you been a bit more anxious than usual?"

"Yes."

"Have you lost your appetite?"

"Yes."

"Have you been feeling panicky?"

"A bit."

"And when is it worse, Molly?"

"When I am on my own."

"Are you on your own a lot these days?"

"I just don't feel like seeing anyone, I'm not interested."

"Okay. Okay, can I ask if what is happening or has happened to you, has it stopped?"

"No."

"So, whatever is happening, is ongoing, it is still happening to you?"

"Sort of."

"You do know, Molly, that whatever you say in this room, whatever we talk about, it's confidential. That means I am legally bound not to discuss it with anyone else, it is just between you and me. Do you understand?"

I look up at Dr Ericson and nod.

"So, anything you want to share, it won't go any further than this room, and maybe it could even help you. If I know what is going on, I am better qualified to help you, Molly."

I stare blankly at the floor as I begin to talk. I cannot make eye contact with him. I feel too vulnerable, as if he will see into my inner being. I tell him how detached I feel; the isolation that has taken hold of me. I physically recoil when I tell him about my self-disgust.

I relay my listlessness. I mumble, I go off topic, I cry, which eventually leads to a low-level weep I cannot control. Dr Ericson nods and offers reassuring hums on occasion, but mainly he listens. After the room is vacant of my words he slowly begins to explain that he believes I am suffering with post-traumatic stress disorder.

"Post-traumatic stress disorder, Molly, is a reaction to an event outside the range of normal human experience. It is normal to be affected by a trauma, and in your case, this is how your trauma is presenting itself."

The numbness I feel is apparently totally normal. In a sense it is a survival skill. He talks about my self-disgust and tries to reassure me that is normal too, that the fact I froze is also a survival reaction.

"Molly, we are animals. Like animals who freeze in front of headlights, our biological response is sometimes to automatically stay still in the hope we will not antagonise the threat before us any further. You did what many humans do when faced with danger... you simply froze."

The explanation, although plausible, does not help. I do not want his explanations, his understanding. I wanted concrete help; I wanted to sleep. I just wanted sleep. I appease him, and his diagnosis, and then ask again for some sleeping tablets. He sees me as a project now to fix. I do not want him to fix me though, I just want to forget. He places me on the list for counselling, and tells me to come back whenever I feel like I need some help. I find this ironic because the only help I need right now is a helping hand to forget and rest. I ask one more time for something to help me sleep.

Finally, he agrees. "This is just a temporary prescription, Molly. It is not a long-term solution. There are just a few questions I need to ask you first, that okay?"

I answer routinely. It is only when the last but one question comes that I lose my footing. I fall silent.

"Molly, did you hear me?"

I nod.

"Molly, is that a possibility?"

I am silent.

"Molly, is there a possibility you are pregnant?"

I feel sick.

"Molly, when did you last have a period?"

"I thought it was the stress."

"Molly, I'm sorry to ask, but did he use a contraceptive?"

"I just didn't think... I didn't even think." I feel the colour drain from my face. A sick dread swells in my stomach. I think back to my last period. I'd been so distracted, I hadn't noticed they had stopped. I hadn't thought.

"It may just be down to weight loss and stress, Molly. We just need you to take a routine test, just to clarify."

I swallow down my sick. I nod. I feel faint. The doctor seems miles away, blackness begins. Bile gathers in my mouth. Luke always wore condoms – we didn't want children yet. If I was pregnant it was Jacob's.

Richard

Richard has called Molly into the office to run through the court procedure one more time. She has been vacant throughout the meeting. He's not sure she has even listened to any of the information he has tried to relay. He has asked her if she is all right, but she has dismissed him. His doubts that she will make it to court increase as the meeting goes on. He cannot allow the question to remain unanswered. If she is going to withdraw her evidence, he needs to know if she wants to continue with the case.

"Molly, is everything okay?"

"Umm." She barely looks up.

"Is everything okay? It just seems you're very disengaged today."

She ignores him.

"Molly, I need to know that you're still willing to give evidence."

She pauses. She mumbles something. He can barely hear her, the whisper that escapes her lips is hardly audible. He isn't sure he heard her right. He asks her to repeat herself. She just lifts her head and places her hand on her stomach and mouths the word, "pregnant". She is silent. He does not know what to say.

"Jacob?" he asks.

She simply nods. The tears stream down her cheeks.

"Do you know what you are going to do?"

Again, a whisper: "I can't. I can't have his baby."

He understands, but he would have also understood if she'd decided to keep the foetus and let it become a child. Cases such as Molly's are beyond his and all other men's comprehension, so why should he have the right to judge any decision Molly must make?

"Does Jacob know?"

She visibly swells with panic. Her chest heaves. "No, no, no, he mustn't ever know."

He reassures her it is confidential, he will not share her admission, it is purely her business. She begins to cry softly, and against his professional judgement he rises and walks around the table to her. Richard holds her as she weeps quietly on his shoulder.

18

Molly

My body has betrayed me twice. It feels like my pregnancy is a punishment. I have drunk alcohol. I've not slept. I'm in no fit state to carry a baby – another life. A life I'm not sure I want. A life I did not choose. A life I don't deserve.

What would I tell the child if I decided to keep them? What would I say? A child not conceived through love, but in terror. What if something happened to me? What if Jacob lays claim to the child? What if he wanted access? I cannot bear the thought of us being intertwined in the future. I cannot even look after myself. I cannot face it.

I am in no position to have a child. I cannot financially support myself, I'm struggling to function most days. The thought of looking after another living being is terrifying. I am not ready to be a parent; a mother. I still need to be mothered myself. Even with Luke, it was not a consideration: we had other things we wanted to do first: places we wanted to go, people we wanted to become, before we could look after a little person.

I know there is always adoption, but the thought of carrying

Jacob's child for nine months, the thought of standing in court and Jacob seeing my pregnancy, him knowing I was bearing his child makes me feel sick. I cannot contemplate court if I am going to keep the baby. It would not be an option. I do not want to think about it, this child I do not want, this child that may occupy me if I don't make a decision soon. And, if I were to choose adoption, the child would still grow up feeling unwanted, I would be punishing the one person who does not deserve any blame – unwanted at conception, unwanted at birth.

Richard

He cannot help but think of Molly Smith that night. He feels strangely protective of her. In all the rape cases he has prosecuted, she is the first victim of sexual assault he is aware has become pregnant as a result of the rape. Not that it is uncommon: pregnancies arising from rape are common, just beyond his realm of experience.

Statistically one in three women will have an abortion in their lifetime. In England, Wales and Scotland abortions are carried out before twenty-four weeks. Very few abortions are carried out after twenty weeks. The majority of these will be because of a severe risk to the mother's life, or because the pregnancy is not viable. Richard knows these abortions are generally only carried out in extreme cases. It is often only at the twenty-week scan that foetal abnormalities are discovered. Generally speaking, though, the majority of abortions are carried out before thirteen weeks' gestation. Whatever stage of the pregnancy, he cannot begin to imagine how difficult the decision to terminate a pregnancy must be.

Richard had searched the internet that evening, intrigued by the laws of abortion from country to country. He knew the pro-life movement that seemed to be sweeping America was on the rise. In 1973 the case of Roe v Wade set a precedent: it established a constitutional right to abortion throughout the USA. Currently though Georgia, Kentucky, Louisiana, Mississippi and Ohio have banned abortions after six weeks. In Louisiana, the state approved a law that prohibits abortion once a heartbeat is detectable – there is no exception for rape or incest. If Molly lived there, she'd be having this baby whether she was capable emotionally or not. She would not have the choice. The decision over her body would already have been made.

What Richard finds shocking is the stance in Ireland, a country so close yet so archaic in their thinking surrounding women's right to abortion. Up until 2018 in Ireland, under the Offences Against a Person Act 1861, a woman who has an abortion or the medical staff performing the abortion, can be subject to life imprisonment. If that woman was pregnant due to rape, it currently stands she could receive a longer prison sentence than her rapist if she were to terminate the pregnancy. Richard could not believe that a law such as this was still in practice.

19

Molly

In the end, the decision was beyond my control: just like the conception. The trip to the hospital afterwards was just a further violation of my body. It began with mild back pain. The days leading up to the court case were endless and I wonder if I'd ignored the symptoms, so consumed by my anxiety. I'm not sure if I could have stopped it. I will never know. The bleeding came suddenly, and I knew immediately something was wrong. I had been trying to avoid the pregnancy and the looming decision. I was already ten weeks pregnant and I knew that my window of opportunity to terminate the pregnancy was growing smaller.

The blood was crimson. The brightness of it alarmed me more than anything. I passed the clot two days later, what I know now would have been considered the foetus. I remember the pain more than anything. I had been shocked by the physicality of the miscarriage. What I didn't realise was my body had not expelled all of the remains of the embryo. My body had failed me again. I had not passed all the tissue: part of Jacob still remained.

In hospital, I had a procedure to stop the bleeding and prevent infection. The doctors needed to remove all of what they referred to as "the products of the conception" too. I felt a flood of relief when they told me this. Guilt flooded me. Relief washed over me. They rid me of any evidence of Jacob. The doctor performed a procedure called dilation and curettage. It was relatively quick. I was allowed to go home later that day. The ordeal apparently over. All I felt was empty. Only guilt and relief remained.

In the weeks that followed I was surprised at the amount of grief I felt for the unborn baby, the child I lost. Ultimately, I'm not sure what decision I would have made, but whatever it had been it would have been my choice. I would have been in control. I hated the loss of control and ownership I'd felt over my body.

Every day I am on the verge of tears. I try to busy myself around the house, but I have lost all motivation to clean. I used to love decorating. I'd pour through interior design magazines I'd subscribed to; now they just sit in a pile on the coffee table – unread, surrounded by dirty mugs. I mourn the miscarriage, yet I cannot help but feel that my body's decision was the right one: the decision I believe I would have made, and the choice I had the right to.

PART II

20

Molly

I spoke briefly with my mother on the telephone. She wanted me to dress like Jacqueline Kennedy for the trial. I have not. Richard, my barrister, advised a navy outfit. Apparently, navy is the right colour. I did not realise there was a right colour to wear to a rape trial. I find it so strange I am even thinking of something like this. I have not told my mother about the pregnancy or the miscarriage. It was bad enough explaining what had happened to me. I am trying to forget.

I am a ball of nervous energy as I take to the steps of the court. Alison is by my side, holding me up. The building is imposing, the gravity of the law reflected in its strength of standing. It does not help. It only further frays my nerves.

Richard rises as I enter, and shakes my hand. He explains the process as if he has said it a thousand times. He talks me through what today will entail, and briefly covers what I may encounter over the following few weeks, but he is eager not to dwell on what may happen. I feel sick.

Initially, I move as if I am floating. I am not really here. It is as if I am a haze of sedation. I am watching the outside world from under the water. This cannot be life. This cannot be real.

I spot Jacob in the corridor. It is the first time I have seen him since. He is, as always, immaculately polished: his suit sharp, and his smile charming. He senses me before he turns. I can see his recognition in the way his shoulders suddenly stiffen. It is as if he felt my presence. When he turns to look at me I am momentarily disarmed. His stare bores into me. His eyes. Those eyes. I am frozen again. And then, then, he lifts a hand and waves – a little smile dances on his lips, and his eyes flicker up and down my body. I glance around me, not quite sure if this action is aimed at me, but there is no one but me.

The revulsion heaves its way up through my body, and I suddenly turn and run. I reach the toilets in time to retch over the sink, but my body is empty.

My red watering eyes are the only sign that he happened. No one else saw.

Jacob

Jacob is used to formalities, to structure, to authority. It is all he has ever known. Jacob understands this game and gauntlet. He knows how he needs to appear and behave. He knows how quickly these cases can turn if he says the wrong thing, his wording misinterpreted and twisted. He knows his demeanour should be unassuming, polite and humble. He knows not to cry, not to shout. He knows that he must act like the perfect gentleman, the perfect son, the perfect grandson. He will be the man everyone wants as their neighbour, the man everyone would greet on their street, he'll be the man no one would ever fear.

Jacob arrived early, he has always been punctual, and he was uncertain as to whether there would be a furore on the court steps this morning. There wasn't, much to his relief, but then the case has not started yet, so it is understandable the media have shown no interest. He imagines cases such as his occur every day; journalists have better ways to fill their time than covering false allegations.

He is chatting to Stephanie and the court clerk when he smells Molly's perfume. He cannot see her, but it is definitely her smell. The wafts of her perfume make him heady. He feels a mixture of nostalgic longing and anger combined. He has hated her for months, but he has also quite simply missed her.

His shoulders tighten. He should not look, but he is curious. He has not seen her for so long. He wants to look at her, to remember in person what she was to him, and now who she has become. He turns slowly on his heel to face her, momentarily he just stares.

She is a shadow of her former self. She is too slender now, her eyes are hollow and her skin is grey. She looks back, for a moment he thinks she does not recognise him, but then he sees the realisation in her eyes. The acknowledgement she has led them to this place: to this courtroom corridor on a winter's Monday morning. He smiles slightly – he does not know what else to do – and lifts his hand in acknowledgement of their past and the present. He briefly allows his eyes to travel over her. She has shrunk. She appears vacant. Before he turns back to Stephanie, Molly turns abruptly and runs. He does not know why, or where she is going, but only that she won't be able to run in court. There'll be nowhere to escape for her when her story is shattered and her lies revealed.

Stephanie

I love the anticipation on the first day of trial, the impending rush of adrenaline when you begin the fight for your client. I was up early this morning, before five, and I could feel my opening speech wading its words into my conscious, but it was muddled, jumbled. It needed to be heard, but it needed to be coherent. I needed to clarify it, dissect it sentence by sentence and structure my delivery.

I never write an opening statement prior to trial, well not anymore. When I used to they always sounded conceited, as if I'd watched too many American trials on Sky Atlantic. Now I let the words come to me, the pressure of time solidifies my arguments and my understanding. All I need to do then is run. Run until the words slap back up from the concrete in the echo of my trainer's stride.

This morning I ran nine miles. I ran until my shins burnt, and the pain in my chest had extended into my lower body. I ran until I had exerted myself physically just enough to allow my mind to exert itself. I took my time showering when I arrived home. It was still dark and the city steeped in the winter's morning fog. The water was hot, I allowed red welts to develop all over my body. The bathroom was shrouded in mist before I turned the water to freezing cold, shocking my body into life. I could suddenly see clearly again as the mist transcended.

I dress mechanically in my best Max Mara suit. If I look expensive, I feel expensive, and it creates a confidence in me that cannot be sidelined. A confidence that cannot be quashed. Part of winning is looking like you were bound to win all along.

Richard

Richard was flustered. He had already managed to spill half his vanilla cinnamon latte down his suit arm as he took the steps to the court. He had woken up on the back foot. His boiler had packed in during the night so he was barren of hot water. He had left his flat immediately after this discovery, and headed to the gym he rarely set foot in. However, he still paid membership and occasionally he needed to use their facilities.

Thankfully he still arrived at court before Molly Smith, but the rigmarole of carrying all of his heavy files and changing in chambers into his "gown", only exacerbated what had been a terrible morning thus far.

Molly arrived looking forlorn and childlike. She had lost even more weight since he last saw her, and he scolded himself internally for thinking that this may work in her favour with the jury: losing her curves was not necessarily a bad thing, curves were considered sexual and held connotations.

She was wearing navy. He had once read some research that navy was the best colour to wear in an interview situation; court was the ultimate interview so he had extended this theory to his clients. She looked the part. *If there is a part to look for a rape victim*, he thought.

He felt a strange mixture of sadness and relief for her. She had sent him a formal email three weeks before the trial begun, informing him of her miscarriage. He had not pried any further since the moment in his office. It was not his place. She had not needed to tell him anything of the pregnancy in the first place. It was her body, her decision and her choice. In Richard's eyes, it was for Molly to draw whatever line and conclusion she determined right for her.

He had written and rewritten his opening statement. He had read it repeatedly in the mirror, cursing himself for sounding too sensationalist and dramatic. In the end, he had concluded it with caution. He wanted to emphasise that there was a friendship, but that it was irrelevant from the outset when it came to consent. He did not want to paint Jacob as a monster early on, because ultimately Richard knew this wasn't a story that involved his victim being violently attacked. No, it was a story about entitlement and how no one is entitled to something the other party was never prepared to give. Jacob Walker-Kent was never entitled to Molly Smith, and it was Richard's job to prove that.

The morning was fairly slow to begin. The jury had been selected last week, so the formalities that usually took a great deal of time were complete. As the prosecution, it was his turn to call his witnesses first. Stephanie Beaumont could then cross-examine them herself; this did not always work in his favour, especially when it came to the defence maligning rape victims.

Richard had already called a number of witnesses, including the policeman who Molly reported the incident to, and her friend Alison; although her third-party disclosure could not be entered into the court's evidence. He had wanted to call her boyfriend Luke, but Molly had refused, and Richard had agreed in retrospect that he would not actually be of benefit for the prosecution's case.

The text messages did Jacob Walker-Kent absolutely no favours. Richard had relished this upon first reading them. They were mildly threatening in their nature towards the end, and the fact there were so many in succession that Molly had not responded to did not bode well for him.

Richard was mildly concerned about Jacob's initial text message after the night in question, as there was no indication at this point he believed he'd done anything wrong. However, Molly's blanket silence, after her first message where she'd requested he leave her alone, could be beneficial to their case. If it was regretted sex, as Stephanie Beaumont was implying, there was a perception Molly would have tried to cover it up: she may have asked Jacob to keep quiet, not to say anything, told him it was a mistake, stated her regret, but there was none of this.

Richard also called medical experts to the stand. He wanted the jury to realise that Molly had experienced a total normal response, that the symptoms she displayed were characteristic of post-traumatic stress disorder. Her failure to report, and the fact she froze and did not fight back, were entirely normal. He needed the jury to realise there was in fact medical knowledge that supported her reaction; the way Molly Smith had behaved directly prior to, during and after the sexual assault, was normal, and somewhat expected in cases such as this.

The first few days trudged on. The usual rigmarole of the prosecution calling and cross-examining witnesses went on, before the defence had their chance. Richard wondered why anyone would ever consider the formalities and intricacies of this job glamorous. By the time it came to calling Molly to the stand he could tell she was exhausted. Richard worried about some clients taking the stand, but he had confidence in Molly's ability.

Richard's job was not necessarily to be kind to Molly. He needed to prove to the jury beyond reasonable doubt that she did not consent, and to do so this meant there were a number of tough questions he'd have to put her through on the stand, but it was better to prepare her for what was coming next with Stephanie Beaumont. He had warned her that it wouldn't be easy, but no matter how many times you told someone, until they experienced it you could not tell how they would react.

As Molly took the stand, Richard thought back to the Stanford rape case that ignited the global discussion on rape culture; the young man who had been found guilty of three felony counts of sexual assault; the young man who had received a mere six-month sentence for an attack on an unconscious, non-consenting female; the young man who the judge thought a greater prison sentence "would have a severe impact on".

Richard had felt incredulous for the young lady in this case. The female whose life would be forever severely impacted, who could not just complete a sentence and then move forward with her life. A young lady who it seemed the judge deemed somehow less worthy than the convicted rapist of a future. A young lady who was denied justice even when guilt was attributed by a jury of twelve.

Richard was appalled at the case, what it represented, what it clearly conveyed to rape victims everywhere. Of course, there had been a huge outpouring of support for the victim and disgust towards the perpetrator. Her victim impact statement had gone viral, its rhetoric so powerful and brave, yet there were still the rape apologists, those of the general belief that we should somehow collectively feel sorry for the man.

In Ireland in 2015 a man received no prison sentence for repeatedly raping his girlfriend in her sleep. He admitted using her body over the period of a year for his sexual gratification whilst she lay unconscious due to strong medication. He walked free. Richard had found it incomprehensible that a man who admitted his guilt was allowed to go unpunished. Here was the law further validating that males have a sexual entitlement that needs to be protected above and beyond the rights of a female's physical autonomy.

In this case, public comments in the media seemed to empathise with the rapist. Richard had scrolled to the bottom of articles to find comments that colluded with the idea that if the female is your partner it is ludicrous to ask for consent, even if they are asleep. He had read comments by articulate people who believed that the rapist should be shown compassion and helped. He wondered when it was that the rapist had become the victim in cases such as this.

Richard thought back to Stanford. The case had been unusual in a sense. The rapist was caught red-handed. He was chased and tackled by two men out in the open, both of whom had seen him sexually assaulting the victim in public view. Both the victim and rapist were highly intoxicated, and this was an issue of contention in the case: how much should alcohol limits be considered in such cases?

The prosecutor argued it should warrant a harsher sentence as the victim had been increasingly vulnerable, and the man had preyed on her. Whereas the man's family and legal team believed that intoxication somehow negated his decision-making and actions: he was drunk so the consequences should not reflect the crime.

Richard had visibly winced when the man's father had described the rape as "*twenty-minutes of action*", as if this meant the case should be trivialised. The judge in this case said that there was "less moral culpability" for a defendant who was intoxicated. So, Richard thought, what the judge was ultimately saying was if you are drunk it is considered more acceptable to rape someone.

He thought of all this as Molly swore her oath, and he silently prayed for her, as he knew all too well what lay ahead.

21

Molly

There is a deep anxiety that bubbles away every day the trial continues in the pit of my stomach. I cannot eat, and seem to be surviving on coffee and adrenaline. My sleep is restless, and every time I consume even the slightest molecule of food I need to rush to the toilet. The doctor warned me about this extreme flight or fight mode, yet there is nothing physical I can do.

My brother has come every day, and sat in the gallery, a silent supportive presence. I know Jacob must have seen him too, and this reassures me. We are not close, we do not talk much. My brother is a man of few words, more so since he left the Marines. Being here is his way of supporting me, letting me know he is here for me.

Jacob's eyes have bored into me every day at trial. I can feel his intense stare. I have tried to avoid eye contact. I do not want to remember his face. However, as I take the steps to the stand his eyes are all I can feel on me. I tell myself to remain strong, that I can do this, but all I feel is sickness. I want to be anywhere else but here, to run out the room, and wake up five years later when this is all over.

My limited sleep exacerbates my feelings of anxiety. When I do rarely manage to fall sleep, I have the same dream over and over. I dream I can hear a baby crying, but I cannot reach it. I'm in a house with endless rooms, but behind every door I find an empty cot. Still I hear the helpless sobbing of the child. I cannot reach the baby. I cannot decipher where he or she is. I am always looking for a missing baby.

Stephanie

By the time I come to questioning Molly I can tell her energy is wavering. It is beneficial I get to cross-examine her after she has been called as a witness for the prosecution, as she is already tired, and this means she is more likely to slip up. Her counsel has questioned Molly for their purposes, and rightly tried to portray her in a certain light. They have lulled her into a false sense of security, which I now work to my advantage. Richard Clarke I'm sure has warned her about this part since he has prosecuted numerous rape cases and knows the drill, but he is yet to know my drill.

I start my questioning very softly. Molly needs to understand that I am her friend. She needs to see that all I'm asking her to do is talk about the events of that evening. I walk her through, as Richard Clarke already has done, the months that led up to the night in question, their friendship, how things worked between the two of them, shall we say. I make her feel as if I understand. I understood how she had felt, why she had behaved the way she had, that it was okay. I lead into my questioning surrounding the night in question by agreeing with her standpoint of their friendship.

"Well obviously, females like yourself can have totally platonic friendships with men such as Jacob, and I understand that is all you felt it was?"

"Yes."

"And nothing had happened previous to this night?"

"No."

"There had been no previous sexual relations?"

"No."

"And you had never wanted there to be?"

"No."

"And Jacob had never taken advantage of you before?"

"No."

"And Jacob had never suggested there was anything inappropriate between you?"

"No."

"Would you say you ever wanted anything sexual with Jacob before that evening?"

"No."

"So, prior to that evening you had never wanted sexual relations with Jacob?"

"No."

"So, what changed?"

Molly pauses. I had her on a roll of yes and no answers, and it surprised her when I dropped a leading question into my dialogue. Her pause could easily be misread by the jury.

"Sorry, your honour, I'll rephrase. And would you say anything changed?"

"I don't know what you mean."

"What I'm simply saying is, did anything change that meant you wanted sexual relations with Jacob?"

"No."

"There we are, my question was simple enough, wasn't it?" I smile at the jury, as if they understand my confusion. This simple act of body language makes the jury feel that I believe them to be astute, knowledgeable, able to see through things, and it also confuses Molly Smith. It makes her feel small. If she thought she was on solid ground she now realises that she is in actual fact about to enter very choppy waters. I continue questioning. I take Molly back to the night in question.

Jacob

He watches her intensely. He wants her to see him, to realise the impact of these allegations. He does not want to grant her a moment's respite whilst she stands in the witness box. He is determined that she will recognise what she has done to him; how much her lies have affected his life.

He is acutely aware she does not want to look at him. She is struggling, squirming, trying to wriggle out of it, but Stephanie has her in her grips: she is good. He is pleased he is paying so much for the barrister. Molly is faltering, her evidence becomes confused, and he begins to see the colour rise in her chest. It spreads like fire through her cheeks until her voice is quavering. Her lies are unravelling.

He is fascinated by her version of events, the obscure twist she has put on their interlude. He wonders too if she actually now believes this concoction of events, if she has repeated it so many times she believes it to be the truth. A reality rewritten to serve her purpose.

22

Stephanie

I have already succeeded in lulling Molly into a false sense of security, and now she is on the back foot I can see her anxiety levels have risen, and the slight hint of panic in her voice.

"Is it not correct that your boyfriend left the party early that night?"

"Yes."

"Did you not say, I quote: *'you never let me have fun anymore,'* as he went? Was Jacob a bit of fun, Molly?"

Richard calls his objection immediately. He tells the judge it is speculative, but the judge allows the question. Molly shrinks before my eyes.

"Yes, no, well yes I suppose."

"Did you not then approach Jacob at the bar?"

"Yes."

"Did you then drink what is known as a Jägerbomb? For the purposes of the jury this is a drink containing red bull and Jägermeister, a spirit of 35% alcohol."

"Yes."

"How much had you drunk at that point, Molly? Would you say you were drunk?"

"Probably a bit, yes."

"How much, please? Just so we can get an idea of the circumstances here?"

"A few wines."

"How many?"

"Five or six glasses."

"Five or six large glasses of wine?" I raise my eyebrows, my judgement of her clear. Molly barely whispers back "yes", so much so I must ask her to repeat herself louder. I now turn towards her behaviour. I've established she was intoxicated, I now need to prove that her behaviour would be considered loose. "And then you danced with Jacob? That is correct?"

"Yes."

"How would you describe the style of your dancing, Molly?"

Again, Richard Clarke objects. He questions its relevance. I withdraw the question, but it was suggestive enough even if Molly did not have to answer it.

"I understand you continued to drink strong spirits straight?"

"Yes, I think so."

"*I think so?* Are you saying you can't really accurately remember the night in question?"

"Yes, I did, yes I suppose I did."

"You then requested Jacob walk you home, that is right?"

"Yes."

"So, after you had asked Jacob to accompany you home, and he obliged, is it correct you then invited him into your house? For coffee?"

Richard Clarke speaks again, "Objection, leading."

"No, tea. It wasn't like that."

"What time was this? Rather late for coffee – sorry, tea – would you say?"

"No. I didn't really know what time it was."

"I see you were unaware of the details of the night, Miss Smith."

"I suppose." Molly is looking weaker and weaker as I bore my questions into her.

"What happened when you went inside?"

"I made some food, and got changed into my comfy clothes."

"Oh, you went to change into something more comfortable, I see." I raise my eyebrows.

The case is suddenly adjourned for lunch. I couldn't have asked for a better moment for my questioning to pause. The jury has at least an hour to speculate on the facts I had presented before we return for round two.

"For the purposes of the case, and to refresh the jurors' memories, we adjourned for lunch just as Miss Smith was explaining that she went to change into something more comfortable. Is this correct, Miss Smith, you went upstairs to change into something more comfortable?"

"Yes."

"According to your statement you went into your spare room as not to wake your boyfriend. May I ask why it was so important your boyfriend, a Mr Luke Mattingly, should not be woken? Was there something – or should I say someone – you were trying to hide?"

"No, I just didn't want to disturb his sleep."

"Could you tell the jury for the purposes of the evidence what you did then change into?"

"Some joggers and a T-shirt."

"Please see exhibit three: a small crop top and some low-slung trousers." I purposefully alter the wording of Molly's description of the garments. "Is it not right that when you returned downstairs you went into the living room where Jacob was sitting?"

"Yes."

"So, you went to find him in your new comfy clothes?"

"Yes."

"Then what happened?"

"We sat on the sofa, and put on a film."

"Did you not playfully slap Jacob's hand at one point? Did you not instigate touching his hand?"

"Yes, but not like that."

"And then what?"

"We put the film on, like I said."

"And where was Jacob when you were snuggled up on the sofa?"

"Next to me."

"Oh, next to you. I understand you had a blanket. May I ask whether he was under the blanket with you?"

"Yes, but not like under 'under' the blanket."

"So, let me get this straight, you stayed in the bar with Jacob where you continued to get progressively drunker after your boyfriend had returned home. You then requested Mr Walker-Kent, Jacob, walk you home. You then invited him into your home to which he obliged. You then changed into something more comfortable, and you then snuggled up under a blanket together. Am I correct?"

"You're twisting it."

"Just answer the question in hand please, Miss Smith. Am I correct?"

"It wasn't like that."

"What was it like?"

"We were just friends. I didn't want anything more."

"So, do you do this with many of your male friends, Miss Smith? Or is Jacob an exception to the rule?"

"No, I don't, but it wasn't like that."

"Did Jacob at any point make you feel like you couldn't trust him?"

"No."

"Did Jacob at any point make you feel uncomfortable?"

"Yes, he tucked a bit of my hair behind my ear."

"So, let me get this straight: Jacob tucked a curl of your hair behind your ear whilst you were snuggled up next to each other, and this made you feel uncomfortable?"

"Yes."

"Did you tell him you felt uncomfortable?"

"No."

"Did you move?"

"Yes."

"But, did you move off the sofa?"

"No, I moved up, closer to the arm of the sofa away from him."

"And yet you felt so uncomfortable you then fell asleep next to Jacob. Is this correct?"

"Well, yes I must have."

"Tell me what happened next please, Miss Smith, in your own words please."

I watch then as she unravels, as Molly's words jumble and fall out on top of themselves into something incoherent and rambling, and I simply nod, and then stare straight at the jury and smile, and say: "We have no more questions, Miss Smith."

Molly

I crumple. As I stand in the dock, I crumple. There is nothing left for her to break. She has beaten me. The blows were delivered so expertly. She was timely in her questioning so it confused me. I suddenly felt like I had to defend myself, but the more she asked the more I questioned myself, the more I questioned my actions, and I stumbled. I stumbled over the facts. I could not cope with the pressure. I had not known it would be that bad, I had not anticipated she would be so nasty. She was like a viper – her tongue so sharp and cutting. And, all the while I could see him. I could see Jacob sitting in the dock, his eyes intently fixed on me, and he was shaking his head slowly, incredulous that he was sat in that chair.

I did not want to look at him. I did not want him to have any power over me, but I could feel his eyes boring into my head. And her questioning, this woman who had pretended to be my friend shortly before, was firing questions at me now, so quickly I had no time to think. She twisted what I said, she turned it into something it wasn't, and all the while I could feel his eyes. I was breaking, and I wanted it to stop. All I wanted was it to stop. And, I could still feel his eyes, his scathing disapproval and contempt for me, even though it was him. It was him who was the wrongdoer.

She is quicker now. The questions are shorter, sharper, faster. She asks me to repeat myself, but she mangles my words so it all sounds wrong. I know as I am speaking that I have lost. I know as she continues to intimidate and abuse my vulnerable position that it was not worth it. I know immediately that I made a mistake, that I should have let it go, I should have forgotten and moved on. I should not have gone to the police. I should not have let it get to court. Because, this is worse, I am on trial, not just the night in question, but everything about me: my job, my social life, my clothing, my history, my relationships, my alcohol consumption, the way I dance, the way I construct friendships. I am on trial in front of everyone, and I can see now what a failure I am. I should have expected this. What else could I have expected? And the worst thing? It is like I am being raped all over again, only this time with an audience.

Richard

Richard may as well put his head in his hands. It is hopeless. He tries his best to remain composed, but he watches on helplessly as Stephanie Beaumont tears apart whatever part of Molly Smith's case he had left. She is very good, he will give her that. By the time she is finished the jury appear to have made up their minds as they watch Molly sob on the stand. They are watchful of her, already assessing her guilt, even though her guilt was never actually in question.

The judge is also weary, and Richard wonders if he too has grown despondent with the way these cases are tried; either that or he wonders why they even make it to court in the first place, as they all knew how the system was aligned. Richard has noted the judge's underlying illness all week, he has spluttered and coughed through his deliveries, and he worries for his health. Not that he is suffering severely, but Richard wants nothing more than the case to be over. An illness that may suspend the hearing would be catastrophic.

He is relieved when the judge adjourns the court for the day. The last thing he wants is to call Jacob Walker-Kent to the stand, not whilst Molly's testimony is still ringing so strongly in the jurors' ears. It is better for Richard if they have an evening to forget some key points Stephanie Beaumont raised, so he can manipulate them for his own purpose tomorrow.

As the judge dismisses the jury, Richard glances over at Jacob Walker-Kent. He has been assessing him all day in court, trying to figure out how he ticks. He is a man of surety. He holds his torso with authority and a calmness only the wealthy possess. As if all the worries in his world can be solved by money and his standing in society. *Sadly, in this case*, Richard thought, *he is probably right.*

23

Stephanie

The journalists arrived slowly to begin with. Yesterday morning I noted only one shyly standing on the steps of the court, a slip of a woman she barely registered: she just appeared fragile and lost like a fledging out of its nest. She was unassuming and delicate in her presence. It was only the notepad and camera that gave it away. This afternoon was a different story. They swarmed around the doorway as I left court, their cameras peering through the crowds. The buzz of their words, their incessant repetitive questions, their elbows rotating in a small aggressive dance; rampant for the first quote, the best snippet of information.

I am unsure why the sudden interest. I have represented cases like this before, and they have sailed by unnoticed, merely leaving a ripple in their wake, but this case suddenly seems different. I wonder whether it is the sheer good looks of Jacob Walker-Kent that have caught their attention. I imagine he is known in certain circles due to his previous successes. The golden boy fallen from grace. I can see why they would have picked him up as the lead in the story. What I cannot understand, though, is the strange fascination with myself. The birdlike journalist I spotted first has a peculiar interest in me. She followed me quietly as I left, and whispered statements in my ears, trying to persuade me to affirm or deny them.

The following morning the court's audience has swelled further. As I arrive they dive on me, their questions aggressive. I hear the tail end of their comments: *rape apologist, anti-feminist, bully, hard-nosed bitch.* I wonder why I am suddenly the target of their motivations, what is fuelling their hatred of my role in this case.

I enter court quickly and see Molly ahead. Her shoulders are shaking and she is pale, for a moment I stop and stare at her, and I am awash with guilt for my part in her breakdown yesterday, but then I remember myself. It is a job, and this is simply my role.

Molly

After yesterday I am unsure how much more I can take. I lay in bed last night staring mindlessly at the ceiling until 3am my mind overwhelmed with the questions I'd been posed on the stand. I replayed it over and over again, desperately disappointed in myself that I had not answered differently, that I had not seen what she was trying to do. My mind whirling, I knew I would not be able to sleep, instead I rose and drunk a glass of red wine – quickly I glugged it back, desperate to forget. I woke up this morning on the sofa, the glass still in hand. It was 6am. I had managed two hours restless sleep, I dreaded the day ahead.

The case has stirred emotions in me that I have tried to suppress. After my miscarriage, I did not want to think of the unborn child again. Maybe the miscarriage was my fault? The child could sense it was unwanted. I had been so concerned the child may have grown up with certain mannerisms. Mannerisms that are hereditary. Jacob's mannerisms. What if the child had found out it was a product of rape? Would they have felt unwanted? What if I hadn't had the maternal capacity to care for the child? What if all I'd seen was Jacob, and I had wanted to repel the baby?

I do not want to think about any of it, but I cannot help it. I keep thinking about whether my family would have rejected the baby. A child of shame. When I have these feelings, I have the compulsion to climb up on a high building, take a step and let the ground swallow me up. Instead I attempt to feign sleep. It never works. I'm still consumed by the child that will never be. I wish I could switch off these thoughts. None of it matters now anyway, I'm just torturing myself.

When I arrived outside court I could not understand the commotion, why there was so much fuss and flurry on the steps. They launched at me before I realised what was happening, the microphones were flung in my face, and the sharpness of the camera flashes momentarily blinded me. I spun around wildly looking to escape. I did not know what they wanted with me. Alison grabbed my hand and pulled me forward towards the court steps – I could see Richard ushering us to come in quickly. As fast as they preyed upon me they left, their interest waned when they saw Stephanie Beaumont. They surrounded her immediately, the shrill sound of their voices echoing across the court's entrance as I ran inside.

24

Stephanie

The stress of the media interest is dragging me down. I cannot so much as breathe without them jumping on it and writing an article on my alleged tactics. The sensationalism they employ, the downright ignorance of their articles, and the facts they throw around are an insult to rape victims across the globe. The media has done more to harm women than to help them. It is because it is a juicy story they are now interested in how I represent alleged rapists. It is not because they deeply care about rape victims. They care about money, and shock value, and creating a storm that does nothing to prevent future incidents of rape. They do not create solutions, or offer support: they are vultures.

That is not to say that there are not sensible reporters, those who instil morality and justice into their articles; that is not to say that there are some journalists who want change, who write for a better society, who would print a well-considered article. I am talking about the tabloids, the papers who target the uneducated and naïve, the readers, who then become more and more misinformed, and believe everything they read: the BNP voters, the anti-Islamic, the bigoted, racist, judgemental readers who are that way because they believed what the media fed them.

That is not to say that there is no truth in some of their reporting this time, but their accusations are too harsh. I do not practice harassment in rape cases, as has been written. If harassment is considered overt bullying of Molly, purposefully making her cry, no, I would say I refrain from this. Of course, certain views come out loud and clear in my questioning, I know that plain bullying would lose me the jury. But, ruthlessness, well, ruthlessness does not lose me the jury: it helps to secure an acquittal. There is a difference between bullying and a no-holds-barred approach.

It is not my brief to take Molly Smith's sensitivity into account. I adopt my approach based on the assessment of the complainant. It is easy to tell if a more aggressive approach is appropriate, or if a softly, softly approach would fare better with jurors. It really depends on the alleged victim, someone who appeared more brazen I would dismantle on the stand. I do not determine how I am going to treat a complainant based on sensitivity. My decision is simply based on what method will secure my success.

One of my methods is what some would describe as trapping the complainant; I lull the complainant into a false sense of security. If I can establish a common ground with the witness I can normally get more information out of them. I try to get the complainant to agree with the first five or six propositions, then when I come in with the seventh there is a psychological tendency to be agreeable, even if at this point the witness does not agree. In Molly's case, it would be easy to lead with five or six statements about her and Jacob's friendship, simple propositions covering the length of time they've known one another, a day spent together, a moment of shared history, and then I would imply that they partook in consensual sexual activity together.

I like to keep the complainant calm too. I ask neutral questions to begin with: the jury is far less inclined to believe someone has experienced deep trauma if they relay the experience in monotone. If Molly appears together and relaxed, people are far less inclined to believe a rape occurred. I leave the fatal blow until the end, so if she does break down it appears she is doing so because I caught her out – I simply exposed her lies.

It is of course essential I undermine the witness in the eyes of the jury. I need to make Molly sound and appear less credible. If I align her facts alongside Jacob's, and make it sound like her version continually contravenes his, I appear to be reasonable, but I am playing a game. I'm trying to make the jury think that Molly's vulnerable act is just that, and underneath it she is simply a manipulative woman.

There are several strategies I can use here to discredit the complainant. Firstly, there is maligning the victim's behaviour. Juries are prejudiced, and if I can make them see that the victim, at the time of the incident had put herself in a compromising position, well then, juries tend not to convict. If they do not trust her character, or see her behaviour as unwise they often tend to acquit. My cross-examination in large focuses on the complainant's behaviour, and how "foolish" she could be perceived to be. The subconscious message I relay is, *you brought this on yourself.* I question Molly's motivation; I make the jury question why Molly ended up in this situation. I make them suspicious of the amount of time Jacob and Molly spent alone together. I imply that sex was always on the cards, and it was Molly who laid them there.

The notion of political correctness goes out of the window when it comes to juries. They are just going to see a woman who says she didn't consent, but whose behaviour suggests otherwise, and if they are confused by her behaviour then so was the defendant. I make them see that Jacob's assumption of consent was reasonable. "Foolish behaviour" is key in cases such as Molly's and Jacob's. We use it not only regarding consent, but independent of it. It helps to engineer our overriding message that this is her fault, her actions led her to the situation she now finds herself in.

I use comparisons between foolish behaviour and common sense. I suggest that the way Molly behaved would invite the jury to believe she may have consented, or that Jacob believed she had. I may even go as far as to suggest Molly's behaviour meant it was partially her fault, therefore Jacob should not be convicted, even if he knew she wasn't a 100 per cent consenting adult.

It will be hard for Richard Clarke to present Molly as having the right to decline Jacob's advances even though she was drunk. Whether it is right or wrong, the attitudes ingrained in people make them believe women should act in a certain way; a way in which Molly did not act.

Jacob

Jacob finds the case so far altogether embarrassing. He can tell Richard Clarke knows where this is heading, and he pities his simplistic arguments somewhat. The truth is the prosecution has no medical evidence and no witnesses, and Mr Clarke is hanging on by a thread as he attempts to weave a viable argument. He relies too strongly on opinions about why so few women report, why cases are acquitted, why the stereotype is wrong.

Mr Clarke makes a good argument had we been in a

sociology class; but the law does not rest on attitudes and mistaken beliefs. It is concerned with facts, and Mr Clarke appeared to have few of these that proved even an ounce of possible guilt on Jacob's behalf.

He called an expert in rape attrition rates, a medical expert in post-traumatic stress disorder to try and support Molly's claims, but it was quite clearly desperate. Jacob could not even comprehend that the prosecuting counsel was trying to argue that Molly had developed post-traumatic stress disorder. PTSD affects people after combat. It affects people who've lived through the most horrific experiences, not girls who have had regrettable sex.

"Oh, good God! This is ridiculous, what a silly thing to claim." Jacob could faintly hear his mother's constant dialogue from the public gallery. "PTSD – how dare she compare herself to those who fought in the war. Honestly, what a waste of everyone's time."

As the expert witness began to speak his mother had stood and bellowed at him: "You should be ashamed of yourself speaking on behalf of girls like this – ashamed. It's all lies about my son. PTSD – I've heard it all now..."

The judge had promptly shut her down. "Order! Silence, Mrs Walker-Kent, or I will be forced to remove you from court. Need I tell you again?" Jacob had turned to look at her and saw her begrudgingly sit down, she was still mumbling under her breath. It was not the first time the judge had promptly shut her outbursts down.

Jacob is almost looking forward to taking the stand. He wants Molly to face him. To understand the enormity of her false claims. To look him in the eye, and realise how much she has ruined his life.

This is one of the reasons Jacob is so incensed when the case is adjourned. He is indignant. He cannot quite fathom that the courts have adjourned the case due to illness. He now faces Christmas in limbo, still unaware of how his future is to be decided. He had desperately wanted to get the whole sorry mess out of the way before the festive period, especially now there was the added media presence. He was meant to take the stand today; he had prepared himself, but now he must wait.

The jurors have been warned not to discuss the case, which Jacob finds wholeheartedly laughable, as if this was even a feasible possibility. He watched each member of the court exit, after the clerk had informed them of the judge's illness and the adjournment. He watched these twelve strangers walk away, most probably to their relief, and struggled to comprehend that his future fate lay in their hands.

Jacob knew the type of some of them: uneducated, ill-informed, slovenly. He imagined the majority of them were bitter *Daily Mail* readers, fuelled by misleading stories and propaganda. How could this type of person ever be judged appropriate to decide such cases? It was like a Jeremy Kyle show, but they weren't the audience. Instead they were in charge of determining his innocence.

25

Richard

Richard used the judge's illness as an excuse for a holiday. He had not realised how involved he had become in the case until the enforced pause in the proceedings. Molly Smith had become such a focus, as the case had in itself, especially with the media coverage. The controversy made him feel like he had joined a one-way crusade, without remembering when he bought the ticket to the ride. He supposed there had been a tipping point, as with everything in life, when suddenly things tilt that little too far, and all that has been resting and balancing on that precursor comes crashing down.

He had not anticipated that Molly would be the one to knock things off kilter, but looking back over the years there had been a multitude of cases that could have easily done so. It was as if all the ludicrous comments, unjust sentences, irresponsible reports concerning victim responsibility and misogyny surrounding rape had imploded on itself, leaving a dirty mess, a filthy secret of society's attitude to rapists and victims, sprawled out before everyone with Molly at the centre. Richard was exhausted from it all and he needed a break.

Cornwall was beckoning again. He had found himself, the night before he had packed the car up, searching the definition of "burn out" on Google, and had suddenly realised how deeply he had allowed his lifestyle to be affected by his work. He had known for a long time that a drastic change, a shake-up was needed, but that scared him, also. Where did he go from here? If he didn't have the law he did not know what to be. Suzie had helped him realise his happiness to a certain extent, but it had become an elusive, unobtainable source out of his reach in the past year.

Am I happy? Richard wondered. *Is this what happiness is and I don't know it?* Was happiness merely moments that washed over him, not impacting long enough to change his constant state of mind, or was he too busy, too consumed by work, challenges, chores in his mind to feel any extreme emotion: good or bad, apart from tiredness.

The journey to the coast was monotonous, but he managed to drive without remembering most of it. Arriving at his destination he was slightly concerned at how robotically he had driven for five hours. It was blustery and wet in Porthleven this time, and it was just what Richard had hoped for. He wanted to hole himself up in the The Ship Inn for the weekend, and drink his sorrows away. He wanted to look out as the waves battered the harbour wall, and sigh with delight that he was warm and snuggled away from the elements. He wanted time, responsibility and age to elude him. He wanted to become ageless, timeless, just a man in a pub on the Cornish coast reading a newspaper and drinking a pint. He wanted to be nothing but that, if only for one weekend.

Stephanie

Bayonne is beautiful at Christmas. It holds just the right amount of tradition and class, very much like the French themselves. The music dimly drifts into the streets as the smells of delicious delights waft through the air. I have always thought Bayonne much more romantic than Paris or Venice, both of which I have always found too big and cumbersome for a weekend, when you want all the joys of a city within footfall. The difficulties involved with public transport, undergrounds, even canals had always put me off – I just wish to walk carefree through the streets knowing that losing my way would be pleasant, rather than a logistical nightmare.

I found the bar I frequent when visiting the city, and ordered a hot wine. "Je voudrais un vin chaud." I noticed him before he saw me across the bar. He was wearing black, I liked him in black, it was smarter than his usual attire for trips, but I liked that also.

He merely raised his eyebrows when he caught my attention, and that was all it took to surrender to him. I had not anticipated inviting him, I had not even known why I had chosen to ask him on a whim. Nothing could ever happen between us, I had never wanted anything to happen between us, yet recently he had caused a new physical reaction in me. It was confusing, scary, exciting and enticing all at once.

It had been just what I needed to get away, especially after all the fuss and furore of the past few weeks. When the judge had become unwell, and the case had been adjourned, the media had become fixated on the case, and particularly my role in defending rape cases.

I was exhausted by it all, and I had leapt at the chance of a European break. I have spent the morning meandering through the Christmas market next to the cathedral and the town hall; the small wooden houses filled with Christmas crafts, carriage rides and an ice-skating rink in the centre: it is idyllic. I forgot myself amongst the huts, I bought Christmas gifts that I needn't give, I tried food that I was not hungry for, but I soaked it all up. I was intoxicated by the French, by the beauty of their everyday life. I have always aspired to live in France, but I have often felt too inadequate in my beauty and my skills to do so. I am not effortless enough to settle in this country. I am a worker, a grafter, everything I do is meticulously planned and executed, I cannot enjoy the sheer moment as the French can; I cannot successfully just "be".

He stares across the table at me as I place my bags of shopping on the floor. I smile, he nods. "Stephanie." When he speaks my name, it sounds almost like a question, but he goes no further in his greeting.

"You came? I didn't think you'd make it, but it seemed like a waste of the hotel room and ticket. I'm glad you could make it: my friend cancelled so last minute, and I don't mind holidaying by myself, but I'm so glad you did, you know, it's nice you came…" I realise I am skittish in my speech, but I feel nervous around him suddenly, and I can't understand why.

"Stephanie, we need to talk."

I am not used to him addressing me like this. He is formal in his manner, which is unlike him, and he is yet to smile. I notice he has not even ordered a drink, so I stand to approach the bar for him.

"Where are you going?"

"To get you a drink, you look like you could loosen up a bit." I laugh gently, but he does not respond. "A beer okay?"

He nods.

I return to the table after I have his beer in hand, and I can see him scanning through his phone. His leg is twitching, his leg only ever twitches when he is anxious. During our finals, I had sat behind him, and been astonished at how much he jiggled his left leg during a three-hour paper.

"Do you remember our criminal evidence lecture, Steph?"

I nod. This time it is my turn to stay quiet.

"You remember that speech she gave us on our last lecture?" He looks at me expectantly.

"Yes, I do, I remember."

"You remember what she said, Steph. What she tried to teach us?"

I think back, and I am transported to a day over a decade ago. We are sitting in a small lecture theatre, Matthew to my left. We have just finished our last class on bad character evidence. We are in an amphitheatre so we are all looking down at the lecturer. She is slowly packing her papers as the first person goes to stand. She pauses then breaks into a passionate dialogue.

She tells us of fairness, she talks of the failings of the law, of miscarriages of justice, of lives ruined. She tries to instil one last lesson. She warns us against the profession if all we wish for is a sports car and nice bank account. She talks to us of change, of practising law for the right reasons. She continues until she gets so passionate she wells up, some of us stand, we are clapping her when she finishes. I can see Matthew by my side, whistling her as she leaves the lecture hall. It was inspiring; it was what we had all studied for, or so I thought. As the rapture died down I looked around at my fellow students, and saw the ones who were unimpressed, who had not registered what she was saying, who had no interest in justice or fair representation, but who were just there for the money, the power, the status.

"Of course I do." I come back to myself, the memory vanished. "How could I forget."

"You'll understand then..." He pauses. "You'll understand

why I did what I did – why I spoke to the newspapers about your tactics."

I am confused. I stare at him blankly.

"You know it was me, Steph. You must do. Who else would have known your tactics so well."

I do not understand what he is saying. "What was you, Matthew? What are you talking about?"

"It was just– just– You had forgotten. You forgot why we did this, why we got involved, why we wanted to do what we do now... It was like you had become just like them. It was all about the game and winning. You would skip from murder to talk of Habitat sofas without a sigh... It was as if it all stopped mattering: those people, those lives you have the power to change or destroy. It was like innocence or guilt became an afterthought, and I could not watch it anymore, Steph. I couldn't bear to stand by knowing what tactics you all use, and not speak out, to not say, because it needs to stop, Steph, and if you're not going to try and stop it, I am, Steph. I am."

I raise my glass and try to take a sip, but I realise my hand is violently shaking. I cannot steady it. The room I am in becomes blurred: the lines that structure my life suddenly wobble. I go to stand, but I stumble. I need to get out of the bar. I need to get out of the bar now.

It is late when I return to the hotel room, it is late, and I am drunk. Drunk and angry. Angry at Matthew. Angry at myself. Angry at a whole pile of situations I have failed to fight when I should have. Angry that the fights I always set out to take on have become skewed, the conflict present, but I have found myself on the wrong side. Matthew is right, I can see that now. I know he has his reasons, his own moral compass that he uses to justify what he did. I know he is merely trying to use the media as a useful tool to secure justice, but he does not understand them, or how it works; by highlighting the game of barristers in these cases, he has just given rapists insider knowledge. He has allowed them to know the tricks, the behaviour, the appearance of victims to look out for, the ones to prey on, because they are less likely to get convicted or caught.

26

Stephanie

Matthew and I had met for breakfast the next day after his revelation. Ultimately, I knew I could not bear a grudge for him speaking publicly about an opinion he had always voiced privately to me, but nevertheless I could not bring myself to pretend that our relationship had not been damaged by his actions. I had struggled to keep conversation, or make eye contact over our croissants. In the end, I had stood and left, and told him I needed some time, and that'd I'd see him on my return to the UK.

The remainder of my holiday had been sombre: I was angry and hurt. I knew Matthew had never been comfortable with my tactics, or those of any other barristers when it came to rape cases, and maybe he had felt compelled to speak out. However, this did not stop the sense of betrayal I felt.

The anger had disintegrated into mild annoyance as the days went on. The media attention was unnecessary and not, in my opinion, in the interest of justice, but I knew it was only temporary. Molly Smith and Jacob Walker-Kent would become history, and the case would be soon forgotten. Yes, Matthew had exposed my tactics, but they were not just mine; they were the tactics of the majority of barristers in such cases. It was the way the machine worked.

We had fallen out before when it came to our ideas on professional conduct, but never did I think he'd go to the media.

He had tried to message briefly, but it was fruitless. He would have known that, he always knew when he needed to give me space to calm down.

If it wasn't for the reminder about Matthew and Annalise's festive gathering arriving in the post a week after my return, I think I would have actively avoided more contact with him, but then I knew shunning him at Christmas could send out a permanent message, and for that I was not prepared. By then I quite simply missed him too.

27

Molly

There are forums online I never knew existed; whole worlds of virtual cyberspace dedicated to the accounts of victims of inappropriate sexual touching, rape and harassment. There are pages and pages of accounts by girls and women who are confused, shocked and disgusted by what has happened to them. There are hundreds, if not thousands of females trying to decipher whether what their friend, date, colleague, boss or boyfriend did was rape. I never realised how grey the area was, how confused we all are about what constitutes rape until it happened to me.

I see the same questions over and over again in the forums: *Was it my fault? Did I lead him on? Do you think anyone will believe me? Was it rape? What if I've remembered it wrong?* I recognise myself in the other women's accounts – the denial, the questioning, the confusion. I wish I was brave enough to respond to these women, but I just read through their experiences.

I want to reach out to these girls: telling them that they

should report, telling them not to be ashamed, telling them we must stand up and stop these men, because it is wrong, but deep down I would feel like a liar, a coward, because I did not report Jacob initially. And, I too am deeply ashamed, and I am also so terrified that I cannot even describe it as frightened or scared, because it is so much more physical than that. The thought that Jacob will get away with what he did, that all these men will continue to go unpunished, and this abuse will continue to happen is too much.

I do not for a moment believe that by standing up to Jacob I will change anything, but I did it because there is nothing else I can do. I have such little control over what happened to me that I desperately wanted to gain some back. My barrister, Richard, is encouraging, but I see the worry in his eyes, the look of pity that comes when someone is humouring your hope. He seemed to know about the absence of justice in my case before it had even begun.

Jacob

Regretted sex was all over the media these days. Jacob couldn't seem to turn the TV on without reading about another campus rape in America, the campaigns that featured alongside them were just as tiresome. "Rape is Rape" posters filled his Instagram and Facebook feeds; he thought this term was somehow ironic: when so many women claimed that regretted sex was rape.

It seemed to Jacob that many women were reporting sexual assaults and rapes as acts any normal, reasonable person would assimilate as simply morning-after regrets. The problem in Jacob's eyes was this want to be promiscuous, to celebrate free-sex and experimentation, the desire to be reckless, but then the goal posts of what is too reckless changes. The man is suddenly caught off guard, because what was fun last night is now cast in another light come morning.

Jacob could recall so many occasions where girls had presented him with misleading signals. It was a minefield trying to decipher what was okay and wasn't these days. When it came to consent, Jacob could remember times when he and his friends in university had sex only not to remember the act the next day. Is that really to say it was rape?

Jacob had recently read an article by a writer based in LA that discussed the validity of "rape accusation culture", not "rape culture", but "rape accusation culture". This ridiculous notion that just because you are a male you are somehow by-proxy a rapist, Jacob was appalled at the lack of media coverage on the impact this had on these men; the lives that were irreversibly ruined, the reputations that were forever lost, the futures extinguished, simply because these girls could not own their drunken behaviour.

If drinking too much with a female friend, before having drunken sex together, which you may or may not remember, made you a possible rapist, well then nearly all of the men Jacob knew would be considered rapists. It was, quite simply, a joke.

28

Stephanie

It is a week before Christmas and the festivities and cumbersome annual dinners are suddenly upon me. I do not have the energy or the inclination to attend, yet I am obliged to, or so society dictates. The only invitation that I have received from friends is from Matthew and Annalise. I am acutely aware of the tension between us since his revelation in Bayonne, and I have only seen him twice since I received the reminder about this evening: once in passing by Harrods, where we both found ourselves suffocated by the London crowds, and for a post-work drink, which was awkward and stilted in retrospect. But I want to attend their party. I would like to instil some normality back into our relationship. I am not in favour of spending time with Annalise in their "darling home" as she calls it; but I would like to see him, to laugh with him, and celebrate a whole week off work.

I arrive at Matthew and Annalise's early. I hate arriving late at parties I feel unsure about attending, I never settle into the night, as if I missed out on the crucial joke that everyone else seems to know about. There is only one other guest: Albert, a pompous surgeon who purposefully raises his chin when he speaks to me, just to make it even more apparent he is looking down upon those around him. I have met Albert before, and find him significantly irritating. He has delusions of grandeur, and he cannot help but steer every conversation back to his occupation, which I do admire but I find the fact he solely discusses his career rather sad.

Annalise loves Albert: she is in awe of his position, and obviously believes that his status as a surgeon impacts upon her social standing given they are friends. I watch her giggle and open her mouth in wonder at his stories concerning the hospital, and occasionally I note she grabs his upper left arm to emphasise quite how impressed by him she is. Albert laps it all up, and slaps Matthew on his shoulder whilst peering at Annalise's chest. I am sure Matthew notices but he does not say anything.

"Oh, Stephanie, I'm so sorry, darling. I did not realise you didn't have a drink." Annalise opens the fridge and produces a bottle: "It's Chablis of course, hang on let me get the nice wine glasses from New York. You'll have white, won't you? Oh, of course you will." She raises an eyebrow at me, Matthew can't see but I know it is a subtle dig at my drinking.

"Yes, white is fine, Annalise. Thank you," I say through gritted teeth.

"Here you are." She passes me a glass. "Matthew and I bought those wine glasses last year, you remember when we went to New York for a romantic weekend, Steph." Annalise loves to assert ownership over Matthew when I see her.

"Yes, I remember. They're lovely."

"I know, I saw them in *Macy's* and I said to Matthew: *I just have to have to have them.*" I smile and feign interest. "Every time I drink out of them I just think of our time in New York."

It does not go unnoticed it's the third time she mentioned New York.

"I'm so glad you've come, Steph. What with you being on your own. I said to Matthew, *you must invite Steph.*"

I nod and smile. It is like this between us – Annalise does the majority of the talking.

"So, anyway, how are things, Steph?"

"Yes, good. Work, work, work. I won't bore you with the legal talk, best save that for Matthew." I know she is deeply threatened by mine and Matthew's shared intellect and this comment will irritate her.

Matthew comes to join us and kisses me on both cheeks. "Sorry, I didn't get a chance to properly greet you when you arrived."

"It's fine, too busy listening to Albert's stories of heroism." I smile at Matthew, he's aware I am not taken in by Albert's stuffy didactic tone.

"I was just saying, Matthew, doesn't Steph look great. Have you done something new with your hair." She actively seeks to compliment me when Matthew is in the vicinity.

"No," I reply curtly. I know I'm being rude, but I struggle with Matthew's choice of partner. It is not that I don't like her as such; it is just I cannot understand her.

I cannot fathom why Matthew would choose to be with someone so vacuous and self-consumed. The woman doesn't even vote; she actively avoids current affairs; and everything she discusses revolves around money. I have, on many occasion, heard her brand drop during a conversation.

I could understand the initial attraction: she is glamorous and pristine, her beauty is undeniable, but there is not much else to give. I always imagined their relationship to be limited, that Matthew would grow weary of their conversations, at the lack of mental stimulation, but now I wonder if this is what attracts him. Maybe outside his job he wants to shut off. He wishes the world was not complex, and when he is with Annalise he can pretend just that.

Richard

Richard was dreading the next week or so. He knew the rest of the country was looking forward to time off, to long, lazy lie-ins and sumptuous dinners; but he could not bear the thought of it.

Two years ago, it had been an entirely different story. He and Suzie had been invited to her parents' in Cornwall for three nights. He had reluctantly agreed at first: he had yet to spend an extended time with them, and he was nervous.

His parents had feigned agreement when he floated the idea that he was going to be doing something different over the festive period, but he knew they were devastatingly disappointed he wasn't spending it with their family beneath the understanding façade.

Suzie's parents' home was what Richard aspired to owning. He knew whilst he stayed in London he would inevitably live in cramped bedsits and flats that cost an extortionate amount, but in the future he hoped to live in a house that he felt proud of, that reflected the person he wanted to become.

The house was a sprawling great mass of red bricks and plants weaving up its sides. The doorway was grand and inviting, with a mass of holly and fairy lights. From every window warm yellow lamps glowed onto the enclosed lawn. It was a secret haven of tranquillity and beauty, and Richard loved how it reminded him of country homes in the movies. For all its quirks and eccentricity, the house was a thing of beauty. It enveloped you in its warmth and history. He could almost sense the happy memories that had occurred under its roof when he first entered. If buildings could talk he was sure this one would tell tales of happiness. Suzie had taken on the energy of her teenage years when they entered, her limbs almost too excitable and big for her body. She threw herself around from sofa to sofa laughing with her siblings, and play fighting with their long-haired spaniel, Ludo.

Richard had initially been timid around Ludo: he was jumpy and yappy, and altogether an irritant, but after a long muddy walk and a bath, he had been endeared by him. As Richard snoozed on the sofa Ludo had approached him, and snuggled in for a long, warm sleep. He struck up a strange relationship with Ludo over that period. The dog would never leave his side as if sensing he was in need of a companion, and Richard had found himself searching him out in the house should he disappear from the room for more than twenty minutes.

Christmas now was just a timely reminder of what he had lost, days he had still hoped to enjoy. Suddenly the memories of Suzie flooded back: it had always been a time they spent together, a happy time, yet all he wanted to do was delete the halcyon days. He wanted to forget the happiness they had once shared, because it made his sadness now more apparent.

Last year Richard had taken Suzie to Florence after Christmas. He had booked the first weekend in January to avoid the hike in prices over the New Year. It was much quieter then, and they could enjoy the city without barging through the crowds.

Richard had never visited Florence, but Suzie had. He found her endless dialogue about the last time she had been there, and the tales of other, Italian men infuriating. He did not wish to hear about her wild, fun and free days from a time before he existed on her horizon. He knew she had been a waitress outside of Florence, but the trip seemed to re-ignite her passion and memories of that period, and he could not stop her manically reliving her youth there. It had been meant to be romantic, but he found himself enraged with jealously when she told him of Antonio, an old flame, and Richard became increasingly possessive of her whilst the men gawped unashamedly in her direction.

Suzie had finally understood his feelings after he had a few too many red wines and had exploded in a fury of rage at her. She had become quiet, and then promised not to talk of her experiences in Florence again. In retrospect, it had been selfish of him to make her deny her past, to silence her memories for his benefit, but the thought of Suzie before she had met him had this effect upon him. He could not bear to think of the men that came prior to himself, or the nights out, or the jobs, or the friends. He had wanted too much of her, but never given her enough of himself.

They had spent the days wandering the streets, gazing at the Duomo and the Ponte Vecchio bridge. He had been enchanted by the city's beauty and art; for him the city of Renaissance had woken him from the drudgery and morbidity of his job. He had felt a rebirth whilst he sat in the Café Gubbe Rose overlooking Piazza Della Repubblica. A sense of perspective and calm had overtaken him, and he had felt inspired to change things. His work had all but extinguished his relationships and his downtime, and he promised to slow down, to let the cases wash over his head.

He promised Suzie as they watched the carousel in the square, the lights fading into one another as the city buzzed around them, that he would prioritise her. He would make sure she came first more often. He had promised not to lose touch with what was important. His promise had lasted less than two weeks.

When they returned home he had tried. He had lamely suggested walks in the park, he had booked a spontaneous meal in a high-end restaurant, he had bought her underwear, he had even discussed going on a long holiday that summer, maybe island hopping around Greece, but it had not been enough. Suzie was already despondent. She was angry with him, yet he did not know why; she would spin into a rage at the slightest comment from him. Looking back, he'd already lost her.

29

Jacob

Christmas for Jacob was a lavish affair. This year more than ever, as his mother had succeeded in spoiling him with no end of gifts due to the current court case. He had rather hoped the case would have been thrown out by now, or the judge would have seen Molly for what she really was, but he realised now that all hope of that was fruitless. It appeared the case was going to run until the bitter end, until the jury had their moment, and could convey what a conniving whore Molly actually was. He had found his anger level rising immensely recently. He would be out with friends having drinks, and find himself lost in a world of confusion as to how he had ended up in the current situation. He would watch men and women flirt and become suspicious of where the interludes were leading. He became concerned that what one party may interpret as a come-on, the other may see as harassment.

He had been overwhelmed with rage at the grey mass that clouded his mind when he tried to make sense of these relations. It was as if the whole dating, male/female dynamic, had been altered, and no one knew what was appropriate anymore. Girls could go out, flaunt their bodies, dance provocatively, even rub themselves up against men, yet as soon as men reciprocated or mimicked the behaviour they were ridiculed, chastised, even arrested in some cases, as he now knew first hand. It was as if society had become based on some obscure feminism that seemed to think it was okay for women to act as sluts, but not okay for them not to be treated as such.

He wondered what his father would have thought of Molly's preposterous allegations. He would have thought the world had gone mad, Jacob was sure. He could hear his booming voice in his head explaining that it made absolutely no sense. Gender equality was a notion Jacob particularly struggled to come to terms with. He found it laughable: genders could never really be equal, because there are so many variations between male and females. If gender equality really existed, and was the ideal, why did women still want to be looked after financially? Why did they still innately become the primary caregiver for children? Why were women more than happy to take Jacob's money? Why did they revel in the enjoyment of him taking control? Jacob knew men and women were not equal. Women have always wanted men to be powerful, to provide, to protect them. You need only read up on the basic evolution of the human species to understand this, and no amount of fraught debate between women, whose mothers were dope-smoking student artists in the sixties and seventies, was going to change Jacob's opinion on this.

Jacob and his mother had spent Christmas Day at another inanely boring restaurant, which fancied itself too much, and spent so much time being exclusive it forgot to actually provide anything of substance. He longed for the days when he had to undo his trouser button he was so full of Christmas dinner, when he had lounged on the sofa all afternoon slowly snacking on more and more food, until he felt nauseous with greed.

Since his father's departure his mother had not allowed them to spend a Christmas Day in either her house or his. He imagined it was because it made her too sad, but she pretended it was because she liked to dress up and flaunt her fortune around the city's eateries. No matter how many tables were filled, how many people dined around them there was still a sense of loneliness to Christmas. Wherever they were there was always a feeling of loss. He had never wished for brothers or sisters before, but on days like this he believed he may have found a sibling some comfort: another body, another voice to quash the inevitable silence as they quietly ate their meals, and made small talk. He drunk brandy on Christmas Day, a lot of brandy to be precise. It helped numb the mounting pressure to have a good time; and he found it often helped him have a good time.

His mother had arranged that they attend the home of one of her friends, Amelia, in North Islington for evening drinks and nibbles after dinner. The only reason Jacob had agreed to this was because he was mildly aware of this particular friend's daughter. Sofia, the daughter, was twenty-five years old and fiercely pretty. He had seen her out and about in the clubs and bars he frequented, and he had always thought her a bit too cocksure. She was loud and carefree, not the type you wished to settle down with but a bit of fun. Jacob was on the lookout for some escapism, and Sofia seemed the perfect candidate for his affections.

They arrived at Amelia's house just shy of six o'clock. His mother greeted her warmly with a hug, and Jacob politely kissed her on both cheeks before she drew them into the belly of the building. Amelia had decorated the house with taste and enthusiasm. The decorations were the perfect mix of class and tradition. Across the table was a spread of nibbles, canapés and blinis. He had champagne thrust in his hand, and watched as his mother disappeared into the sea of guests. He knew he too should mingle, but his thirst was not yet quenched enough to keep up the fitful pretence his mother required of him at such events.

He found a bottle of champagne, and carefully placed it on the fireplace to his left. The guests were in the long open-plan dining room and kitchen; he was near enough to the door, should he need to slip away from any unwanted attention. He assumed Amelia's friends would have heard of his current court case, but he was not certain, and he knew his mother's friends were not accustomed to discussing such matters in public, so he hoped the subject would not be raised. He had spotted Sofia across the crowd, and watched her movements carefully. She was not self-conscious, when she laughed she threw her head back with gusto, she placed her arm around guests as she spoke, and was not ashamed to fill her mouth with food. She did not seem to fit here, but then Jacob wondered if any of them did, or whether some were better at pretending to be reserved and proper.

Jacob did not get to converse with Sofia until the clock had chimed eight o'clock, and by that point he had consumed the whole bottle of champagne he had piffled away earlier, on top of the wine at dinner and brandy. He was outside smoking a cigarette when she appeared, a scarf thrown over her hair and an oversized coat shielding her from the bitter cold.

"Jacob, what a pleasure." She smiled at him with one side of her mouth. He knew she was a minx, and she had the ability to sound seductive with a mere greeting.

"Sofia, Merry Christmas, and all that."

"Full of the festive cheer, Jacob." She threw back her head as he had seen her do earlier and laughed. He stared at her, perplexed by her joviality.

"Oh, Jacob, relax. I hate these things too, we'll just get pissed together. We can creep upstairs soon, they'll all be too sloshed to realise we aren't playing the game with them. There is a good series on, and a blanket I want to snuggle up in."

Jacob smiled, and nodded back at her. He had expected her to suggest a party, another debauched evening of alcohol and fun, but he was now glad of her proposal. He had wanted to spend Christmas in front of the TV for years, and now he had the opportunity to do so, albeit at someone else's house, but TV nevertheless.

By nine o'clock they had managed to slip away to the sitting room on the third floor of the townhouse, and Jacob was comfortably laid out on the chaise longue ready to watch *Call the Midwife*. Sofia was cross-legged on the floor with a beige cashmere blanket over her legs. She leant back against the chaise longue and sipped on her champagne.

"Jacob, can I ask you a question?" She had twisted her body and was looking up at him now.

He nodded in response.

"What they are saying, about that girl... it's not true, is it? I mean, I don't mean to pry. I never believed it, but I just wanted you to know that."

He stared back down at her, briefly annoyed she had mentioned Molly and spoilt the moment of relaxation he was enjoying. "No, Sofia, of course it isn't true. Do I look like a rapist to you? I was her friend for God's sake, but I suppose I didn't know Molly at all. I just can't believe women can get away with making such things up. It could ruin me. She could ruin my life." He tried to quash the anger in his voice, he did not want to appear too forceful on the matter.

Sofia was silent, she rose after a few minutes and sat down

next to Jacob, placing her hand on his leg, she smiled. "The jury will see the truth, Jacob. They'll see that you're not capable of such a thing, trust me. Of course you're not a rapist, everyone can see that."

Sofia rested her head on Jacob's lap, and they watched the rest of *Call the Midwife* in silence. It was only later when Sofia had fallen asleep that Jacob moved her body so he could leave. When he reached his mother downstairs she was inebriated, and he could barely make out her slurring words. He had not drunk much over the remaining hours of the evening, probably too much to drive, but he knew Amelia would lend him her car. The wait for taxis would be too long and he was impatient. He would drive his mother back to his. She was in no fit state for a hotel room now, not on her own anyhow.

Molly

I had always spent Christmas surrounded by friends and family, desperately trying to fit everyone in, driving from one household to the next. Luke had a big family and the day was always full. We rarely had time to sit back and relax. Last year I hadn't even managed to watch one programme on the television, what with grandparents, nieces and nephews, and of course Luke's parents (my mother rarely made an appearance). We only really enjoyed the lazy indulgences of Christmas on Boxing Day.

I had thought about calling my brother this year. I had floated the idea for days of asking if I could join him for the day, but I never quite gathered the courage to ask for an invite. I knew he had assumed I had plans, otherwise he would have asked me to join them. My mother, as per usual, was abroad. She had never really celebrated Christmas, so it wouldn't occur to her to ask what her children were doing. Alison had asked me to hers, and a few of the girls had half-heartedly offered up their company, but I would be an awkward presence for them. I didn't want to impose. It was easy really: I told them I was staying with my brother; they didn't think to check, and they did not know him to ask; and as soon as they assumed I had company the topic was not mentioned again.

So, this year I had spent the day on my own. I had not left the house. I had not even changed out of my pyjamas. I had eaten a bag of Doritos and a few Roses chocolates, nothing else. I had drunk a bottle of red wine and four gins, and I had been thoroughly drunk throughout the day as I watched the programmes and films on offer. It had been liberating briefly, not fulfilling any other family commitments, but as the day wore on I realised how alone I was. The baby would have been twenty-weeks now. I wondered if circumstances had been different if I would have been showing by now, how I would have felt if I'd decided to keep the child. It seemed incomprehensible that I could have been carrying Jacob's child. Life seemed incomprehensible.

I spent the later part of the day scouring Facebook, searching through happy faces and large family gatherings; images of copious amounts of food and presents filled my screen. It was towards the bottom of my news feed I came across the image of Luke, all smiles and joviality. He was wearing a reindeer onesie, and he was sat beside his sister and a girl I did not recognise, he looked so carefree, as if our break-up was years ago. I fought back tears as I imagined this Christmas had Jacob never happened.

Stephanie

The sweet smell of warm currants and cinnamon filters through my door. I glance at the small pile of presents on my dresser, five in total, three of which are for myself. I have treated myself to a pair of Louboutin heels, Jo Malone perfume and a cashmere scarf. The remaining two gifts are for Matthew and Annalise.

I hadn't wanted to spend Christmas here, but then I never really wanted to spend it anywhere. Matthew had suggested it when he had discovered I lacked any specific plans for Christmas Day. Annalise had kindly insisted I spent Christmas Eve with them too, so I would not wake up in an empty house.

I had spent the previous Christmas by myself, convinced that you could make such a day special for one. When I awoke I had run myself a bath. I'd drunk champagne from the bottle, whilst I soaked in the tepid water. I'd cooked myself scrambled duck eggs and smoked salmon. I'd put on a dress and lipstick, and desperately tried to convince myself that it was enjoyable. I had not anticipated how cumbersome my loneliness would be, how crippling the empty seats at my table were. It only magnified how alone I truly am.

I do not dwell on my situation, but it is days such as this that the gap of my parents' departure from this world is intensely apparent. I had lost them both in quick succession in my mid-twenties to differing forms of cancer. Their deaths had highlighted the fact that I was an only child, forever desperate for a sibling to share the magnitude of my loss with me. Since then it had been altogether easier to remain solo. The thought of further devastation through loss was something I feared I was too fragile to bear. Christmas had since then represented everything I no longer had; everyone I no longer had.

I am sure Annalise appreciates sharing the festivities with me as much as I do with her. I am trying my hardest to maintain pleasantries, because, despite my feelings towards how vacuous she is, ultimately what she is doing for me is kind. She has enabled me to have company when I need it most, and I recognise this.

The day was perfectly pleasant in the end. Matthew was attentive to both of us, and jovial throughout. His sister and her husband joined us for dinner, so I did not feel like too much of a third wheel. I had met Emma and James previously, and enjoyed their easy company, something I noted made Annalise prickle. We ate lobster bisque to start, followed by a plump turkey and chocolate roulade. At one point, I even managed to forget what day it was, and I actually found I was enjoying myself.

Matthew has always known how difficult Christmas is for me, but he does not question or console me as he knows I would despise this. He quite simply "is", and that is enough of a distraction. I retired early to bed that night. Annalise and I just about managing to cope with the prolonged contact.

I awoke hours later to the sound of the bed creaking on the floor above me, and I lay there and listened as a silent tear ran down my cheek.

Richard

In retrospect Richard knew it had been the wrong decision. He could have quite easily spent the day with his parents, his sister, her partner and their children. He would have by this time already been asleep on the sofa full to the brim with Cathy's home-cooked turkey, a glass of wine ready on the side table to drink when he awoke, and a cheeseboard in the evening to enjoy. But this had been his old life, the life he partook in before he had met Suzie, and to return to it was a step backwards. He saw the invite as a regression.

In order to move forward Richard had chosen to return to Cornwall, which was ironic in itself, as this was also a step into the past, but he craved the isolation. What he had not factored in was the fact that when you booked yourself into the local pub, a table of one for Christmas dinner, you would not remain in isolation.

Three tables already had invited him to join them, one had even sent a compensatory whisky over, and smiled at him with pity. He wished he'd ordered room service. The Queen's speech was surely even better than this. The only day of the year worse to dine on your own was Valentine's, and he'd accidentally done this once too.

He was aware in the eyes of society choosing to dine alone on such a day is a heretical tragedy. His empty diary fills the people in the pub with unease, he can see that. Richard wished he could forget it was Christmas Day altogether. He longed for solitude, yet he did not want to be judged because of it.

The pressure to be jolly in the build-up to Christmas seemed insurmountable. He could not muster the enthusiasm or positivity required, the decision to opt out had been somewhat cathartic. Richard had been genuinely shocked at the disbelief his decision ignited in some of his friends, some of whom had been fairly hostile at his choice to be independent of company.

As he ate his slightly chewy, overdone turkey, his mind swam with thoughts of Suzie. He wondered what she would be doing, who she was with. He thought back to last year, and once again allowed the endless regret to wash over him. How could he have been so foolish, so lazy, so complacent that he had not even considered her departure an option? He ate his food quickly, before retiring to his room and the television, overcome with everything he wished he could change, and the devastating knowledge that it was already too late.

30

Molly

The courtroom was lighter than I remembered. In my memory the room was darker. The length of time since we were last here means my memory is somewhat absent, but now the strip lights glare down upon us. I can see the public gallery if I twist my head around to the left, but I try to avoid looking. I don't think I can bear to see their reactions as Jacob takes to the stand.

I have seen his statement, and I know how it already looks; what I am not prepared for is the force of the bitterness on the edge of his voice; the power of his resentment for being placed in this situation. If I didn't know better I would have thought he truly believed his innocence. There is no remorse. I wonder if he even regrets it? He is so arrogant, he stands there as if he doesn't have a care in the world; as if he is above me, above all of this.

As he swears the oath on the stand he stares directly at me. I try to maintain my composure, but his gaze is too intent, and I dip my head. I notice some members of the jury have picked up on our brief connection, and I hope that my inability to keep eye contact with Jacob does not make me look as if I have something to hide. Why would I want to look at him for too long? I cannot bear those eyes. I know I could have requested that I testified through video link, or that a screen be put up between us, but there was a part of me that wanted to face him, if only for a moment, that wanted him to know that I was not going to hide from him any longer.

Jacob

Molly looks tired. He is not surprised as he looks down at her from the stand, she must be exhausted from keeping up the pretence for so long. He wonders whether she can sleep at night, whether she lies awake thinking of how much distress she has caused him. He has heard through friends that Luke left her. He is not in the slightest surprised: he for one could not make love to a woman who he knew had another man's member in her whilst they were together. He is not surprised she is single. She should expect nothing less considering what she has done. He feels for the next man she traps with her soft, big, brown eyes and cascading golden curls; her persona and skin both like honey. She has the features and façade for the perfect ruse. She had easily fooled Jacob into thinking she was someone she was in fact not: honest and kind.

Jacob was prepared for questioning today. He had been prepared for months. He had wanted to take the stand as soon as the trial began, so he could have his say. He wanted to tell everyone the truth of the matter. He wanted to show Molly Smith for what she really was: a liar.

31

Richard

Richard begins with Jacob slowly. He wants to get the measure of him. The way he answers questions is often with a question: he is obviously extremely competent under cross-examination. His composure is unwavering. Stephanie Beaumont has already laid into Molly about her drinking, and how inebriated she was on the evening in question, and Richard knows he has some catching up to do. The jury are quickly making judgements as to whether she was what might be called loose.

"How many drinks would you say Molly had that evening, Mr Walker-Kent?"

"Six."

"And, how many of those drinks would you say you bought Molly, Mr Walker-Kent?"

"Three."

"And, would you say you drunk the same amount as Molly, or did she maybe drink a little bit more?"

"She drunk more."

"And who bought her that extra drink?"

"She bought herself the first three drinks. She'd drunk a bottle of wine: the glasses were 250ml measurements."

"So, you estimate that Molly had a bottle of wine, before you bought her a drink. You then proceeded to buy Molly two Jägerbombs, and a further large glass of wine, even though you were not drinking. Is that correct?"

"I did drink the Jägerbombs."

"Would you say Molly was drunk, Mr Walker-Kent?"

"Yes."

"So, you thought Molly was drunk? That is correct?"

"Yes."

"So, knowing Molly was drunk did you suggest that you'd walk her home?"

"No, she asked me to walk her home."

"Molly suggested it? Is that what you are saying, Mr Walker-Kent?"

"Yes."

"And, what were your intentions at this point?"

"Concern."

"But, you told me earlier you bought Molly another large glass of white wine and shots knowing full well she was drunk. So surely you would have known that would get her drunker? It doesn't sound like you were entirely concerned then for her well-being."

"Molly often drinks a lot. She didn't seem that drunk until we went to leave the pub."

"Oh, you didn't know that increasing the amount of alcohol she was drinking would make Molly more drunk?"

"No, that is not what I said."

"It seems rather confused – what you are saying, that is. Was she or wasn't she too drunk to walk home alone?"

"She could have been, yes."

"Now, Mr Walker-Kent would you say someone who is

clearly too drunk to walk home alone is too drunk to consent?"

"It wasn't like that."

"Tell me what it was like, in your version of events then, Mr Walker-Kent."

Richard sees the glint in Jacob's eye as if this is what he'd been waiting for. He begins his dialogue with Molly asking him in for a cup of tea, word for word his account is nearly exactly the same as Molly's until the point that she woke up.

"So, she sobered up – is that what you are saying?"

"Yes."

"How exactly did she sober up?"

"She slept."

"And what makes you so sure she sobered up whilst she was sleeping?"

"It is a well-known fact that when people sleep over a period of time they sober up. She'd also eaten toast and drunk cups of tea."

"So, are you saying Molly was no longer intoxicated?"

"No."

"So, she was still drunk in your opinion, Mr Walker-Kent?"

"I'd say she still had alcohol in her system but she didn't appear drunk."

"Surely if she had copious amounts of alcohol in her system she was incapable of consenting." Richard words this as a statement, rather than a question.

"She consented."

"How did she consent?"

"She didn't say no. She didn't say stop..."

"But, did you not have your hand over her mouth? So, how could she?"

"That is because she was moaning with pleasure, and I didn't want her partner to hear that."

"So, you didn't want her partner to hear, but you didn't mind having sexual intercourse behind her partner's back?"

"It was not like that. Molly and I had been falling in love for months."

Richard wanted to avoid Jacob going any further. Declaring his love for Molly on the stand would not work in their favour.

"So, after you had intercourse with Molly what was her reaction?"

"She wanted me to leave." Jacob looks forlorn. He pauses. "I imagine because Luke was upstairs she felt guilty."

"Did she say this?"

"No."

"So why have you imagined this? Was it not the case that Molly had not agreed to sex with you whatsoever, you had forcefully pushed yourself on her against her will, you had then silenced her by covering her mouth, and as soon as you were done raping her she wanted you as far away as possible?"

"No."

"I put to you, Jacob Walker-Kent, this was in fact the case. You had wanted Molly Smith for months, so you waited, you preyed on her by plying her with alcohol. Then you waited until you were invited into her house when she was vulnerable, and you forcefully raped her. You were of the belief you were entitled to her, that she should be yours. You wanted what you couldn't get so you took it anyway."

"No, that was not the case. I loved her. I loved Molly."

Richard stops the questioning, he has implied enough, and there is no need to say anymore. Sometimes it is better to stop earlier than you wished. He wasn't prepared to give Jacob airtime to talk of his love for Molly either.

Molly

There have only been a number of incidents in my life where I have found myself so off kilter, so far removed from where I knew I should be, that I have been totally silenced by the pure shock of the realisation. Today is one of those incidents. Nothing seems to correlate: the itchy three-piece navy suit I am wearing, the rigid chair I sit in, the barrister to my right, the courtroom, the case, the miscarriage, this life.

I have no idea how I got here. It is as if the previous six months I have been shrouded in heavy fog and suddenly it is lifted, and I can really see the situation for what it is. Jacob is so collected as he takes to the stand, he is unwavering, he does not appear nervous whereas my legs have shaken violently since the court case began. I cannot control them; these violent spasms seem to be my body's physical means of coping.

The thing I have discovered during this court case is how removed I feel from the whole procedure. I suppose I have felt removed from all my recent procedures – that is how I coped with the pregnancy and miscarriage too. As each expert witness has risen to take the stand I have further felt like I am watching a TV drama unfold. The consequences of the trial seemed entirely removed from my life.

Now as my barrister questions Jacob about my drinking I feel even more foolish. Who allows themselves to get that drunk? Who drinks so carelessly? I know what the jury will be thinking, what they already are thinking. Stephanie Beaumont has already ensured that they consider me loose, and as Richard runs through how much I'd drunk, it only compounds this idea.

I know Richard has already discussed with me the fact he will be arguing I was too inebriated to have the capacity to consent. I understand. But just because I understand it does not make it easier to hear your behaviour, your lifestyle, your choices dissected bit by bit.

Jacob

He knows what Mr Clarke is trying to do, but he too is a master of manipulating words. He had wondered what tack the prosecution was going to take when it came to cross-examining him, and it was now clear their focus would be incapacity to consent. *A little obvious*, Jacob thought.

Whereas Stephanie rightly focused on Molly's loose morals and hedonism, Mr Clarke was trying to present to the court that Jacob intentionally plied her with alcohol to take advantage of her vulnerability. He questions how many drinks Molly had, how many Jacob bought. He is trying to twist his generosity at the bar into something sordid. Molly had drunk more, but then Molly had always drunk more than him, most people did. Jacob preferred to maintain an element of control. He had learnt in his teenage years how to control the booze. He was far too considered to ever allow it take hold of him.

Mr Clarke focuses on the fact he bought Molly a number of drinks when she was clearly already intoxicated; he goes on and on. Jacob can feel his frustration rising. He understands he must keep calm. Stephanie has warned him not to get riled or angered by the prosecution. He is aware that this is their job, they want him to flare up, to demonstrate some signs of aggression. Of course, an angry man is far more likely to commit rape than someone calm and placid.

Jacob does not allow himself to be coerced. Mr Clarke cannot determine that buying your friends drinks repeatedly constitutes a clear intention to rape. He calmly explains that there had been many other nights he'd bought Molly drinks, many other nights she'd been drunk. When Mr Clarke implies he was taking advantage of Molly by walking her home to enter her house, Jacob answers with a question.

"So, walking your friend home, who is highly intoxicated, so she is safe, is a predatory act?"

He sees Mr Clarke tense, clearly uneasy with the manner in which he is responding. Mr Clarke comes back at him, suggesting if he was that concerned why did he buy her more drinks. Jacob is getting bored of his line of questioning, he is implying Jacob got her too drunk, but he is also implying that after he got her too drunk he shouldn't have walked her home. He is trying to rabbit hole him so nothing he says will look good.

Jacob is astute and can defer the line of questioning before Mr Clarke has the opportunity to trap him. He can see Stephanie looking intently on, a look of curiosity on her face that he cannot place. Maybe it is intrigue, maybe it is something altogether different, but he catches her eye all the same until she drops her stare, and for a moment he sees a flicker of unease in her expression as if she suddenly sees him through Molly's eyes.

Stephanie

It is always a worry when your client takes to the stand. I can explain to them what to expect but I cannot train Jacob Walker-Kent; I cannot practice the possible lines of questioning the prosecution may undertake.

However, as I watch Jacob on the stand it is as if he knows exactly what is coming, where Richard Clarke's questioning is leading and precisely how to answer. He answers as knowingly as a barrister. I knew he was clever, but I had not realised quite how sharp Jacob was until this point. I imagine he could quite possibly argue his way out of anything. He remains controlled and calm. I had warned him not to anger, not to concede when counsel tries to wind him up, but he is emotionless. His confidence so great he just appears arrogant to me. I note the jurors do not appear to notice, but then they are not attuned. They do not see the courtroom as I see it.

Jacob catches my eye, I see a slight raise of his brow as he focuses on me. I see him telling me he is in control, and I have a moment of doubt. I look at this man before me, and suddenly question what kind of person I am defending. He does not drop from my gaze, and it makes me uneasy. I quickly look down at my notes, but as I do so I see a flicker of recognition. He knows that I have seen him for what he is.

32

Molly

I look down at my skirt as he speaks, focusing on a small thread that has come loose. I had not noticed it before. I debate pulling on it, but fear it may unravel further. I do not have scissors so I cannot even snip it. Instead I place my hand over it, but then I'm acutely aware it is still there, it is just now I cannot see it. This tiny thread bores into me, it occupies my mind as Jacob speaks on the stand. All I can think about is a tiny, loose navy thread that no one else can see.

Stephanie

Sentencing in rape cases I often think may be a deterrent in securing rape convictions. Unless a jury can be certain that rape has occurred, which is near-on impossible in some cases, I understand why they do not wish to convict a possible innocent man, who would then face a stretch in prison; as it stands under sentencing guidelines the minimum recommended sentence is four years.

I have often thought about a sliding scale of convictions when it comes to rape. Not that any type of rape is currently considered lesser or greater, but maybe there is a need to look at intention more closely, like we do in cases of murder for instance.

When it comes to rape the act (*actus reus*), and the intention (*mens rea*), must both be present. It is not just the *actus reus* that is important in criminal law, but also the *mens rea*.

In cases of rape the *actus reus* is satisfied by the penetration by a penis of the vagina by the defendant, and the victim did not consent. The *mens rea* of rape is satisfied if the defendant intended to penetrate, and the defendant did not reasonably believe the victim consented. Now, whether the belief is reasonable is determined having regard to all the circumstances, including any steps the defendant has taken to ascertain whether the victim consents. The difficulty arises because sometimes there is confusion between the difference of consent and submission; because the victim submitted the defendant reasonably believed this constituted consent.

I have discussed on numerous occasions redefining the *mens rea* of rape to include levels of intention. I'm not suggesting it makes certain rapes less traumatic, but it may help with conviction rates and sentencing, if the law could further define the confusion in the area.

Not knowing you are a rapist is not an excuse to commit rape, but we must address society's failings, and those are that, whether we like it or not, we live in a world where some men are unaware that the way they behave when it comes to sexual relations could constitute rape. I know that rape is rape, but should the rapist who carries out a violent attack also face additional charges?

When we look at the *mens rea*, there is an immediate problem: "The defendant did not reasonably believe the victim consented." But rape can still occur if the defendant believed there was consent. It just means the defendant did not know or intend it to be rape. It does not mean it isn't rape though, it just means they had a mistaken belief it wasn't rape. If there is no intention in murder, the charge is manslaughter if the victim died. What if there is no intention to rape, but the victim was raped? Many men claim they did not know it would be construed as rape, so could there be an alternative charge in these cases?

It is not controversial for one to hold the opinion that a murder that involves torture, is carried out over a number of hours, and is meticulously planned, is somewhat more gruesome and disturbing than someone who shoots a gun and kills someone instantly. The intention of the later perpetrator is maybe blurred because they did not realise at that moment what they were doing? Should these two acts hold the same sentence? No.

So, the question is, should the man who plans to drug, beat and repeatedly rape a woman, and then leaves her for dead, face the same charge as the man who went to bed with a girl at a party, and had sex with her using force after they had committed sexual acts on one another prior to this, yet he had failed to take reasonable steps to ascertain whether she had consented to actual intercourse? It is not an argument I advocate, or am particularly comfortable with, but it is an argument, and when I have talked to many of my female friends it is thought to be a valid argument at that. It is not only men who think that there are different degrees of rape.

What the media don't assert is that it is not only MPs, judges and rapists who are unclear on rape. It is society. It is an area where people are so one-sided when faced with the issue that the proper discussion, the discussion that involves really re-assessing how we can change things, how we can alter perceptions, the law, the conviction rates, well this discussion never really happens because "rape is rape". Yes, "rape is rape", but by talking in black and white we're just dismissing the enormous grey area in the middle, that is not yet gaining a resolution.

Richard

Richard cannot believe the furore on the steps of the Crown Court again that morning. The camera lenses create a wall of large black eyes as they enter the doors. He fends off the reporters shouting his name, and demanding statements, as the flashing lenses momentarily blind him. He has nothing he wishes to contribute to the rising debate that he will not be heard to say in court.

He had not expected such an intense reaction from the public. It is strange the cases that the media and the social networking sites pick up on. He has prosecuted much more hideous, depraved sexual assault cases than this one. He has over the years prosecuted, often with failure, hundreds of rape cases where the victim knew the perpetrator, all of their stories similar to that of Molly and Jacob, yet for some reason there is something that has harnessed the public's emotion with this one. There is an avalanche of opinions daily on Twitter as the case develops. Richard reads these comments every evening. He is trying to gain insight into the public perception of rape. He wants to understand the extent of rape culture in the country, to decipher where these opinions come from, how to field them.

The majority of the comments are negative towards Molly. The support for Jacob is expected, and altogether predictable in its nature. The usual uproar that such allegations ruin men's lives, that Molly led him on, another case of one-night-stand regret on a female's behalf.

Richard is dulled by the monotony and lack of originality of these arguments. He wonders if one sole person who has commented has actually ever read an academic paper on the prevalence of false rape allegations, or the psychological reasoning behind the women who do falsely accuse. He strongly suspects not.

Richard wishes the media would truthfully indicate how common false allegations actually are, because research suggests that false allegations of rape are actually extremely rare. There is not a high incidence of cases, and it is a rarity that any such false allegations ever reach the courts but the papers love to sensationalise the impact of unjustified accusations. In the process, they have demeaned the notion of rape within the law.

By the time the weekend came Richard was relieved. After the commotion in and out of the courtroom this week he was purely exhausted. He had left chambers last night at eight o'clock, and collapsed on his sofa as soon as he arrived home.

He awoke at 3am, dribble smeared down his cheek, and the imprint of a zip seam from a sofa cushion on his forehead. He had managed to drag himself to bed without even taking his clothes off, or washing his face. Now he lay there, the sunlight streaming in and the sound of the city at the weekend trying to beckon him outside. It took all his might to even consider rising to make a coffee. His limbs felt drained from the mental exertion he had endured. He had never felt so acutely observed as a barrister before, but now he had the nation's media as a platform he really wasn't sure he wanted it. He preferred the background, the lull of his cases quietly streaming by. He hated the fuss, the furore that Molly Smith's case had attracted. It would do nothing for justice but only made it more difficult for Molly to move forward once this was all over.

He had been questioned endlessly by the media vultures as to his belief system on matters of rape. He agreed that rape culture needed uprooting, but he had no coherent formula that would achieve this. The journalists seemed concerned with how to better protect women. They had asked Richard his opinions on freely given pepper spray at universities, on the anti-rape female condom and anti-rape underwear.

He was baffled that the focus was still substantially perpetuated by the myth of rape being committed by strangers. Richard knew the truth was that the majority of girls who were watching a film, working late in the office, at a party with friends wouldn't employ these strategies, because they are not going jogging alone in the dark, walking home down a secluded lane, in a foreign country travelling alone. No, they are in places they think they are safe, they are with people they feel secure with, they do not perceive themselves to be at risk. He knew that rapes mostly happen when people feel safe, when women are with people they know, in environments they trust. Until the media, for one, changed their campaigns to focus on this, until people were educated correctly, and the awareness was shifted and instilled within society, rapes would continue to happen in places society still denies they do.

As he lay in bed his mind was a continuum of thoughts. There were things he needed to be doing: household chores, shopping, renewing his tax on his car, ring the electricity company, check his voicemail, reply to emails, speak to his parents, change his sheets, speak to the window cleaner, transfer money between accounts, eat, clean. But all he wanted to do was lie in bed, switch off the world and watch *Friends* on TV on repeat.

He knew he was stressed when he craved *Friends* episodes

back to back, but they took him out of himself. He wondered whether it was because the sitcom transported him back to days before he was a barrister, when he could go out at the weekend and his biggest concern was whether he could be bothered to go for a fry-up the next day. He missed those days.

He knew that the world was watching, and this would also make the outcome even harder for Molly Smith to deal with, but she was too far in now, and they both knew that they had no choice but to continue. Richard had his own opinions on the case, but these were irrelevant where a jury was concerned. They would go with the most plausible explanation in their minds, and the most secure. And, Richard realised where their decision already lay.

It was easier to side with the alleged perpetrator in cases of acquaintance rape. It was safer. It was so difficult in these cases to determine where the truth lay. Jurors did not want a wrongful conviction on their head. How could they really be sure he had raped her? They couldn't. But, Richard knew in cases such as these to follow his gut. To date, he had never come across a case where he believed the victim had made a false allegation, but he could not say that in court.

He had found himself watching Jacob Walker-Kent avidly in court, he was intrigued by his character – his façade. Richard knew straight away what kind of man he was. He could tell he came from money. He could also tell he was an only child. He had the air of someone who thought they deserved the best, were entitled to the utmost privilege, just by virtue of being born. Jacob Walker-Kent was innocent in his own eyes, and Richard was sure that he believed himself not to be guilty of any of the charges laid before him, but that was not because he did not commit the act in question. It was because Jacob Walker-Kent did not believe for one second that what he did was wrong. He was a man used to getting what he wanted, to getting his own way. If he laid claim to something or someone, he achieved his claim. And, if his claim was Molly Smith – as Richard believed it to be – Jacob had just achieved his aim. He had just failed to take into consideration anyone else's feelings in the process, including Molly's herself.

33

Richard

Richard stood before the jury, took a deep breath, and delivered his closing statement. Jacob's chances of acquittal were high, but he wanted the jury to understand the gravity of the crime, to focus on the violation that had taken place, and not everything that surrounded it.

"It is not a crime to socialise: to drink, to dance, to be friends with the opposite gender, to walk home with a friend, to wear a dress, to make a cup of tea, to invite a friend into your home, to change into something more comfortable in your home. It is not a crime to fall asleep, to be friendly, to fear for your safety, to be quiet initially and not report – but it is a crime to rape.

"Miss Beaumont has twisted the night in question. Suddenly all those innocent acts done by Molly have been twisted into a crime in itself.

"Trusting a friend becomes a crime, having fun becomes a crime. Every little thing Molly Smith did that night, every minute detail that surrounds her behaviour has been scrutinised. But that is not what this case is about, nor was it ever. Rape is defined by the Sexual Offences Against the Person Act as the penetration by a penis of the vagina by the defendant, and the victim did not consent. The defendant intended to penetrate, and the defendant did not reasonably believe the victim consented.

"So firstly, we need to ask, 'Did Jacob penetrate Molly?' The answer is clearly yes. There is no disputing the first part of the crime. But, what you the jury need to look at now is whether Jacob believed Molly to consent, and is that belief reasonable? When you look at whether that belief was reasonable, you should have regard to all the circumstances, including any steps Jacob took to ascertain whether Molly consented.

"In our opinion there is no evidence, nothing that clearly or even remotely suggests that Molly consented. There is no indication that Jacob took steps to ascertain that she was consenting. No, as far as the evidence suggests perhaps entirely the opposite. Now Jacob may argue he thought she was consenting, but how can he argue he took reasonable steps to make sure she was? He did not ask her. He did not check she wanted sexual intercourse. No, he went even so far as to push his hand forcefully over her mouth so she couldn't make a noise.

"Molly Smith did not commit any crime that night. Far from it. She was instead the victim of a crime. A crime of entitlement, shall we say, a crime where Jacob Walker-Kent took full advantage, because he wanted something, and he thought he had the right to just take it. It is up to you as the jury to make sure that a clear message is sent, that Molly Smith has the right of autonomy over her body, that it was not Jacob Walker-Kent's to do with as he pleased. Regardless of what Miss Beaumont has told you, Molly Smith's life is not on trial here. It is Jacob Walker-Kent's actions, and that, members of the jury, is what you need to deliberate on."

Richard sat down. He was absolutely spent. He assessed the

jury. He was not even sure they had listened to what he had to say. A trial is long and laborious by the time it comes to deliberation, Richard imagined they were just as fed up as him. He glanced at Molly. She nodded at him, a small acknowledgement that she knew he had tried his best.

Stephanie

"You are not guilty if you get drunk; if you look after a friend; if you make sure they get home safely; eat toast; stay the night; engage in consensual sexual relations; even, fall in love. Mr Clarke is right: that does not make you guilty.

"Some could say Jacob Walker-Kent is guilty, and maybe he is, but what is he guilty of? Forcefully having sex with Molly Smith? No, there were no bruises. There was no sign she even struggled. Raping Molly? No, she did not once express an aversion; she at no point asked him to stop, or attempted to push him off. By her own admission through text messages she doesn't even suggest the word 'rape'. Falling in love with Molly Smith? Yes. Trusting Molly Smith? Yes. Being naïve to Molly Smith's game? Yes. Being led on by Molly Smith? Yes. Not seeing through Molly Smith? Yes. Being used by Molly Smith? Yes.

"Richard Clarke would have you believe that none of the information you have heard leading up to the event in question is relevant. He'd have you believe that the way their relationship developed is insubstantial. However, their relationship prior to the night in question is crucial. In terms of context you cannot just look at the night in question. Jacob reasonably believed Molly was consenting, and this belief was reasonable with regard to all the circumstances leading to the night. What we quite clearly have here is a lie that has gone on too long. Molly Smith had developed a relationship with Jacob Walker-Kent that was inappropriate. By her own admission she herself clearly stated that her boyfriend, Luke, was no fun. She danced provocatively with Jacob; she got drunk with him, she spent a disproportionate amount of time with him, and then she had sex with him. She had consensual sex with him, and then when she regretted cheating on her boyfriend she spun a line to cover her guilt. And, it spiralled. Molly Smith was not raped. The only person who has been raped in this case is Jacob Walker-Kent: raped of his reputation."

34

Molly

As I wait outside the courtroom for the verdict to come back I can feel myself shaking. I want it all to be over, yet I don't want to know the verdict all at the same time. I can see the way people are looking at me. I can see the media deciphering whether I appear nervous, or upset, or regretful. I can see them trying to navigate how to paint a picture of me already: the false accuser or the poor rape victim. Black and white: wrong versus right. There is no in between here, it is a case of two sides.

I did not put myself through the aggressive questioning and maligning by Stephanie Beaumont because I made it up. I would never have put myself through the questioning if it were not true. I even questioned dropping the case because the interrogation was so upsetting. I can understand now why rape cases don't come to court, why women don't come forward. It is too hard to go through the courts. It is beyond distressing to be torn apart on the witness stand. If I had been burgled I would not have to prove that my house had been robbed, or justify my behaviour prior to the burglary. I do not understand why in cases of rape it is acceptable to put forward these questions.

It is hard to be repeatedly accused of being a liar. It is hard when you are trying to tell the truth, and all Stephanie Beaumont was trying to do was catch me out. I can't remember how many times she asked the same question in a different way to trip me up, I still feel anxious when I remember how easily I could have said the wrong thing, how easily she would have misinterpreted it. I felt enough shame already, I felt revolting and dirty before the court case, and it had just been an extended humiliation for me.

I know I had come across as hard, almost aloof, but I was trying to remain composed. I was told to contain my emotions as much as possible: to not get angry. I was trying to remain dignified, but it had the opposite effect, I ended up looking emotionless, hard-faced, when all I was just trying to do was keep it together.

When they brought the photos out, I remember thinking "do not shout, do not shout", instead I mentally removed myself from the room. My mother had once told me to do this: "If it is too much, shut down, Molly, take yourself away in your head." It had been the day of my grandfather's funeral.

I did, I took myself away. I pretended I wasn't there as the jury looked through the defence exhibits: endless photos of Jacob and me smiling, sitting in pub beer gardens, over lunch, at weddings, on the beach. All the time I wanted to scream: "Was I not allowed to be happy? Was I not allowed to smile? I did not know he planned to rape me."

I felt so helpless. I had laid all my fears, my darkest times before the jury, and I trusted they would believe me, but Stephanie Beaumont, she just kept on at me. She picked me apart bit by bit until all she had left was the threadbare, and I had nowhere to hide.

I do not hear the announcement that the jury is back, but I just lightly feel Richard's touch on my back.

"They are in, Molly. Follow me."

It feels like I am floating as I trace his footsteps before me back into the courtroom. Jacob is in the stand. He has his head held high. He is looking out directly at the jury. He is so certain, so sure of himself. I already feel sick, and they are yet to return the verdict.

I hear the voices in slow motion. The sound of my heartbeat, the rush of my breath amplified.

"How do you, the members of the jury, find the defendant?" It sounds as if the judge bellows, but it could be a whisper for all I know. Noise is suddenly heightened.

"We find Jacob Walker-Kent on the count of 'Rape'..." I can hear my heartbeat faster now, my breath quicker. I can feel him on my skin. I can feel his weight on top of me. I can see the glint in his eyes. I can feel the power of his strength, his hand over my mouth. I can feel the burning in my groin as he takes something from me all over again. I can feel the sick in my mouth. I can feel the race in my heart, the cold sweat on my forehead. I can feel the fear, the pure fear as I hear the words, "not guilty." I can feel all of that as Jacob turns to me smiling, and I am sick.

Richard

He had allowed himself a momentary element of hope. As they re-entered the court he had imagined the reaction as the "guilty" verdict was read out. He had envisaged hugging Molly, exuberant at their success. He thought of his interview with the press where his rhetoric would largely centre on the beginning of a shift in attitudes towards rape, the need for an open dialogue and improved justice in the area.

The case had attracted such a great deal of media attention that should he secure a conviction his profile would sky-rocket. He could possibly leave the full-time office of the CPS and work on an ad-hoc basis, determining what and when he took cases. Of course, Richard realised these were all selfish reasons. Ultimately, he did want to secure a conviction for Molly. He wanted men like Jacob to understand that they weren't entitled. He wanted a clear message determined by the courts regarding capacity and consent. He wanted clarity in an area that had for so long been muddied. But what he wanted was not guaranteed.

As the jury re-entered he felt a rush of adrenaline. He never had quashed the apprehension he felt at these particular moments despite it being an event that was repeated regularly in his career. He glanced at Molly. She was still shaking. He had noted her shakes throughout the trial.

Stephanie Beaumont looked unperturbed. He imagined she believed the case to be her success as a forgone conclusion.

Jacob stood straight in the dock, his shoulders back, his chin raised, still with an air of indignation as to his situation. The foreman of the jury stood, and the judge asked him to relay the verdict. As he spoke Richard wondered why he'd ever hoped for anything more. He heard Molly retch, and registered the splatter on his shoe, but by the time he turned she was already running out of the court.

Jacob

He partly knew that he would get off. He had a knack for understanding where the judgement of others lay, and he had seen the manner in which the jury had looked at Molly. He had noted the look of pity of the two elderly ladies when he had taken to the stand. He had seen the way the young man – in his late twenties Jacob estimated – had smirked when the video of Molly dancing with him was played, as if he had the measure of what type of girl she was. And that was the thing, they only needed reasonable doubt – just one of them – and he would be acquitted, and he knew before the foreman of the jury stood that he had done enough. Molly had lost her little twisted game, and he was going to be a free man. He could tell by the way they looked at him and the way they then looked at Molly. That was not to say that Jacob did not recognise the disdain of the faces of a number of them, the utter contempt for him, but it did not matter because he was a free man. He'd been found "not guilty".

Stephanie

I felt no pleasure when I won this time. I loved the chase, the idea I may lose keeps me on my toes, but when the verdict came back it was as if all the excitement faded. Normally by the evening I had almost forgotten what the day's case had entailed, already under a new mound of papers and concentrating on a different client, but occasionally clients stayed with me. They floated through my thoughts as if I was still trying to compartmentalise them. They did not sit comfortably with me, as if I was still hoping to decipher the facts. Jacob Walker-Kent was one of those clients. It was not that he had ever done anything to compromise my position; he had never disclosed information that may jeopardise me representing him, but I had a gut feeling. A feeling that had swelled as the case had progressed that Mr Walker-Kent wasn't as honourable as he seemed.

I hadn't been able to pinpoint it, maybe it was the way he looked at Molly Smith on the stand, or the subtle smirk on his face when the not guilty verdict was returned. Maybe it was the manner in which he conversed with females, as if he was entitled to their company and attention. I had noted how he paid extra attention to those in a position of power or authority. He wanted to impress them and, equally, them to be impressed by him. He did not bother with those he had no use for; I had seen the way he spoke to the court clerk or the girl who made him coffee. Jacob Walker-Kent was quite clearly manipulative and devious, and someone who liked getting what he wanted: and Jacob Walker-Kent had wanted Molly Smith.

In that space between night and day when the truth slides into your bed and there is no way you can escape those dreaded innermost thoughts, I had been honest with myself. I had been honest with myself about who and what kind of a man I was representing. Jacob Walker-Kent had wanted Molly Smith, and Jacob Walker-Kent got what he wanted whether Molly Smith wanted it or not.

I do not sleep easily. I am aware I contribute to the safety of our streets and not in a good way. I know that every time I get people like Jacob Walker-Kent off I am putting another innocent woman at risk; I too have my part to play in the future crimes he may commit because being successful at my job will enable him to commit them.

PART III

35

ONE MONTH LATER

Molly

I would like to say that after the trial my life went back to normal, that I fell into a routine, and now the case was over I could move forward. I would like to say I forgot all about Jacob, the court case and the miscarriage. I didn't.

After the verdict, I slipped out of the court as quickly as my legs would carry me, the splatter of sick fresh on my skirt. Richard had tried to help me, but I was overcome with embarrassment. Jacob's attitude had only added to how exposed I felt. The first night I had returned home and washed myself with such vigour that my skin had peeled. I had not eaten anything. I had downed three tumblers of whisky – which I do not usually drink – and then collapsed into bed, absolutely drained from it all.

Much to my surprise I had slept for thirteen hours that night, the longest I had slept in at least six months, my mind silenced ever so briefly, long enough that my crippling anxiety did not bubble to the surface and wake me again. I woke the next morning and lay there – my entire mind listless. I thought of the days ahead, the weeks ahead, and I was filled with an overwhelming feeling of nothingness. A flat, empty blank space lay before me, my future seemed barren. Any hope that the case may have ignited for a resolution now extinguished. I had no job, no boyfriend, my friends were sparse, I had isolated myself in the past few months, and my family were a rare frequency: my brother had attended the trial but he too had his own life he wanted to get back to.

Everything felt so pointless. I was so angry. Angry at myself for putting myself through the court process just for Jacob to get away with it. I should have known it was impossible the jury would take my word against someone like Jacob.

I spend the first two weeks after the trial aimlessly walking the busy streets of London. I prowl the area, my head down, my heart empty wondering what the hell I am now to do.

I wake suddenly in the middle of the night, my dreams forcing me to the surface. I had been in court again, but this time I was holding a baby and surrounded by laughter. I could not escape the callous cackles: the courtroom corroded with a macabre sense of humour. My sheets are drenched, and my heart thuds quickly inside my chest. My fear is palpable.

I sit up. My bedside lamp is still on. It is always on. I glance over to my bedside chair. The navy dress I wore three weeks ago in court remains there; sick splatters are visible on the hem of the skirt. I cannot bring myself to wash the physical remains of the day away.

Jacob

There was a serenity on the slopes that Jacob had yet to replicate anywhere else he had ever been in the world.

As soon as the verdict had come back he had gone out for the evening with his mother. He did not feel like celebrating. He was just relieved that the nightmare was over. She had, as usual, chosen a preposterous restaurant, greatly overpriced to be under-fed. Jacob had not been interested in food though and had sunk champagne like water. His mother was emotional and overbearing, and she was still incredulous about the whole process, but he could see her shoulders had eased, and she appeared more relaxed than he'd seen her for months. He seized the opportunity to instigate her departure.

"I've been thinking I need a break now the trial is finished."

"I totally agree, darling. I think it'd be good for us. Where do you want to go? I can speak to Celeste today, get something in the diary, my treat."

Celeste was Jacob's mother's cleaner who she treated as her PA for life, even though she did not work and Jacob was her sole purpose as far as he could see. He did not intend to upset her, but a week away with her was the last thing he desired. He knew she hated the mountains though: a holiday where you needed to physically exert yourself in anyway was her idea of a punishment.

It wasn't that he actively didn't invite her – he just made it clear that he was going skiing, something he knew she would never do. Jacob was aware that his mother also would not reside in London whilst he was away; this way he was certain she would also return home.

Two days later Jacob found himself on the mountains. He spent hours carving the freshly fallen snow, he went faster and harder than he ever had, and his body ached with an intensity he had never experienced. It was good to feel something though, at least now his pain was physically palpable.

He liked the exclusivity of skiing; he liked that it wasn't overcrowded with uneducated working-class louts. It was a holiday where he anonymously mingled with his type: an unspoken acknowledgement that locations such as this were only appropriate for the wealthy middle and upper classes.

Jacob gained as much peace as he possibly could that week, mainly purely due to the fact he was able to switch off from the reality of the last year. The altitude, the scenery, the unworldly light, all a welcome relief. He realised how much he had desperately needed to escape what his world had become.

Stephanie

I am meeting Matthew this evening at a small French bistro for dinner. He has reached out to me this week through text. I suspect because he is feeling so awful about the media circus he has helped to create. Matthew more than anyone knows the stresses of the job, and how unhelpful the pressure of being under scrutiny from the country's press is when you are struggling with the client and case in hand as well.

I have calmed with my feelings towards him of late. Maybe it is because I have not seen him as much: our contact has been limited since the New Year, particularly since the incident in Bayonne, which we have both tactfully ignored.

I have reserved a table for eight o'clock, the restaurant is small and only seats eighteen so we were lucky to get a place. I love it there: you immediately feel like you are entering a little eatery abroad, the music, the rustic decoration, everything about it is typically French, even the menu is written in the country's language.

Matthew is perplexed by my French obsession. He likes France, but he does not understand my passion for the culture. I have always daydreamed of owning a house there, a beautiful Provencal house with duck egg blue shutters and creeping bougainvillea. I have a book full of cuttings that details the designs, from the large farmhouse table seating fourteen, to the colour of the walls and the prints for the individual bedrooms. I do not have anyone to share my dream with, but nonetheless I hope one day it will happen.

Richard

He felt so jaded, he had no energy, he was beaten down by all of it: by living. The endless slog of bills to pay, cleaning, work and cooking had left him deflated. He felt like he had had all of life's zest knocked out of him. He had tried his hardest to be positive recently, but he just could not muster it. He wanted to throw everything in, he wanted to book a flight and leave all that his life represented in the UK: the work, the hours, the stress, the clients, London, commuting; he wanted to banish all of it from his daily existence.

Monday was just the beginning of what had become a monotonous routine for Richard. He craved something new, a week you could not predict, places he had not yet been. He knew what lay ahead of him before time had even begun ticking that week: clients; cases; his office; court; maybe the gym; a few lonesome meals for one; two excessive nights of drinking to numb the reality of the working week; a hangover that made him hate himself, and then start all over again. Next week: Repeat. Repeat. Repeat.

He knew things had to change, but he just didn't know how to. When you are in something secure it is easier to remain still. He had so many questions about a change of direction that he could not answer: what would he do? Would he like what he chose to do? How would he afford to live? Would he have to leave London? What about his friends? What if it was a big mistake? Richard knew these questions were just the rational part of his brain deciphering where to go next, but the questions were so big and cumbersome and confusing it was easier to not answer them and continue as he was, albeit unhappy and unsatisfied.

36

Molly

I log on to my Twitter account and feel the bile begin to rise in my mouth as I await the avalanche of abuse I am about to endure from complete strangers. I wonder whether, when these people write their comments, they think of the person at home opening their computer screen? I wonder whether they envisage the reaction they cause in complete strangers? I wonder whether in other parts of their lives they like to make people cry? I wonder what has caused them to think they have a right to direct such vile comments towards others?

The messages and comments to my Twitter account began slowly at first, I would receive about five or so a day from men and women alike, they would have the same theme embedded throughout them: I was a whore, a liar, even if he did rape me I deserved it, I should die. The comments were horrible, these people hated me; I was totally shocked. I would feel shaken every time I logged out.

My identity was not meant to be revealed, but once the newspaper article ran on the techniques barristers, such as

Stephanie Beaumont, use in rape cases, the media clung on to her latest rape case, and that case so happened to be mine. My anonymity is allegedly protected by law: I was promised that, but it did not stop the photographs on Facebook or Twitter. It did not stop the speculation, the question mark surrounding the girl with the golden curls. It was not long before they had discovered who I was, it was not long before the questioning Stephanie used against me was national news, and my answers were spread across the tabloids and broadsheets ready to be dissected.

The Twitter trolls and anti-feminists did not take long to find me online. It was almost a strange relief when it finally began, because the anticipation of it beginning was making me extremely anxious, but the extent, the sheer volume of people who felt so strongly against me was such a shock.

I had not prepared myself for the number or content of the tweets. I had not prepared myself for the women and men who told me I deserved it, who told me it was not rape, who told me that they hoped it happened again. I was not prepared for that.

Jacob

Jacob had bumped into Sofia Calcott three weeks after he returned from skiing. She was shyer than she had been at her mother's house. Jacob sensed she may be embarrassed for falling asleep on him. Jacob was all too aware of the irony that this is what Molly had done shortly before waking up and accusing him of rape. He was perplexed that one woman could say such things about him, yet another could be so trusting to put herself in a vulnerable position with him. He was relieved that Sofia felt she could: obviously she was not lying when she said she did not believe the accusations against him.

Sofia was drinking at an inner-city trendy bar with a table of girlfriends when he spotted her. She had raised her hand and smiled when he entered, but he wanted more of an interlude: he wished to talk with her, he wanted to make her throw her head back and laugh from deep within. He had sent a bottle of champagne over to her table with a note, which simply read, "On me, Sleeping Beauty".

He knew not to approach her directly. It made the chase all the more interesting and charming. She had sashayed over to his table a little under an hour later. The effects of a few glasses of champagne had increased her confidence, and she seductively sat on Jacob's knee: much to the delight of his three friends, who he caught peering at her legs enviously.

"Jacob Walker-Kent, may I ask why you are buying me champagne?" She half-smiled, portraying that look of naughtiness he found so tempting.

"Can one friend not buy another friend a drink after spending Christmas together?" He placed his hand dangerously high on her thigh, before smiling back.

She glanced at his hand, unsure momentarily at his game, and then realised he too was teasing her. She threw her head back and laughed as she slid from his lap onto the space on the sofa next to him.

"A friend can indeed buy me a drink, Jacob, but only on the condition we can go somewhere so I can buy him one back?"

"That could be arranged, Sofia."

At that she stood and grabbed Jacob's hand, pulling him to standing.

"Okay, let's go."

"What, now? But I'm just having a drink with–" She had transfixed him with her half-smile, and he knew he no longer had a choice in the matter. "I'll grab my jacket. Sorry, lads." His friends laughed at his female escapades; not that he had indulged since Molly: it had been too risky considering. He knew how females jumped onto things like this, especially when he had money. His friends barely raised their eyes as he excused himself. They, too, regularly jumped at the chance of a pretty lady on their arm. They had no problem understanding his departure, or in drawing assumptions as to his intentions with Sofia.

Sofia had already asked the waiting staff to order a taxi by the time he retrieved his jacket. He did not ask her where they were going, as it only added to the excitement of their unexpected date. As they exited the bar he heard the boys cheer behind him. He did not correct them; he could not care less if they thought he was going to take things further than a date with Sofia. After the past few months he deserved some distraction, and she was certainly that.

He found her dress intoxicating, if not a little revealing. He liked to see what was on offer, but he thought she could have chosen something slightly more demure. He could not deny she had a great pair of legs and a pert chest, but he thought she didn't have to show it off so readily. She was a pretty girl, no one could deny that, she just did not need to dress so provocatively.

It was quickly apparent to Jacob that Sofia had consumed a substantial amount of alcohol. She was louder and crasser than she had been at Christmas, and he found it slightly irritating. However, he could not say that as she stroked his thigh in the taxi he was not turned on. Their taxi journey came to a halt outside of a club known for its famous clientele, Sofia smiled: "Jakey, don't look so scared, I'm paying."

Jacob did not know how to deal with Sofia, for a start his name was not *Jakey*, he was not off some CBeebies programme, and secondly, how dare she imply he could not afford to pay.

"Sofia, it's Jacob, and money is not a worry to me. I'm just surprised you brought us here."

"Jacob, you need some fun. You need to let your hair down a bit."

"Sofia, I'm aware I may need some more fun in my life, especially considering the past couple of months, but I'm not sure going to London's most exclusive club, where all the media can pass comment, is my idea of fun at the moment."

"Jacob, are you forgetting I work in PR?"

"Yes, I'm aware you work in PR, Sofia."

"Exactly, so yes, the media will see you; they'll probably go to print with photos of you tomorrow, but you are also forgetting you are standing next to me in those photos: a well-known upper-class London socialite, who knows a lot of important people. The media will print us, and they'll play it just how I want them to. By tomorrow they'll be talking about 'Sofia Calcott and Jacob Walker-Kent'. Not Jacob Walker-Kent the suspected rapist. I know what I'm doing, Jakey." Sofia winked at him, and he could not help but fall into line alongside her.

As he expected the media went berserk, the flashes of the paparazzi shrouded them in white light. All the while, Sofia said: "Head up, don't smile, I'll smile, keep calm." They shouted his name, they asked crude questions: implied that he may take advantage of Sofia. For all her brashness, she dealt with the media so very elegantly, and Jacob could clearly see why she was so successful at her job. She was a master of telling the story she wanted portrayed.

The evening, for all his initial doubts, was an immense amount of fun. Sofia was a wicked flirt, but he respected the fact that tonight she was only paying attention to him. She had managed to get them a private booth: out of the view of prying eyes and gossips.

He found he forgot himself whilst they spoke, thoughts of Molly disintegrated. She had the eagerness of a child: she was wildly excitable and appeared to look on the bright side of everything. It helped she looked like she'd walk straight out of a 1920s Hollywood movie: her lithe body and smooth silky hair were set off by her smoky feline eyes. She was a divine creature, and he was sure to enjoy her further at some point.

By the time they emerged from the club they were a little worse for wear. Jacob had consumed more than he realised, but he was managing to keep it together. Sofia had suggested a plan for their exit strategy, and he had been more than happy to go along until he realised he did not want the night to end. He did not want to play the media game any longer. He wished to carry on their evening without fear of judgement. He knew he could sway Sofia, he just needed to be a little more persuasive. She entered the waiting taxi, the plan being Jacob would kiss her on the cheek, close the door and wave her off before getting a ride home himself. He managed to do just this, the trustworthy gentleman, putting his date safely on her way.

Jacob had got in a taxi right behind Sofia. He decided upon a new strategy that the media would not detect. He would follow her taxi home, where he would then surprise her. As the cars weaved in and out of each other under the night sky he felt himself ignited with excitement.

Stephanie

Matthew is late. I have been sitting at our table for twenty minutes, and he is still to arrive. He has texted to say he got caught up in work. I have ordered some olives and a glass of Shiraz that I enjoy whilst I browse the internet on my iPad, looking for nothing of need, but it is my guilty pleasure to purchase household items of limited use. I like things to look pretty in my home even if I don't have anyone to share it with or any reason to buy it. I have just found a beautiful set of tea, coffee and sugar holders when Matthew approaches; I hold the screen up to him so he can see.

"What do you think? Too kitsch?"

He smiles and nods, which only encourages me to place the items in my virtual shopping basket before I close the screen and return the iPad to my bag.

"Perfect, that is what I was going for."

"Stephanie." Matthew leans across the table and places two small, soft kisses on each of my cheeks. I can feel myself blush at the thought of his lips. I really need to get a grip on my feelings. I worry I am going through early menopause, to even be considering Matthew in this manner suggests something is awry with my hormones. In all the years I have known him, I have never once considered Matthew in this way, until recently that is.

"How are you? Already ordered wine I take it? That's not like you..." Matthew raises his eyebrows as he says this. That is what I love about him, he knows me so well, there is no mystery, no hiding places. It is straight forward and comfortable our friendship.

"Yes, of course, I'm not in court or the office so what else would I be doing?" I laugh and throw my head back to get the waiter to serve us another glass for Matthew. "So how have you been? Annalise okay?"

"Yeah, yeah fine." I notice he bristles as he replies to me.

"Are you sure?" I smile knowingly at him, he knows that he cannot hide anything from me.

"It's, oh it, I don't know how to say, let me get the wine first, Steph."

"Okay, I'm intrigued." I stare at him smiling until his wine arrives. He looks nervous and I can tell my determination to get whatever he is keeping from me out of him is irritating him.

"Well?" I raise my eyebrows inquisitively at him as he takes the first sip of wine.

"It's Annalise. It is, you see, well Annalise is... How do I say this? Annalise she is– Well she– I mean we... We are going to have a baby... It's Annalise – she's pregnant."

My mother always said I should have been an actress. And my skills now prove to be proficient, I manage a smile: a wide smile. I was determined not to be abashed. I stood from the table and gave Matthew an enthusiastic hug and told him how pleased I was. I stuck my hand up in the air and once I gained the waiter's attention I ordered champagne: to celebrate. I asked him a dozen questions, questions concerning her health, whether she had morning sickness, the due date, whether the baby was planned, did they have any names, were they going to find out the sex. I was surprised at how easily I had managed to feign delight when all the time I felt sick. I wanted to scream and cry, and shout at him for making such a dreadful mistake.

"It wasn't planned – you know I would have told you if we were planning it – we just kind of stopped not planning it and then it happened so soon, and I just didn't really expect it, and I'm going to be a dad. I can't believe I'm going to be a dad, Steph. It's mad..."

"It's fantastic news, Matthew. You're going to be brilliant, it's so exciting." The waiter brought the champagne over, and I welcomed the distraction. He popped the cork and I let out a little yelp: I was maybe overdoing it now on the joviality, but Matthew didn't seem to notice. He seemed dazed as if the news of his impending parenthood was yet to sink in.

"You okay, Matthew? You seem a little distracted."

"Yeah, yeah, I'm fine, I just can't get my head around it, I mean we found out almost a week ago, but it still doesn't seem real. Annalise is over the moon, you know already spending thousands on the nursery and buying endless baby clothes."

"Isn't that bad luck... baby clothes before the baby is born?"

"You don't buy in to all that, Steph? Whether we buy the baby clothes or not isn't going to change whether the baby arrives safely or not."

"You're right. I just– I mean are you happy about it? Happy about the baby?"

"I think so..."

"What is 'I think so' meant to mean? You either are or you aren't?"

"It's not that I haven't always wanted to be a dad, because I have. I have always wanted to have children, I just... I don't know, maybe I just wasn't sure I wanted to be a dad with Annalise."

I cannot believe he has said it, after all my years of suspicions that she wasn't the one for him, hoping that it would fizzle out, he has finally admitted what I suspected: that he was not as keen as Annalise herself is on their relationship.

"And now?"

"Well now I'm going to be, so it's pointless dwelling on it, and they say parenthood changes people, don't they? So, I'm sure she'll change and all the materialistic things she thinks are so significant will pale in comparison to the baby. It'll probably be good for us. Ignore me, I don't know whether I'm coming or going, Steph. I'm just having one of those days. Anyway let's drink, we've got champagne and that is reason to celebrate in itself."

We toast our glasses and smile, knowing full well what the other is not saying.

I look at Matthew and our eyes meet for just a moment too long. It is not what is spoken in that moment that matters: it is what is not and maybe that is all I need to know, there is no need to say anything further now. It is already too late.

Richard

Richard is fielding phone calls when the email comes in. He is simultaneously hanging up his mobile and his office line to the cockroach journalists that won't leave him to do his job, when he sees his screen refresh and her name pop onto the centre of his screen: "Suzie sent you a message."

His hands begin to tremble, he can feel his heartbeat increase and his nerves become raw. He has not heard from her since her last message detailing her new relationship and pregnancy. She always used to send him messages when he was in work. It would keep him going: titbits of her day, insights into what she planned for their evening.

Suzie would send the menu of a restaurant she randomly picked out of the *Time Out* guide to eating in the city every Thursday. She would scroll down the page, close her eyes and place her finger on an eatery for them to try, before emailing it over to Richard. At around three o'clock he would receive a downloadable menu that he would salivate over whilst having his coffee break – if he had the chance to get to the depressing corner in his office where the jug of warm stale filter coffee was kept: sometimes he was just too snowed under by paperwork.

He would delight in choosing from the menu. His favourite was the exotic foods he had never heard of or tried. He liked Vietnamese, Indonesia, anything with an Asian twist really. He always was mildly disappointed when he received a French or British menu. He liked to try foods he would not himself cook, not that he did much of that, Suzie was always the one behind the stove. It was not that he had not wanted to cook; it was just she loved it. She said it relaxed her at the end of every day. It meant she could switch off from whatever had been troubling her and concentrate on the simple pleasure of making dinner.

The screen takes a while to load but he can see there is an

attachment. The photo gradually fills the screen pixel by pixel until the chubby cheeks of a fresh baby's face fills his screen. There is a line of text underneath the image: "Meet Lawrence, he's amazing".

Richard shuts down the screen instantly. The face of the baby is just a hollow reminder of the child they'd once planned they'd have. Of all the things Suzie could have done... Richard could not believe how insensitive, self-absorbed, unwanted and inconsiderate her contact was.

37

Molly

Alison suggested I start an online course. It is my first lesson tomorrow and I am excited for the first time in a while. I used to love decorating and upcycling furniture. I know I need a focus whilst I try and find forgiveness. Alison says it was not my fault but I cannot switch off the voice that holds me accountable for what happened, that blames myself. I need to learn to forgive the situation, the circumstances, the person. I need to forgive what happened as a whole, not just Jacob, not just the person who committed the act, but everything that led to it happening and what occurred afterwards. I need to forgive my body for betraying me.

My thoughts come in rushes. I am learning to create a dam for my feelings, to let a little in at a time so I am not flooded with emotions. I saw Luke again last week. We passed on the street. I did not know what to do. I stopped, but then felt stupid so continued to walk. He had passed me without a second glance. I could feel the tears welling inside of me, threatening to burst into the public sphere. I picked up my pace and was just rounding the corner when I felt a hand on my shoulder. When I turned Luke was bent before me trying to get his breath back, his face red from the exertion of running to catch me.

"Molly, I didn't realise it was you. I mean, I didn't recognise you. What have you done to your hair?"

I had not spoken to him properly for months, or seen him for that matter, yet the first question he posed was about my hairstyle. I had gone to the hairdressers after the court case. I wanted to rid myself of my past identity, anything that represented my former self I wanted gone. The person Luke had known no longer existed and I wanted to look like someone else. I had shed nearly a stone and a half in weight, my skin had lost its glow and my eyes looked hollowed; my mass of golden curls had just upset me, reminding me of who I had been before.

When I entered the salon, and told them what I wanted the hairdresser had stared at me, her mouth wide open. She had then tried to dissuade me. She had tried to reason with me, she had complimented my dramatic hairstyle like so many others often had, but I had refused to listen. When she had finished, and the dark brown crop was complete, I had smiled at my reflection whilst she just sighed.

I had succeeded in ridding myself of my femininity. I no longer looked like a woman with her sexuality on show: I had made myself asexual, my breasts had disappeared with my weight loss, as had my hips and now with my hairstyle I could be mistaken for a boy for all I cared. I am sure a psychologist would say that my image change was a way of protecting myself from unwanted male attention. I am sure they would love to psychoanalyse my decision to change how I look so drastically.

All I know is that when I walk the streets now I do not receive disapproving looks anymore, I can go by unnoticed as Molly Smith. I do not have men ogle me, wolf-whistle, shout in the street, I do not receive attention in bars or clubs. I am not asked out on dates. I look off limits to the male of the species and that makes me happy.

"I wanted a change," I reply, my voice shaking.

"It's different. Yeah it's certainly different. When did you have it done?"

I answer his questions about my hair, all the while wondering of what relevance it really is to him, it is as if me changing my hair holds an insurmountable significance to him that I am yet to pinpoint.

When he finishes his questioning, he sighs, he looks defeated and tired, as if the next question is too much to ask. "How are you?"

For a moment, I am dumbfounded. This is the first time Luke has asked me this question since before I broke the news to him, after returning from my first visit to the police station.

"I am different."

"Different?"

"I'm not the Molly you used to know, Luke, so I wouldn't bother trying to find her by having a conversation with me now."

"I'm sorry," Luke whispers.

"You're sorry?" I spit the words back at him. I had not realised how angry I was, how deeply hurt I had been by this man, in a sense more so than Jacob. As I stand on the corner of the street, the light fading, the rain slowly pelting down on my shoulders, my childlike figure shivering with anger and pain, I look at Luke for what he really was, what he really is.

"I am, Molly. I am sorry. Can we... can we go somewhere to talk?"

"To talk?" I cannot control the disdain in my voice. "What would you like to talk about, Luke? I'm not sure you're comfortable with the truth so I don't know how much good talking is going to be."

"I wasn't ready, Molly. I wasn't ready for the truth before, but I believe you now. Please can we just talk."

I don't know whether Luke thinks that sentence is an absolution for him, that I will sleep easy now because he is prepared to listen, to understand, to face the things and the reality of what happened to me. I cannot dispel the laughter as it bubbles up in my throat. "Thanks for that, Luke, it means a lot." I begin to laugh, I laugh so loud in his face that he looks around him searching for the joke, which only makes me laugh louder. I know I must look hysterical as I stand in the pouring rain now unable to stop myself. I see him take a step away from me, obviously concerned for my mental health. It is only when I have finished ridding myself of the strange comedy of the situation that I become calm again. "Okay."

"Okay what? What is okay, Molly?"

And then I surprise myself: "Okay, Luke, let's talk then, but not here."

Jacob

Jacob had followed Sofia in his taxi, but he had been careful to get the driver to drop him two streets away. He knew Sofia would be angry if she thought the media had seen him returning to hers. No matter how careful he thought he was – she would think him not careful enough. He knocked at her door roughly ten minutes after she had arrived home. He was surprised to see she had already removed her make-up and put her nightclothes on. She looked more beautiful than she had earlier.

"Jacob?" She looked confused, and there was a hint of annoyance in her voice.

"I didn't have the chance to give you a kiss goodnight."

She leant against the door frame and smiled politely. "Jacob, you are not coming in, just so you know, but I am not averse to a goodnight kiss." She laughed coyly.

Jacob leant forward and kissed her lips gently. He felt her soften ever so slightly, and he pushed his body towards her in the hope she would succumb and let him in.

She pulled back and smiled at him. "Jacob, I said no." She was still smiling, and he knew she was just teasing him now.

He started to kiss her again. She did not resist. He nibbled on her neck and held her hands. It was easy to hold her arms and enter her flat: he used his groin to manoeuvre her up against the wall. He was much stronger than Sofia.

She pulled back again. This time she appeared flustered: "Jacob, I am serious, you are not staying."

"You say that now, Sofia..." He began to kiss her neck forcefully again.

He could feel her slight curves underneath her camisole. He could feel himself beginning to get aroused. He could not help it when girls teased him like this. She had been teasing him all night.

Sofia pushed him back once again. She looked a little more alarmed now. "Jacob, you need to go. I'm not doing this... it's just too fast, okay. Please, let's just call it a night."

He tried to kiss her again, but she was forceful now. She shoved him towards the door with her hands. "I said no, Jacob. I've asked you to go. Don't make me ask again."

He pushed her hard against the wall. In that moment, he hated her. She represented everything he despised about Molly. She was a cock-tease. She had played him. She had led him on all night. He held her against the wall, his hands squeezed her upper arms to her torso. She could not move. He pushed his hard penis into her groin and groaned. He slid his hand up her slip, pushing her knickers aside he inserted two fingers. Leaning forward he whispered in her ear: "You're just a cheap little *bitch*, like the rest of them. I wouldn't want to waste my time fucking you anyway, Sofia." He released his grip and pulled his fingers out from inside her. Sofia stood silent. He smiled at her and laughed, before he turned, exited and shut the door. He heard her murmur *goodbye* from behind the door as he walked down the steps and into the night.

When he arrived home, he had punched the wall of his kitchen in frustration, irritated that he'd let himself be the victim of such behaviour again. Sofia had just succeeded in spoiling the end of their evening. He had thought she was different. He realised now that they were all the same. They led men to the point they wanted, and just expected them to be amenable when they decided to stop. They didn't consider his needs. They did not consider how it made him feel. They did not consider what it was he wanted.

Stephanie

I lie in bed all day. I do not rise to shower. I do not eat. I do not dress. I do nothing but watch the monotonous daytime TV. I turn my phone off. I keep the curtains shut. I bring the kettle, some milk and teabags from the kitchen to my bedroom. I only rise to use the bathroom. At six o'clock I make my way to the larder and find a bottle of red wine. I return to my bedroom where I drink straight from the bottle. I have chocolate chip cookies for my dinner. I order a film from Sky Box office. I watch the film with not one ounce of suspense. I do not care.

Matthew is going to be a father. And I am not going to be the child's mother.

I knew before the invitation came through the door that they would marry. I knew that whatever story we may have become had ended. I knew that the story of Matthew and Annalise no longer needed a Stephanie.

Richard

Bridget and Nathan were in London for the weekend at some wedding fayre or another. Richard hadn't been able to decipher their exact plans, but he had managed to arrange to meet them for some dinner before they caught the Eurostar back to Paris, and they went onwards to their French home. He envied their lifestyle, but knew perfectly well that he would get tiresomely bored of planning extravagant weddings for couples with more money than sense. Bridget was enthralled by the details: the flowers, place names, canapés, orders of service, whereas Richard just saw it all as a pointless waste of time and fuss.

Nathan adored Bridget, so of course went along with whatever she wanted and was more than happy to tend to their land whilst she organised the weddings. They had been endlessly trying to get Richard to visit them, with promises of pretty single wedding guests and days in the gardens with Nathan on offer, but Richard just could not bring himself to spend his holiday time with them. It was not that he did not like him – of course he was fond of them, they were old friends – it was just the older they got the more and more removed their morals and values were from one another. All the things of importance to Richard paled into insignificance in Bridget and Nathan's eye. They were concerned with objects, how much someone possessed rather than what they were about.

Richard knew they would have seen the news, so he was more than prepared for the conversation to be peppered with questions regarding Molly's case, but they were the last people Richard wished to discuss the case with. He knew their stance, and no matter how uneducated they were on the matter they seemed staunchly stuck with certain unsubstantiated beliefs, which he had always failed to influence, despite his job and vast experience in law.

They met in a trendy eatery in Soho, that served minimalistic French cuisine, basically not much in Richard's opinion. He would much rather have a pub lunch, but Bridget insisted on the place as part of her "research". The usual pleasantries preceded dinner and they discussed mutual friends, the weather, the upcoming weddings they had booked in France, before focus had shifted to Richard's job, as he was all too aware it would. Bridget voiced her disdain about the case when Molly Smith was mentioned, Nathan had winked at him and said, "You shouldn't have to defend those types of girls."

Richard floated the idea of correcting them. He considered informing them both: a) he wasn't a defence lawyer, and b) everyone had the right to a defence, but he thought both tasks fruitless.

Instead he simply nodded as they continued to speak. He glazed over, he knew he should speak, he should argue, he should advocate, but he no longer had the energy for this fight: the law and his moral compass no longer aligned. As he sat eating his miniature steak with sour blue cheese parfait he found himself longing for an escape. He dreamt of Cornwall, and as the afternoon drifted on, and Bridget discussed the best time of the year for peonies, what the future wedding colour schemes were and which Pinterest boards to follow, he discovered he'd already made up his mind.

38

Molly

I take a seat at the table in the window. There are plenty of distractions in the Islington lanes outside if I do not want to listen to Luke. He orders at the counter. He does not even ask me what I want, which irritates me. He is making the assumption that he knows me still, that what I would have requested is the same as before. It is not. He will have ordered me a skinny cappuccino, I know this before he even takes a seat. I do not drink coffee anymore, though: it makes me jittery and only heightens my anxiety.

I stand and walk to the counter, where I alter the order Luke placed moments before. "I would like a green tea instead," I say. Luke raises his eyebrows, but he leaves it at that. He does not question my decision, but he does not like that I have changed my habits and he didn't know these things about me anymore.

"So how have you been? You know, really been?" Luke fixes me with his eyes.

I try to look away, but realise that he has seen the flicker of emotion already. I try to muster a smile, a shrug, a simple movement to display my indifference to his new-found interest in my well-being, but I can already feel the heat overtaking my body as the panic sets in. It has not happened for a few days and I know I need to leave before it properly envelopes me; but I am suspended between Luke and the door. I have frozen with fear, and it takes everything in me to remain as calm as possible.

I have never suffered with panic attacks before. I had read about them and spoken to friends who had experienced them, though I had always thought there was an element of dramatisation on their parts when they described the overwhelming feeling that gripped them. But since finding out I was pregnant I have begun to experience them first hand, and I know how crippling they can be. It is the intense pain in my chest that gets me first, I am sure I am having a heart attack. I try to reassure myself, but then the shortness of breath begins, and I cannot stop the swelling inside of me: everything feels like it is going to implode. My mind and my body simultaneously erupt, and it is such an intense feeling I am sure it will never end. I see Luke's face as I grip my chest and begin to hyperventilate. Luke looks confused as he watches me fall apart. My breath is short and raspy and it takes all my will power to mouth "paper bag" to him.

He pushes his chair back so quickly he knocks the table behind him, sending salt and pepper dispensers flying.

We have the other three tables' attention now, and I can feel their eyes boring into me. I need to get out of here. I need them all to stop looking. If only I was in my bedroom, or at home, where no one would have known, but I am here of all places, somewhere starkly public and with Luke: the man I have wished so many times to never see again, the hurt he inflicted was so profound.

He rushes towards me with the paper bag in hand, I take it from him and try to regulate my breathing using it as an apparatus: I can feel my lungs begin to inflate and deflate, the rhythm is too fast but it is regular, I concentrate on the breath, it helps. I can feel the heat start to disperse, and the pain in my chest eases. I am no longer crippled by panic, and although I have not relaxed I have moved away from the precipice of fear, I can still see it and feel it, but I am no longer peering down right at it, ready to be pushed into it at any moment.

It is only as my breathing slows that I become aware of Luke's hand rubbing my back. It is a strange sensation – I have not been touched by another human being for such a long period of time, except in a medical manner. I find myself allowing him to continue so I can explore how I feel about physical interaction. The colour in his face has drained and he seems shaken.

"I'm fine, sorry about that, just happens sometimes these days."

"What happens, Molly? What was that? Are you ill?"

"No, I'm not ill, well it's not an illness, it's just this thing I've been having where I get too panicky, but it's fine, I'm fine. I think I may just head off though. I don't think this was such a good idea, Luke... you and I talking, I just don't think, well I don't think there is much point anymore."

"Molly, please, please just stay for the tea, we've ordered it now, just stay until you've got your energy back and then go, just ten minutes, that is all I ask, ten minutes." He tilts his head and stares right back at me. I have seen him make this gesture so many times, he always used to tilt his head to the right when he was apologising to me. I always thought he looked more vulnerable. It made him easier to forgive. But not now, I cannot forgive him. I am not sure whether that is what he is asking of me, but if it is, he is going to be sorely disappointed.

"Okay, ten minutes but that is all, Luke, and then I am going."

"Molly, I am so sorry. I am so sorry about all of this. It is such a mess, but I just wanted you to know that I've been in a state. I didn't know what to do, what to say, I just couldn't bear it, you know, it was just so hard to imagine you with someone else."

He had told me twenty minutes earlier he was ready for the truth as we stood in the rain on the street, but now I realise he does not get it at all. He speaks as if I had made a choice to be with someone else, as if there had been a one-night-stand I had a decision in. It is as if he is offering his forgiveness for not being more understanding of a mistake I had made. He does not realise it was not me who made the mistake. I did not make the decision to be with someone else. Jacob made the decision to be with me; it was forced upon me, I had no choice, no power, no control: that was all taken from me that night.

I realise that Luke is entirely ignorant. He has no idea what really happened, because he has chosen to come up with his own version of events. He has created a scenario that will help him deal with the event. He has no idea what I have had to suffer in the aftermath. For him maybe it is easier to believe that I cheated on him than the actual reality of that evening, because if he did face up to the truth he would have to live with the fact he was upstairs sleeping whilst a monster was in our house destroying me ten feet below him. And, whether he likes it not he didn't protect me; he wasn't there to stop it or prevent it, and for Luke that would be unbearable.

"I didn't want to be with someone else, Luke."

"I know, I know you didn't, but maybe you did and then you realised you didn't, but it was too late, you'd gone too far and then it got out of hand. I know these things happen but it is okay, Moll, it's okay now."

I cannot believe what he is saying. I am dumbfounded. Luke

actually thinks I led Jacob on and then changed my mind halfway through. "Do you even know me, Luke? Did you even know me at all?"

"Yes of course I do, Moll. I know how fun and kind and caring you are, and I know you didn't mean it when you flirted with my friends, but I think you couldn't see, you know– you know– how other men could have taken it, and I know you wouldn't have set out for anything more than coffee with Jacob, but I also know what you're like when you're drunk. And, you two were getting close..."

I cannot listen to it any longer. I push my chair back and stand up, I do not utter another word to him as I sift through my purse to find a £2 coin. I place it on the table and leave without even saying goodbye. His ten minutes were up.

Jacob

After the case was over the relief had been immense, but now Jacob just felt exhausted. It'd been two weeks since his misunderstanding with Sofia, and he was feeling increasingly frustrated. He carries around an innate anger at the injustice of the process, a deep resentment towards Molly for twisting the evening between them into something it was not, but also a paranoia that it would happen again.

He need only think of his night with Sofia to realise how likely it was that this could happen: another female who regretted their drunken actions so tries to pin the responsibility on the male. He was perplexed by the manner in which these women behaved. Sofia had flirted, led him on, then suddenly changed her tune. It was confusing and a minefield to decipher what women wanted.

On Saturday night Jacob decided it was time to escape his hovel of excess: takeaway boxes and empty beer cans. He'd not been out and he fancied a change of scenery. Notting Hill was already awash with young drinkers crowded outside pub doors and scantily clad young females propped up against cocky males.

Jacob took a seat by the bar. He was drinking alone, but that didn't bother him: he needed the release. The hours led into one another. Females became faceless, just flashes of material and flesh occupying the establishment. A lone woman tried to engage with him, but she was too drunk and common for his liking; her lipstick clung to her two front teeth. He could see her dress was obscenely short even though she was seated. He did not have the energy to entertain her.

He continued to drink old fashioneds and the whisky soon took effect. The lone woman had disappeared and now in her place were two attractive twenty-somethings. He bought them drinks, turned on his charm, but he wasn't convincing: he was too preoccupied with how they would misinterpret his behaviour. He had one more drink and then made his excuses and left. He was no longer concerned for the complexity of relationships.

On his way back home, he slipped into Bunny's 24-hour massage parlour. He would simply have to find other ways to fulfil his needs.

Stephanie

I can tell which male friends of mine found Jacob Walker-Kent's case uncomfortable. I can see immediately in their faces a look of something similar to guilt, not because they have raped someone, but there are question marks about their previous sexual behaviour. They are unsure whether there have been occasions when they were too drunk, too forceful, too abusive; occasions they groped girls; said lewd comments but dismissed it. It is only now this case is in the public sphere that the discussion is broached, and it is making them think. I can see it in the subtle flicker of their eyes when I tell them what constitutes rape. I can see it in the panic when I ask them if they've ever questioned their sexual behaviour the morning after. I can see it when they talk about "bad sex": not rape, but "bad sex".

Jacob's innocence or guilt is not something I dwell on. For the purposes of my client I have presumed his innocence and that is the position I will take on the matter, but it does not mean I will not discuss the issues it raises. It does not mean I am pro-rape culture, that I believe the system works.

Richard

It didn't happen immediately. The idea after his meal with Bridget and Nathan grew organically. He had had to acknowledge he was burning out to really realise he needed to make a change. He'd asked the Crown Prosecution Service to lessen his workload; he'd taken a much-needed holiday abroad, where he'd finally managed to turn his phone off. He'd allowed himself to slow down. He knew it wouldn't happen overnight, but at least now he knew it would happen. He could no longer go on as he had been.

Bridget and Nathan had again offered him the chance to stay with them in France, but he knew he needed a fresh start. He needed to begin again. He had not prosecuted any more sexual offence cases in the last year. He had requested that they were only put on his caseload if there was an emergency. Since Molly's case he thought of her often. He thought of all the women he'd failed, all the women who had been through the ordeal of the court system. He often thought of contacting Molly, but then he imagined he was a reminder of a time she didn't wish to relive.

39

Molly

After the miscarriage and the court case I needed a holiday, an escape and a rest from what my life had become in London. I barely recognised myself and knew I needed time to recover and rest. I had lost. I had not just lost the court case, I had lost me, my sense of identity. When I had looked back through old photo albums I did not recognise my former self. She had this twinkle in her eye I have not seen for over a year now, a smile that reached further than her lips. I have none of that now. I have hollow eyes and a mouth that permanently downturns. I am not trusting, I am guarded, I do not let my hair down, I have become reserved – isolated. I am no longer the Molly Smith my mother knew. I can see her face drop as I walk towards her in arrivals. I can see her trying to comprehend the difference in my appearance, in the way I hold myself.

There is a photo of me on my fridge. My mum pinned it there when she last visited: a rare gesture of maternal love. A memory of my childhood. In the photograph, I am on a boat, my hair wind swept to the side, I am smiling widely at the camera. I look so happy. I'd found myself in front of the fridge last week staring at the photo crying. Crying for the child who had no idea what she'd have to endure. Crying for the child I feel like I failed. Crying for the child's future. I wanted to dive into the photo and hug her. I wanted to swaddle her up and keep her safe. I'd looked at my seven-year-old self, and I'd cried for her. And then I'd booked a flight.

"Hi, Mum."

"Oh, Molly!" she gasps. "Good God, girl, what have you done to yourself?" She drags me into an embrace that is too dramatic and tight for my liking, but she is always overzealous when she sees me: trying to make up for the fact she neglects her children for the most part of the year, except for these visits.

"Just fancied a change." I automatically become morose around my mother. It is an age-old reaction to her company.

"It looks awful, Molly. You look awful, good God – look at you..." She pushes me back to arm's-length and stares up and down at my body: "You are so thin, like a boy, Molly. Oh, you haven't got an eating disorder thingy, have you? I can't be dealing with that. Oh, look at your poor hair, what were you thinking? I can't get over this... where are your bags? Is that it?" She looks down at my hand luggage, I have not packed much: some books, a bikini and a few pairs of summer shorts and vests.

"Yes, I packed light."

My mother sighs. She rolls her eyes, turns on her heel and walks towards the exit. I am used to her dramatics, so I just follow her lead. She is wearing a white blazer with a black vest and a matching white skirt. She has always dressed younger than her years. My mother loves to exercise and you can tell. She's never quite left the 1990s in terms of her fashion.

She and Colin live at a resort in Spain, so the accommodation was free and the sun was shining, and it had seemed the best idea. I had spent so much time by myself over the past two years, I needed company, someone to cook for me, remind me to get out of bed. Maybe I needed my mum, however dysfunctional she was, and despite the fact that the parental role was often reversed between us. We drove to their self-catering apartment, inside a complex. The apartment had two bedrooms, so there was plenty of space.

Colin was lazing by the pool when we arrived. The apartment was on the ground floor so a swim was only a mere 100 yards away. He lifted his hand in the air to greet me before casually coming over. He was wearing small black speedos, and I tried to avert my eyes: it all felt a little too familiar. He was politer than my mum and told me I looked well, which I knew to be a lie, but let the comment wash over me. My mother wanted me to join them for a drink, but all I really wanted to do was swim for a little while.

She let me go. She'd booked a tapas bar for the evening: "Nothing fancy, Molly. We like more simple food these days. 8pm – it is early for us here, but I suppose you're not used to Spanish time yet." I'd waved in acknowledgment and gone to get changed.

I slipped into my bather and entered the pool. It was bliss to be submerged in water, the sun beating down on my face. As I closed my eyes I could see that wonderful red light through my eyelids that was only ever visible under foreign sun.

Luke had texted me before I had got on the plane. I had not replied to any of his advances of friendship since we saw each other last year. I was perfectly happy to leave him in the past, but he continued to contact me with questions, suggestions of meetings and offers of help. I could not go back.

Jacob

Jacob always knew that Molly had played the drunk card. Of course she had: he had seen it so many times before. Obviously not to this scale, but the number of times Jacob had witnessed people blaming their behaviour on alcohol, as if becoming incapacitated was reason enough to act however one wanted. Her drunkenness had cost him two years of his life.

In retrospect, he wished he'd left when he had realised how drunk she was. He can see now how vulnerable he had made himself. It is quite clear he should have either tried to stop her drinking any more, or he should have left as soon as he had walked her home. Because now the perception is twisted, he can see how easy it is to twist things: poor drunken Molly taken advantage of when she was too drunk to know what she was doing. He understands now why men need to be careful too, why he, too, needed to protect himself that evening. Jacob knows that when alcohol is involved it is so easy to distort memories, to alter the events in one's mind. He knows how people begin to question what really happened and how, and Jacob can quite clearly see how Molly has executed the distortion of this particular evening. He just wishes he'd left before she had the chance to.

He just had to look at what had happened with Sofia last year to reaffirm that had Molly at any point asked him to stop, or said no, he was more than capable of doing so. He wasn't an animal after all. Yes, he was a man with needs, but Molly had seemed more than willing to fulfil those needs until her guilt kicked in.

He has not seen Sofia. She has not been in the usual clubs or bars and she has not replied to his messages. Maybe she had moved away. He has heard previously she is fitful and restless when it comes to men, and he knew it would only be a momentary fling between them anyway: he never expected or wanted anything more of her. She was a good-time girl, not wife material, and he was not looking for anything more than meaningless flings at the moment. After Molly, he had had enough drama to last him when it came to females. He had a new way to satisfy his urges, and it was far less complicated.

Stephanie

As I lie awake in the middle of the night my thoughts run like treacle, I jump intermittently between all aspects of my life. Occasionally I become stuck on a thought, and I must lubricate my mind to let go of an image or feeling. I am used to this level of stress, this constant whirling of worries only briefly numbed by my nightly self-medication of wine, although the machine that is my mind is unleashed a mere few hours later when the effects of a few glasses have worn off. I know I need time off, I know I need to stop, to reassess, I am aware of this, but it is difficult because work and this life is all I know. My job is my contact with the outside world, once I forgo chambers and clients I will have to release the impression I present. I will just be Stephanie and that is a very daunting prospect when you have spent your whole life defined by your ambition and career. Since losing Matthew I have thrown myself further into work. I have nothing else.

Richard

His cottage was part of an old farmhouse. There were still remnants of the working farm: the neighbours still had the company of three cows although bar milking the cows for their own needs they did not work the land. He had seen the place for rent in a local newspaper last time he was visiting Cornwall and had cut out the advert – not that he intended to move or relocate so soon, but maybe in the recesses of his mind he had been considering taking the plunge sooner rather than later.

His job search had taken on such an urgency he had subsequently realised quite how much he needed to escape London. In the end he had chosen to leave without a job in place. He was sure he would find somewhere soon enough given his experience and qualifications. He had checked the newspaper clipping of the cottage in his wallet every day for two weeks, before he finally plucked up the courage to ring the landlords and ask for a viewing.

He had made the long drive to just outside St Austell the following weekend, where he had booked a quaint B&B for two nights. On the first night he had enjoyed fish and chips on the harbour wall and a bottle of beer, whilst defending his food from the overzealous seagulls. Saturday morning heralded his visit to the cottage, and he was surprisingly nervous – as if it was all resting on the cottage.

Richard needn't have worried because he quite simply loved the place, the exposed brick walls, the fireplaces in the majority of rooms, the small windows and quaint features. The garden overlooked fields of nothingness and the blooms in the garden meant spring was thoroughly present in the surroundings. He felt revitalised and was certain that he would take the place as soon as the owners allowed him to move in. He did not have much in London: his flat was sparsely decorated so he estimated that it would only take one car journey. He would leave the bulky furniture and sell it as part of the flat. He would have more than enough from the sale to refurnish should he need to.

He had scoured the criminal law firms within commutable distance, but found he was uninspired to apply or contact any of them. The excitement and drive he once felt for this line of work seemed to have dried up. He wasn't entirely sure whether it was a by-product of the Molly Smith case. He certainly knew that it had contributed to his decision to leave, but he suspected that the burnout had been brewing for some time. Maybe it was that Molly Smith's case had made it glaringly obvious that he disagreed with the system: the snobbery, the judgement, the process, the injustice, and the game.

He had feared the change, but he also knew that fundamentally it was the right thing to do. He understood distance created perspective that could enhance his happiness, and he was desperate for some happiness. It had not been a hard process leaving the CPS. He had handed his notice in and they had not begged him to stay. Richard knew that it was only the most arrogant who believed themselves indispensable in the workplace. He understood that there was always someone fresher, younger, cheaper and harder working around the corner, someone who had the drive and enthusiasm he had long ago relinquished.

Within three weeks of his first viewing of the cottage he had relocated his whole life. The CPS had allowed him to tag on his remaining holiday to the months' notice, so he was able to leave earlier than his contract initially agreed. His flat had sold for a substantial amount, so he had enough money in the bank that he wouldn't have to worry for four months, so he was planning to relax and weigh up his options. He was aware he had given up a respected, well paid job that would have set him up for life. He had left his friends and everything he knew behind, but he felt released, as if all the baggage, the ties, the emotional guilt that lay heavy on his shoulders in London had gone. He felt lighter, exhilarated almost. He did not know what would happen, where he would end up and this excited him no end. It suddenly felt like he had opened his life up to possibilities.

40

Molly

I lie by the pool for days on end, the weeks blur into themselves, and I become blissfully unaware what day it is. I do not see my mother and Colin much, they have their own routine. In all fairness I do not see them for most of the hours of sunshine. I have become a very early riser since sleep eludes me. I wake at 5am. I tend to read in bed before fetching my towel and a strong black coffee and heading to the pool. I have read eight books already and I have only been here sixteen days. I intermittently read chapter by chapter in between dozing in the sunshine, waking every hour or so to see my skin become a deeper shade of mahogany.

There is a small cafeteria in the complex. It sells iced apple juice and foreign crisps: two of my favourite things when I am abroad. I have developed a slight habit, and it seems to be the only thing I eat and drink throughout the sunlit hours. A fifteen-year-old girl works there. She has started practising her English whenever I enter, and I have become quite fond of seeing her. I wonder what she thinks of me, a young British girl alone doing nothing but lounging and reading. She must think I have no friends, no one to holiday with: I wonder if she feels sorry for me.

Two years ago, I would have never dreamt of going on holiday with my mother, let alone spending days by myself. Before Jacob I had never enjoyed my own company. I was what some would call a social butterfly. I found it difficult to be still in my own company. My previous holidays had been busy, endless parties, filled with friends and Luke. I would spend the days chatting and sightseeing I loved going to all the places the locals went. Once I had exhausted an area, I would suggest hiring a car and we would drive on to other towns, villages or beaches and explore. I never sat still. Now all I do is lie horizontal, the sun healing my soul, the last thing on my mind is movement – it is as if every inch of me is craving rest.

Jacob

The messages Jacob receives on Twitter are mainly from raving feminists or lesbians. He thinks, their thinly veiled hatred of men and his sexuality is quite clear. He cannot understand why they think his and Molly's relationship still concerns them. What he cannot understand is the total lack of tolerance of these women. If they want to cover up and not have casual sex – fine, but it is not their concern if other women wish to do so. The tweets began with the expected "rapist scum" style, but quickly escalated to tweets about men in general. Jacob apparently is the scapegoat for women to vent at.

He replies to some of the tweets mainly explaining to them that if they do not want to go to bars where they may receive male attention that is their choice, they do not have to. Jacob cannot understand these women. It is as if they are living in a parallel universe where women do not make the choice to be treated the way they are. The world has changed. Jacob clearly sees how society is a different place. It began with the ladettes of the nineties, girls who wanted to be on an even footing with men: they wanted to be treated the same, drink the same, speak the same, they wanted to be interacted with as if they were male. Jacob believes women lost a little self-respect around this time. He remembers when he first trawled nightclubs and pubs and it was frowned upon for women to let loose, roll around, drink copious amounts. It is boasted about now as if it is some kind of achievement to lose yourself altogether.

He cannot understand how these women behave. Take @Victoria666 for instance, one of his biggest abusers who regularly tells him via social media he should die, regardless of whether he is innocent or not. She is a man hater. He predicts she was cheated on by her boyfriend and this has caused the monumental anger she holds towards the opposite gender, but nonetheless she is a contradiction in terms. On one hand Victoria hates Jacob, tweets irately about how women are treated and advocates women's equality and rights on an annoyingly frequent basis; yet she also posts selfies of her duck-face pose suggestive of blow job lips in the hope that she is sexually alluring to men. You want men to want to have sex with you? Yet you don't want men to actually want to have sex with you?

Jacob cannot understand these women: they don't seem to consider that males are hardwired to instinctively want to procreate with females, and when females are offering this on a plate, why is it so hard to understand that they are confused when the plate is removed suddenly? Jacob didn't have to major in science to realise that having sex is part of a human being's genetic make up: it is instinctive to want to procreate.

He could only imagine a Naturalist attempting to commentate on the patterns of human mating: "And, here we have a female dressed in next to nothing, grinding her hips up against the male. She is quite inebriated, her body relaxed. She pushes her bum towards the male's groin and licks her lips simultaneously. The male can see her breasts moving. The male is beginning to get aroused, he places his hands on her hips. She can tell he is interested in a sexual manner, she turns and grabs his hand and they suddenly slip away from the crowds, off to somewhere private, the female willingly leading the male. The teasing lasts half an hour. During this time we can see the female removes her clothes, and the male becomes more excited. But, as the male goes to penetrate, oh what's this, the female has changed her mind: she no longer wants the male for sexual purposes. She is pushing him away. The male is frustrated that the promise of sexual intercourse has been so suddenly removed and is now confused, for the female showed all the signs she was initially interested in mating. In some cases, the male leaves the female feeling down-beaten, but in others it appears the male does not listen to her last-minute rejections, quite clearly carried away sexually from her earlier teasing."

Jacob thought that when it came to nature, if they were merely animals they had a more complex and confusing emotional and mating pattern than any other species.

Stephanie

It is Sunday morning. I'm despondent as I put the kettle on for my coffee. I think back to Sundays gone by when Matthew would arrive at my door. "Steph, it's me. Croissant delivery." He'd shout through the letterbox. He'd welcome me with a hug and a handful of papers, before rushing through to the kitchen where he busied himself making brunch for us both. We'd read each other the headlines and playfully argue over current affairs. I long for those days, before Annalise came along.

I still have the newspaper delivered but only *The Guardian* now. I fetch it from the porch before moving to the sofa. I'm intrigued to see if my letter made it to the comments section. I'd responded last weekend to an article they'd featured. I suppose it was slightly depressing how I spent my spare time now, but for me my work wasn't just a job.

The article had concerned the prevalence of rape in any given demographic. The journalist argued that the occurrence of rape happened across all ages, cultures and classes in equal measure. Now, I do not think we can isolate rape culture to one given demographic of people, I think this culture of rape is ingrained across a broad spectrum of people within society, no matter their class, their jobs and their background. However, I do believe that there are certain behaviours that occur within some of the demographic groups that significantly impact this culture of rape, particularly the student culture in our country.

It is well documented that there is an increased occurrence of sexual assaults among students. Now the optimist in me would say that may suggest an increase in younger females reporting, but I am a realist and believe this is the result of laddism that is instilled in the university culture: the idea that this level of phallocentrism is a passage of partying. We need only look at recent fresher's nights that promote sexual assault: "violate a fresher", the club that installed violation cages, the "lad's" websites that actively promote rape, to realise that this shift in acceptability of the occurrence of sexual assault will substantially negate a shift in some students' attitudes towards the seriousness of rape.

Coupled with commercialism that frequently uses sex to sell, the marketing world is set up to directly contradict the notion of equality.

The script we are giving the children of the future, the ideas of gender and respect need to be positive from the start. Our sexuality should not be the focus or the tool we use to yield power or create success, no matter our gender: male or female.

I open the comments section first and I'm disappointed to see they haven't included my response. I reach for my phone, my instinct is to phone Matthew, as I open the screen I realise my mistake. He is no longer available to me. I would love to meet him, sit in a café, go for a drink in the pub, but I cannot. Instead I put the newspaper down and turn on the news.

Richard

Richard realised quite quickly that the less he had, the happier he was. The sparser his obligations and commitments the more content he was. Every time he visited the tip to offload parts of his previous life that did not fit comfortably in the cottage he felt relief. He found himself able to think of things that did not revolve around his job and work; he remembered hobbies from his childhood that had once excited him. He found himself taking long, tiring walks; cooking sumptuous meals; travelling to the beach early in the morning to practice his surfing; looking for art online; reading a book. He found himself living again rather than existing. He drank red wine on the weekend to enjoy the taste, rather than sinking seven pints to forget the bad taste from the week in his mouth. He realised he was beginning to like himself again.

His finances enabled him to take some time to reassess what he wanted to do, where he wanted to go from here and more and more he was drawn towards teaching. He was attracted to the idea of helping others, the sense of achievement that would afford. He wanted to feel fulfilled in his work, he wanted to bring about positive change, rather than continue in a negative system.

He began to realise that in the end he did not want to be remembered for his appearances in court; he also understood that it was ignorant to believe he ever would. There would always be someone hungrier, younger and more ambitious to fill his shoes. He had a healthy bank balance, a nice car, what others would consider a successful career, but he had no family, no relationship: he was alone and unsatisfied. Cornwall represented an opportunity to change the present. Richard knew that his actions had created the past, and he was instrumental in altering his future.

41

Molly

I dream of him. I dream that our time is running out and that I am chasing him, trying to spend time together before it is too late, before I get caught out. The dreams are so vivid it is as if I am watching a parallel life that would have unfolded had I chosen a different route: a separate Molly, distinct from who I now am, a Molly that would have existed had I chosen differently.

On certain evenings, I would unexpectedly dream of Luke. So vivid and lifelike were these images that my mind conjured that when waking it took me a number of moments to reconfigure where I was and when it was. My mind frequently transported me back to a time when we were together: it was grief. I was still processing the seismic shift of my life. I wondered how long it would be before my subconscious allowed me to forget, how many months I would have to endure these ghostly images in my sleep. I wondered if Luke experienced these moments, if he too was on some level still struggling to process the sudden implosion of our relationship. I hoped he was. There seemed so much injustice in how he treated me. I wanted him to feel the pain that I did. I wanted him to suffer like me.

I have come to understand that my grief is like a fairground tunnel that you don't know you're entering, you don't know when it will throw you down fast and spiralling into its pit or how long it will lift you up only to swallow you again. It is relentless, unpredictable and scary and it is only when you have ridden it repeatedly that you understand what is coming, but that is almost the worst part because you know there is no option to get off.

Jacob

He needed a new challenge, a distraction. He knew he needed to put Molly well and truly in the past. He did not need to work, but then he was not sure what to focus his efforts on now. He still thought of Molly; he still hated her for what she had done to him: how she'd ruined his reputation. All of his time wasted, they had come so close to being together, yet she had destroyed their chances so cruelly. He had wanted retribution for so long, until he realised success would bring him a certain amount of satisfaction again. Molly could look on as he rebuilt his life. He'd show Molly she couldn't ruin him.

Stephanie

I always liked how considerate Matthew was, whether it be making sure he ordered two cups of coffee rather than one, holding the door open for me, offering me the choice of restaurant or film or simply always being on hand to help me should I need him. Matthew had the manners of a generation past, an old-fashioned approach to women that I had rarely experienced.

I sometimes wonder with all our talk of equality and feminism whether we have diluted the male species so far that we have extinguished male chivalry. When I watch old movies I am nostalgic for the men on the screen who I have never encountered, a different nature becomes them that modern men seem to have forgotten. I wonder whether a renaissance of male chivalry is part of the solution, the teachings and practice of respect for the female sex daily, in the smallest of gestures. Maybe we must start at a very basic, minute level of human interaction between male and female to solve the bigger acts of interaction, the abusive acts of interaction.

Richard

Richard had always wanted children, alongside the house he aspired to own in Cornwall, and of late, a dog, but he had always wanted kids first and foremost, preferably a boy to begin. He would love a little boy to play with. He thought he would be better communicating with a son than a daughter. Not having sisters made him a little inept when it came to conversing with females. He did not understand what girls needed, especially teenage girls. The idea he may have to raise a teenage girl put the fear of God into him. He would settle for sons any day.

He thought of all the teachings he had to offer a son. He had spent an afternoon with Suzie once arguing about the most important values you could instil in your offspring. He thought that "to be respectful" was an essential life lesson, although Suzie had insisted that "loyalty" was her priority. He had questioned whether in some cases loyalty could be taken too far, suggesting if their future child was respectful of themselves and others they would not go far wrong. It was one of those arguments that seemed so important at the time, but was a waste of energy in retrospect. Their hypothetical answers were irrelevant in their future lives as it now transpires.

Richard thought of all the cases he had prosecuted and wondered had the defendants been more respectful of others, of themselves, whether they would have ever occurred. If the child with low self-esteem had invested more respect in himself, would he have shoplifted just because he "didn't care"? Would the man who beat his wife have treated another human being in such a manner if he valued others and himself more? Or the girl who glassed a friend in a drunken argument – would her reaction have been different if she thought more of herself and others.

42

Molly

It is late in the morning when I wake, which is unusual: I do not normally have such a long lie-in. I feel exhausted today, and I allow myself to relax into the bed and rest my head upon the pillows. I drift in and out of sleep for a further hour or so, and I only feel vaguely guilty that I have missed my morning swim I am that tired.

My head is swimming with thoughts and fragments of memories today. Sometimes they take me off guard. I think I'm doing okay and then the weight of it all seems too much. I have not had a panic attack for weeks now, not since I have been here anyway. Maybe it is the sun, or maybe the distance has benefited my mental state.

Jacob swarms my mind as I walk towards the harbour, I dreamt of him again last night. He also flits into my dreams without my permission on a regular basis, but I am usually able to shake him off with a morning coffee: today I cannot. It is unnerving this latest dream because in it I am far younger, I am in my late teens and we are at a rundown nightclub I used to frequent. He is speaking to me and I can vaguely make out what he is saying, but my sight is blurred and his speech is slightly slurred. I am trying to understand the message, but I cannot: it is just beyond my reach.

It is days later that it dawns on me. I have dreamt of Jacob every night for a week. I have collected images from my dreams, I am trying to decipher why he is still tormenting my thoughts. It is as I am swimming that I have the first flashback.

It is similar to the dream I had at the beginning of the week. But I know it is real. I am eighteen years old, and I am in the local nightclub. I am drunk. I am wearing a short top, showing off my stomach, which only someone of such youth can do. Jacob is there. He is with one of my friends. She introduces us. I do not pay much attention. Later in the night I comment to my friend that the boy from earlier keeps staring at me. She smiles and says, "He would."

The flashbacks come in waves. Then I am suddenly aware of the enormity of these thoughts.

I am twenty-two years old. I am in Brighton for the weekend with friends. We are having a BBQ on the beach. There is a large group of us, and we are all in good spirits as the sun sets: the promise of summer on all our lips. We are joined by a large group of boys that Charlie, my firm friend, knows. It is dark so I cannot clearly see their faces, but we all chat for most the night. It is only now I recognise one of their voices.

I have just returned from Australia and my skin is the colour of caramel. I am with Luke having a meal in the pub just down from our new home when I bump into a man on the way back from the bar. I knock his pint into him and apologise. He smiles and says not to worry. I remember his eyes suddenly.

I am walking to the wake of a work acquaintance who died

tragically young. As I near the steps a handsome man in a black suit steps aside for me. He gestures with his hand that I should walk before him. I notice him, but not for long enough. He is handsome. I remember thinking, *That man is very handsome.*

I had met him. I had met Jacob many times over the years, but he passed me by. I had never acknowledged him long enough to remember him. He had met me long before I met him. I was already on his radar, already part of his plan: I had always been within his sights. I shiver with the dawning realisation that for him I was never just a coincidence.

I sleep in sweat-saturated sheets, my dreams continue to be disjointed and panicked. Occasionally a baby crying rouses me from my unconsciousness. I awake fretful throughout the evening, worried by the simplest of sounds or possible movements within the holiday apartment. I had begun to relax over the past few weeks, but my night-time stories have awoken a fear in me that I thought I was able to put to rest after I flew here at the end of the trial. It is as if Jacob still consumes me. He still occupies my body however unwelcome. He has become a presence in my mind that I cannot seem to relinquish no matter how heavy my want is.

Jacob

Jacob was thorough with every detail of his life. He could not afford to be complacent. He planned everything meticulously: he liked to be control – prepared. His relationship with Molly had, like everything else in his life, not been a coincidence. It had been part of his plan, he just hadn't anticipated how things would turn out.

He'd first met Molly Smith when she was eighteen years old. She was strikingly beautiful. He had found her allure intoxicating. She had a boyfriend: girls like Molly always did. She was surrounded by friends: boys and girls alike, and he had wanted to be part of her inner circle.

He'd found it harder than he imagined instigating their initial friendship. She'd moved abroad, she'd met Luke. He always kept tabs on her: social media was useful in that sense. He'd seen photos of her life over the years, the birthday parties, New Year bashes, meals and drinks out. He was efficient in his research. He'd invested so much time in their relationship. He was certain she was the girl for him.

He was not a stalker, he'd never actively followed her, he'd just shown an interest in his future investment. The fact she had rented a property off him was a stroke of luck. It'd enabled him to study her intimately before he introduced himself at the wedding. She'd enjoyed the attention at first: he couldn't believe his luck when he'd finally been able to manoeuvre himself next to her at a party. He'd been mildly upset she didn't recognise him, but there had been a slight glimmer of recognition, he was certain of it and this satisfied him somewhat. He hadn't been entirely invisible to her.

His cameras were in all his households; he sometimes removed them when he knew his investments were safe. He would have removed them from Molly and Luke's home had he not worried about her. He only kept the hidden cameras to protect her: he wanted to make sure she was safe. Obviously, there were some benefits to the cameras in the bedroom and bathroom, but he kept these for personal use. He had only ever had her best interests at heart.

Stephanie

I had grown up next door to a man named William Wilde. He had reminded me of a character from a Charles Dickens novel and there was something magical about him. I would try my utmost to speak to him daily. I found him fascinating: he was unlike any other old person I had come across. For a start he wore colours, an array of colours, red trousers, bright jumpers, denim shorts, Hawaiian board shorts too, should the fancy take him. He did not dress like an old man or act like one. When I was in my teens he would make me lemonade in a tall glass and offer me peanuts whilst he regaled me with stories of the war. Unlike others who discussed the war, William Wilde considered it the best time of his life, "full of camaraderie and adventure". I was inclined to believe he did not witness the horrors that other soldiers were exposed to.

As I progressed through university and whenever I returned home to visit he would offer me a beer: an ice-cold pale ale that tasted of holidays and sunshine. I would spend the long, hazy summer nights in the middle of the week out on his decking talking of my future. William would tell me of the travels he had planned for the winter ahead, and the hours would while away.

He always questioned my incentive to study law, he wanted to know what drove me; he would question my determination in the subject every term to make sure I had not lost focus of the importance of my chosen discipline. "When your passion is making money, Stephanie, you have no passion left at all. Making money is not a passion, Stephanie, you must remember this: making money does not leave you without a care in the world, it simply means you care for nothing." He would repeat this to me weekly during our beer evenings, he made me promise that when my job became more about the money than the work itself, that I would leave: change direction, pick another route.

In my sparkling youth, I became intoxicated by William

Wilde's idealism. I swore that I would never end up working in a profession that I had lost hope in. I made a pact with myself that I would jump off the dreary treadmill of bills, mortgages and cars if I did not feel fulfilled. I promised William, and myself, that as long as I continued to believe in justice I would work within the profession, but as soon as I gave up on the law I would find another passion, something that would keep me alive.

William was a comedian: he told me he gave up work to find women, because they too were his passion. He was merely teasing, but a man filled with so much youth at such an age seemed to have a wisdom concerning the holistics of the human health, and I for one listened.

After my parents left my childhood home that I had long ago stopped living in, I did not go back to visit William. I became melancholy with the memories of my youth whenever I was in the vicinity of the village I grew up in, and for one reason or another it was easier not to go back: being reminded of how far you have come from your past is not always a good thing.

I do not know what happened to William Wilde. I suspect he is dead now, he would be pushing ninety-five. He may well be gallivanting in his camper van, still taking trips to northern Africa to search for a Moroccan woman he met when he was sixty years old.

I have thought of William Wilde more and more since the trip to Bayonne with Matthew. His words resonate in my mind as I flick through files and files of clients I am yet to represent. I thought I still had passion for the law; I thought I still believed in justice, but then Matthew's face and his words and William's lessons keep coming back to me, and I cannot help but think that maybe my passion has become about something other than the law, something out of justice's reach: not money, but winning. And I cannot help but think winning without justice being served is not really winning at all.

Richard

Richard began to study restorative justice. The idea that victims had an active role in the resolution of the crime that ultimately affected their lives. He had briefly looked at restorative justice in the past, but then dismissed its merits, assuming wrongly that it was "new age" and "for hippies", rather than acknowledging its proven success.

It was a fascinating construct, derived from indigenous tribes' cultural practices: the idea that victims ask questions to rehabilitate the offenders. It promoted acceptance of responsibility on the offenders' behalf, which was often the biggest challenge especially when it came to repeat offenders.

He considered it an antidote to the failing criminal justice system, one that promoted accountability whilst simultaneously personalising the crime and providing an element of emotional closure for the victims. Richard understood the high level of emotion involved in cases of rape and murder, which may mean restorative justice was not the best remedy, but for every case it may not help he was equally sure there would be one that it would.

Richard could see how it would enable the victim to regain control of the situation. It created a shift in the perspective of the crime and saw the victims identifying themselves as survivors instead. It was not necessarily about forgiveness, but it was a powerful experience nevertheless. Not only this but it would save money. The prison service was overrun; if there was a possibility of rehabilitating an offender whilst saving the system time and money, surely that was a better alternative. Richard thought jail time was an empty form of justice if there was no understanding or acknowledgement of the gravity of the crime at the end of it.

Richard understood that the current system was one based on denial, manipulation and a veil of deception, which only ever resulted in winning or losing. How could anyone argue that a system that focused on accountability, acceptance, empowerment and resolution was not a favourable alternative?

43

Molly

The realisation Jacob had known me previously shook me to the core. Our history took on a darkness I had not realised was present at the time. I did not feel blameless even though I understood on the surface that it was Jacob's fault: I blamed myself for allowing myself to get close to someone who quite clearly did not have my best interests at heart. Someone who just wanted what he could get regardless of the consequences for me.

I had not wanted sex. I had never given him the impression I had wanted sex. My body was not his to do with what he wished: he was not entitled to me. It was not his choice to make: it should have been mine. I was not his property. I knew now I would have never kept his child. It was not a child when I miscarried, it was not even the size of a lemon, it was just a mass that I did not want to be part of me.

Jacob

He wondered if she felt guilty about what she had put him through. He wondered if she denied the existence of their very relationship? Maybe it helps her live with the loss she has caused him. He was taken aback in court by her conviction that she told the truth about the event. He had not expected it of her. He understood she was tarnished now, she was spoilt. She was not what he wanted after all. He occasionally feels sorry for her, but then the anger returns.

He has means of punishing her should he wish: she does not know about the secret cameras he set up, not that he uses them now. There is no point. She is not the woman he thought she was. It was so easy to upload his old photos and videos online these days. Occasionally he'd post one of her masturbating anonymously. It was thrilling that he could expose her for the whore she was. It wasn't what he'd ever intended to do with the material, but she deserved to be humiliated.

Stephanie

The sun shines down upon my bare body through the sash windows. There is a cool wind whipping through the curtains and threatening to hijack the warmth as it always does in spring in Europe. I have nothing to do today except peruse the local food market and bask in the soft sunshine. It is one of the first holidays that I have allowed myself where I have nothing to do. I have no cookery classes scheduled or group tours to historic monuments. I have purely time to do as little as I please. I have spent the past four days considering if the way I am feeling is burn out.

The more time I am away from work the more my feelings of anxiety rise about returning, and I do not like this. I no longer know what I will do upon my return, I am uncertain, and I hate uncertainty. I have always had a plan, an expectation, an organised future, but now I am filled with doubt, with questions, with confusion. I no longer know whether what I thought I had always wanted is what I want at all.

Richard

Richard lounges on the Cornish beaches for the most of September. The temperature is yet to drop and he can continue to enjoy the sunshine. He understands why Cornwall is referred to as the English Riviera, there is something intrinsically Mediterranean about the land and the attitude of the people that reside there: a slower pace and appreciation for the outdoors seems instilled throughout the coastal towns.

He has begun surfing again. He is still very much a novice and his pallor makes him stand out significantly against the honey-bronzed lithe figures that ride the faces of water across the sun-swept shores, but he does not care for the image of the sport. He finds in the moments where he pops to his feet and angles himself into the turn he thinks of nothing but the action he is involved in. He has never lived in the moment quite as much as when he is learning to surf. In those instances, there is only him, a board and the sea. He does not register the external stresses of his life like he does when it comes to other sports he has challenged previously.

He is acutely aware of his sudden and momentous lifestyle change, but it feels liberating, as if he has broken free from himself, from the constraints of London and the life he had created there. It is as if he finally feels like he can begin living, he is entitled to create a universe entirely of his own making, new and freshly removed from the interconnections of his life in the city that he had found so tedious and draining. He had the option to make friends with people whose company he enjoyed.

He had been blighted by school friends in London who still bothered him from his days in Swindon. It was not as if he disliked them, but they just reminded him of a life he had once had, a life that he wished to place in his past, just like he had with his fifteen-year-old self.

He was sure he would miss these connections: these friendships, the certainty of his life, the safety, but he was more aware of how much he needed to escape the city, and it had become apparent that he embraced this new-found freedom more than he had ever envisaged. Richard's life was suddenly an abundance of possibilities, all of which would lead him on an adventure he had yet to realise.

Malika arrived in his life on a drizzly November day. He had been walking the rugged coastal path when he spotted her, her long brown hair flying across her face in the wind as she tried to battle the weather towards the pub. He had just got to Perranporth and was looking forward to a pint in the bar before heading back, when she approached him at his table. He got so used to his own company he had found himself forgetting normal social etiquette and had initially stumbled over his words as she addressed him.

"Can I join you?" she said. She was brazen and confident, and he liked how she held herself.

Richard had nodded and shyly stroked his knees before realising he may look slightly strange, and sat on his hands. He was unsure what to say, how to interact with this woman who he suddenly found sitting across from him.

The shards of light splintered through his windscreen, he squinted as the clouds fought to extinguish the brightness. The journey to Malika's was not far, but he had happened to time it with the sun's afternoon departure.

He had made this winding journey for the past five weeks since they met, and he enjoyed the depth of the hedgerows, as if he was driving through a large maze as he made his way to her. Malika had awoken Richard with ferocious honesty. She was brazen and refreshing: not since Suzie had he felt his spirit lift so greatly.

She reminded him of a raven: confident and present. She had lightness to her approach that he admired and desired. Her name was Arabic for "Queen" and Richard thought it could not be more fitting. He had taken to addressing her as such whenever they greeted.

Her Frenchness only increased her open-sexual disposition. She was not raised in that country, but she had inherited her mother's liberal outlook and approach when it came to nakedness and sex. Whereas Richard worried about inappropriateness and had often shied away, Malika saw nothing of stripping naked and running into the cold, sharp ocean. The human form held no power or threat when it came to feelings of embarrassment for Malika.

An artist, he had found her free-spiritedness fascinating, how she would wallow happily through her empty, free time, hunting inspiration for her next exhibition. They had not discussed finances, but it appeared to be a matter that did not worry Malika. She rode the daily grind of life haphazardly, storming from one idea to the next without an acknowledgement of the future. Richard wondered whether this inability to understand or discuss the future was what attracted him to her so vehemently. He had meticulously planned his future only to discover it did not happen quite how he envisaged it. Malika represented the opposite path.

Their dates had largely been filled with the outdoors, an incessant need to search the cliff tops and beaches as they devoured each other's life to date. Malika was fascinated with

Richard's career, she relished how eloquently passionate he became when he talked of justice and law, but was equally saddened by his disappointment in the profession.

Their relationship developed as most do, in a flurry of sexual tension that eased into a companionable comfort. Richard enjoyed the rhythm of them, the simplicity of their days outside together followed by the quiet preparation of an evening meal in their cottage.

They spent weekends driving to deserted coves. As the summer arrived and the warm scent of flowers floated into the air they would often sleep under the stars or in the boot of his car with the seats folded down, with towels for makeshift curtains. They fell in love in a secluded cove near Penzance, and they would while away hours by the shore reading books and walking through the lush green valley, before heading to Mousehole for dinner in one of the pubs.

Life was for Richard what he had always yearned for.

44

Molly

It takes me weeks to adjust my sleeping pattern again. By the time I am managing to rest for six hours straight a night I have been in Spain for almost two months. My mother has asked me when I'm leaving, or if I have any plans. But, I am only now starting to relax, I have gained three pounds, which although not obvious to others is an improvement for me. I can feel myself valuing my body again. I am physically stronger, what with all the swimming I have done, the monotony of length after length in the pool every morning has paid off.

I am still not right and as I lie on the loungers daily I question whether I ever will be right again. I do not think I will get over what happened to me, but maybe I will learn to carry it with me, to live with it as best I can.

Jacob

It was a drizzly Wednesday when he finally did it. He had been meaning to extinguish Molly from his life for some time, but he had never plucked up the energy to entirely rid himself of her. He'd gathered all the photos, the receipts of meals together, items of her clothing he'd acquired and poured petrol over them.

He stood in his communal garden, and watched as the memories of Molly burnt away – it was time to move on. He could no longer stay consumed by the past: she had taken up enough of his time.

Stephanie

I had seen Jacob Walker-Kent once since the case. I had just left Waitrose and was laden down by bags, when I saw him walking on the other side of the street. I had stopped to rearrange the load and paused to observe him. He had a certain gait, a walk that conveyed his sense of entitlement. He exuded power. I must admit I hadn't thought of him much since the case. Occasionally he'd pop into my mind when I had a new sexual assault case to represent, but he did not occupy my thoughts. I'd done my job: he had the outcome he'd desired. I'd won.

But, as I watched him the unease I always felt when I was reminded of the case grew, there was just something about him, something that occasionally niggled at me, that I could not explain. He disappeared around the corner, and I lifted my bags and resolved to forget all about Jacob Walker-Kent. He was not my business anymore. He was just part of the job.

Richard

Richard rode along the wave, the water laid before him – unbroken, a swelling lump carrying him across the shore, his body balanced on the board as he watched the sea slip away. A seagull flew in front of him, and he felt privileged to share such a moment, the simplicity of surfing, the freedom and fun that it brings, riding the crest of the wave, hoping it will last forever, for in that moment there was nothing but Richard and the water. His mind is a blank canvas from which stress had been erased.

He flung himself backwards into the water as the wave came to an end, he had been practising for so many months now and he finally felt like he'd cracked it. His perseverance had paid off. He could see Malika on the shore. She was waving, he waved back and she clapped her hands, delighting in the moment with him.

One more, he told himself, *before I go back to shore.*

Then they would lie underneath blankets and eat barbecued fish that they cooked on the fire he had seen Malika building on the beach. When the moon was high in the sky and the evening was full of endless stars they would walk back to their car where they would sleep for the night – towels trapped in doors as curtains and a double duvet to snuggle under after they laid the seats down flat. In the morning, they would awake and drink black coffee and eat croissants on the sand before they did it all over again.

45

Molly

This morning as I swim my mind is clear. I do not feel the whirlpool of memories and doubts that Jacob created pressing down upon me. I somehow feel lighter. I have been freed. It is as if he remained partially in control of me but now he is so distant, I no longer feel the hold he had over me.

My swimming has become mechanical. I am so able in the water, my breaststroke is fluid and strong and I intersperse it with front crawl, which is determined and fast. I easily cover 1,000 metres a day swimming. It is as if the chronic repetition is therapeutic. I repeat the movement over and over again until I am exhausted: my mind dulled and my body drained.

My mother generally ignores me now. She and Colin please themselves, which suits me perfectly. I am enjoying the rest – the simplicity of my daily routine. I know that it cannot last forever, that soon there will be a job to think of, somewhere to live, a more permanent state of affairs, but for now it is okay. It suits me just fine. I swim; I read; I eat; I sleep; I am healing.

Life is made up of a series of moments, an accumulation of

moments forming a series that become a sequence of events, these moments are all intrinsically linked to create what we become, whether it be our choices of health, diet, career, or the friends we choose. Life is just a series of moments. Some moments will stick clearer in our mind than others, exaggerated over the years and reinforced to hold great importance in our larger picture. Other moments will disintegrate, we will forget that they happened as quickly as they entered our lives. Some moments take time to process, to recover from: an assault of our senses that is almost too great to assimilate. Some moments only take on significance after the event itself, after the moment has passed. We have no idea how these moments will form us, when they will happen. Life is a beautiful complicated thing full of moments.

I realise now that Jacob was a moment. I cannot allow that moment to define me, and I cannot allow that moment to become bigger than me. He was only a moment. We are all just stories. The stories we live, the tales we tell, the fragments of us, these mere moments create us and destroy us in equal measure, they are the shades of our soul.

46

Jacob

Jacqueline was perfect, his mother had told him. She was from money, she owned a small interior design company, she was quiet, but astute and beautiful.

"She knows her place, Jacob, not like these other girls you have courted previously."

For once his mother was right. Jacqueline had dignity, she was aloof when needed, and perfectly courteous when required. He had been ambivalent to meet her initially, but then his mother's incessant nagging and his curiosity had got the better of him when he had been presented with a photo of her on Google, all bronzed limbs and long golden tousled hair, he could not resist.

She was not as spirited as the others, and he worried his interest would wane. She would present him with no challenges. She was perfect wife material. His friend had laughed and said, "Yeah, Stepford wife material," but after the turmoil and trouble caused by his previous types it was necessary.

They had courted for a year before he proposed. He had, of

course, put surveillance on Jacqueline. He had to be certain of his investment. He had begun work again so his job took him away regularly, but this suited him somewhat, and he was still able to keep tabs on her. By the time Jacob had bent down on one knee they had barely spent more than three consecutive nights together. He did not intend this to change in the future.

They were married in an expensive country house. Jacqueline spent a small fortune of his finance, and she was beside herself with flower arrangements and seating plans. Jacob was disinterested. He walked through the motions, he did as he was meant to, all the while his heart strangely vacant; but then it had been for a long time. He had never really recovered from Molly's betrayal of trust. He did not think he ever would.

Jacqueline adored him the way he needed to be adored. He needed to be the only man in the room, he needed to be the only significant other in her life. Maybe this is why he had struggled so much when the children came along.

They had not discussed offspring, but he assumed Jacqueline must have simply stopped taking the pill. Arabella came first and then Quentin two years later. He did not see the children a great deal. He had no interest in them. His business, as they always did, flourished. He was taken overseas more and more frequently.

He provided fantastically for his family, and his wife was not short of help, with two live-in nannies and his mother suffocating her grandchildren with attention. When he was home, they would attend social gatherings together, have the occasional date. Their sex life was lacklustre, but then Jacob found other ways to satisfy his urges in foreign countries, he always had. His life worked now, he had fulfilled all the requirements.

Jacqueline

He was – in the eyes of my mother – perfect. I had been arrested with attention when I first met Jacob. He was so attentive. The abundance of compliments had been intoxicating. We weren't together long before we wed. I had never wanted a long engagement. Jacob presented me with a world I wanted to be a part of. He was so very successful.

I had the wedding I'd dreamed of since I was a little girl. Jacob was disinterested, but he had allowed me free rein over the finances.

I thought it was just the pressure of the wedding, but the marriage wasn't quite what I imagined it to be. I'd naively assumed that once he was my husband he'd see me more, we'd share our lives together. We hadn't. I didn't realise then that over the years the distance would continue to grow, he'd become more disengaged: especially after the children.

I had always known about the case, of course I had. I knew all about my husband before I married him, but I wanted a certain kind of lifestyle, and a man like Jacob would afford me that. I am not with the man through love, as much as Jacob thinks I'm subservient. It works for me. Initially I thought I would grow to love him, but I quickly realised it was the attention I loved, the endless flattery. As soon as he'd grown bored of me, or got what he wanted – a wife – it had stopped, and I had realised that is what I had loved.

I'd heard about Molly Smith. The circles I moved in meant I was informed about men of wealth: such as Jacob. I had not doubted it to be true. I have witnessed enough men discuss similar situations they'd found themselves in. Jacob had just been caught out. When we met I just put Molly's accusations down to dramatics: slightly truthful, but dramatic nonetheless.

47

Jacob

She was younger than most of the others. There was almost eighteen years difference between them. Jacob quite liked that: he felt powerful. He had approached the matter subtly, he knew better than to rush in, she was one of their nannies after all. Anna had made his brief stints at home more bearable. He was surprised at first that Jacqueline had employed her: she was far too attractive for other women not to notice.

Jacob had begun taking showers in the day when he knew Jacqueline was at her numerous exercise classes. He would walk around the house, just a towel tied around his waist, his torso on display. He had a good physique, and he saw Anna glancing occasionally. He began to compliment her, he'd touch her arm for a little too long, a smile would linger on his lips longer than necessary, and he'd catch her eye and wink. He knew to build the interactions gradually, he didn't want to overwhelm her with attention.

It had been a fairly easy transaction after the weeks of

flirting. He'd come out the shower and found her in the lounge, she was organising the aftermath of his children's play.

"Anna, you wouldn't mind helping me with a knot in my shoulder?"

She had hesitated.

He had smiled his charming smile. And, so it began. She couldn't resist his charms.

Jacqueline

I must admit, I had quite liked Anna to begin. I employed her as a test. She was far too attractive in comparison to the other women who cared for my children. I noticed early on the way he would look at her. I knew he was biding his time. It'd been a risk, but I could see my plan was going to work. I saw how he lorded it about the house in front of her. Jacob saw Anna as subordinate, just like me. He thought he held the power in all his relationships, and I'd learnt to understand that this is how he liked it.

I'm sure Anna enjoyed his advances to begin with, I mean who wouldn't? My husband is extremely handsome; he exudes wealth and power. On the surface, any woman would be a fool not to be flattered, but then they did not know him like me. His behaviour was eroding my future plans, he did not think of anyone but himself – not me, not the children. He thought he was so untouchable, he thought he could control everything, even me.

It'd started with subtle orders, which he masked as requests: to wear certain clothes, behave in a certain manner. I knew when I'd annoyed him at social gatherings, he'd grip my wrist so hard when my behaviour wasn't up to standard that it would result in a bruise. Apparently, my laugh embarrassed him, it wasn't quite *ladylike* enough.

He was not specifically violent with me, no I couldn't say that, but he scolded me, shall we say. The worst punishments were the endless silences, or the removal of my *privileges*, as he called them.

Over dinner, if he thought I was getting out of shape, he'd walk to the rubbish bin and discard my plate of food, before I could sit down. He'd kiss me on the forehead, then say: "I'm only doing it for your own good, Jacqueline. Someone has to make sure you don't let yourself go." His behaviour became normalised over the years.

48

Jacob

The first time it had happened properly she was quiet: shy, slightly unsure. She stood there all doe-eyed, confused as to what to do. He liked the build-up, the anticipation of the finale, that is why he waited – he liked the power of knowing he could at any time, but refraining.

Maybe he was too forceful sometimes, he'd lose himself in the moment, in the sexual urges that overcame him. When he'd finished he would always reiterate their agreement, that she must not tell anyone if she wished to keep her job. He'd made her sign a non-disclosure agreement. He told her he made all the staff sign one, he did not want her to think she was special. He could not have Jacqueline find out about this, it would make things too complicated. A legal document guaranteed Anna's silence.

Jacqueline

The first time I found Anna crying she'd brushed me off, refused to tell me what had upset her. I knew then, I knew. But, I had to build her trust, I had to gather evidence, if we were to get him this time. I knew Jacob would claim Anna's story, whatever it was at this point, was false. I knew he'd tell me she'd constructed a reality to benefit herself financially. What he didn't know was I had already found the non-disclosure agreement he'd drawn up.

He thought he was so clever. That had been my confirmation really, the affirmation that something untoward was definitely going on. I just needed to find out what. I could see Anna was too frightened, too scared to disclose his behaviour. I would have to prove to her that I was on her side: I was willing to help her. I needed to expose him for what he really was; it was all a waste of time otherwise.

We'd had the cameras installed for security. Companies such as Jacob's were targeted, and we had always been aware that the children and I could be considered collateral damage by criminals in the pursuit of his money. Jacob had not questioned it when I told him his security company were coming to test the system, it was part of his security businesses service.

He was always too concerned with his business and "his private affairs", as he called them, to notice my life. He was totally unaware of the extra camera I had installed in Anna's room. His company turned a blind eye to my request, ignoring the gross invasion of privacy. I'm sure they'd done worse if they followed my husband's orders. I would not watch all of Anna's movements, but at least I could check what Jacob was up to. At least then I could be sure what I suspected was true. Once I had the evidence he'd have no choice, he'd have to fulfil my requests.

49

Jacob

Jacqueline was away for the night, some charity event with her female friends. The children were still home sadly, but they'd be in bed asleep in no time if he had anything to do with it. He'd given the other nanny, Brittany, an overweight American girl, the night off. He'd told her not to mention it to his wife as not to arouse suspicion, flattering her with compliments about how she worked far harder than Anna.

Anna had been tetchy since he'd arrived. It had annoyed him: they didn't often have much time together. She had left the rooms he entered, and straight after dinner she'd informed him she'd be having an early night once the children were asleep. This had angered him. She had no right to dictate her hours of employment to him.

He'd let her go to bed... he'd deal with her later.

He sat there with his whisky gradually getting drunker. He scrolled through his Facebook, he searched for Molly Smith, as he often did when he'd had too much to drink. All smiles and blonde curls, she stared back at him from the screen. It had all gone wrong with her. She had been the beginning of his dissatisfaction. Everything could have been so very different if she hadn't ruined it. She looked so happy now; she looked like she hadn't a care in the world. She was still beautiful, but then she was always going to be.

He thought back to their time together and how much she had teased him, how she had led him on. The majority of the time he pushed it to the back of his mind, but the way Anna had behaved tonight reminded him of Molly. Just like Molly, she thought she could lead him on and then withdraw herself. He should have known they were all the same. He drank more whisky. All the while Molly Smith just stared back at him smiling. He was done with this. He'd show them all what he thought of their little games.

He needed Anna to understand she could not behave like this; he needed to show her who she worked for, and what he was capable of should she choose to forget this. He was seething now, his rage was expanding inside his chest, he could feel the anger surging through him. He slammed down his whisky glass and grabbed the bottle, he was pounding up the stairs now, his heart was racing, he had reached his limits. He'd had enough of women behaving like this. It was the last time. It really was the last time he was putting up with it. He'd teach Anna what he couldn't teach Molly all those years ago.

Jacqueline

I knew I needed to give him ample opportunity to see Anna if I were to catch him out. I had started to doubt myself, started to question whether I was reading too much into it. I had to know for certain though. That is why I'm away for the night at a charity ball, when in fact I'm in a hotel five miles away from the house enjoying spa treatments.

I needed to give him the space to either confirm or deny my suspicions. I felt bad I may be sacrificing Anna for my greater good, but I could not go on like this. I realised Anna would find it difficult to get another job amid the scandal. At least I'd know one way or another after tonight. I was sure he'd show his true colours, I just had to wait it out.

50

Jacob

Her body repelled as he entered the room. She cowered in the corner, which made Jacob even more angry. Why was she behaving as if she was scared of him? He approached her and could see she was shaking, a look of disgust in her eyes. How dare she be disgusted by him? He was surprised when he reached her that she attempted to push him away. Who did she think she was?

He dragged her towards the bed. He would just have to show her who was in charge. She needed to learn. He was going to teach her a lesson. He'd pulled her with such force she'd momentarily lost her balance. She tried to regain it, but she crumpled onto the floor.

"Get up!" he shouted. "Get up. Get up now."

She looked terrified now, like an animal caught in the headlights. She froze.

Why would she not get up? He kicked her against the bed frame. "Get up, Anna!" Blood trickled down the side of her face, a river of crimson red dripped from a gash next to her eye. She tried to stagger to her knees. She whimpered in fear. She was still trying to defy him – still trying to disobey him. Why would she not do as she was told? Why would she not just surrender to him? He was in charge! Why did she persist in challenging him?

He thought of Molly; he thought of all the women who'd betrayed him. The days in court came to mind, the frigid little bitches that had tried to push him away over the years. He could hear his mother's overbearing and controlling voice in his head, and Molly; Molly Smith's face laughing at him from his screen, those blonde curls, those deep brown eyes, and Anna had whimpered again, and he just wanted her to shut up and do as he pleased. Why could she not just have obeyed him? She needed to stop goading him, he needed all those women to stop.

He beat her with such force he was surprised he could summon it. Her face was turned to him, so close his lips could touch her if he leant forward a touch. She tried to get to her knees again, but he pushed her down again with his fist. He smashed her head against the floor over and over, until there was just silence.

Jacqueline

I'd intended to remain in the hotel room for as long as possible. I had wanted to give them as much time as possible together, but I found I was restless. I was not used to spending Sundays away from the children, and I usually gave Anna the day off. I hadn't explained that it would be different this week. I hadn't even told her I was going away for the evening.

After a tasteless breakfast, I'd thrown my overnight bag in the Audi and driven back to the house. I called for Jacob and the children first. The children came bounding down the stairs, desperate for attention. "Where's Daddy?" The children told me he'd gone out that morning, this was not particularly unusual: he often disappeared on days he was required to parent or pretend to be an active member of the family. He did not keep up the show behind closed doors, he just kept the façade for his clients.

"Where's Anna?" The children stared at me blankly. I called for Anna, but there was no response. It was very unlike her. Anna for all her faults was always on hand for the children, even on her days off. I put my bag in the laundry room for the girls to unpack later and went to find her.

I took the stairs two at a time, still calling her name. I knocked on her bedroom door. Anna didn't answer. I let myself in.

51

Jacob

When he came around he was soaked in blood; it seemed to have seeped into his pores. He surveyed the room: the scene of a terrible, cruel act. He did not know what had happened. The air was dank and foul: sour. He rose to his feet, he needed to wash the horror off. He showered, but he couldn't cleanse himself of Anna's blood, it permeated his soul. He knew he should ring for an ambulance. He hadn't meant to inflict so many injuries. She had begged for mercy. If only she had remained silent.

After he dressed, he found the children downstairs watching TV with Brittany. How was it the morning already? He knew he had limited time, he needed to get away, he needed to clear his head. He informed Brittany that Anna was feeling unwell, so not to disturb her. It would buy him some time.

London seemed different that morning as he travelled along the M25. There was an umbrella of darkness over the city. He was agitated; suspicious eyes everywhere. He held his passport tightly. It was not long before he would be on different shores. He stared at his hands. There was blood under his nails.

He reached Heathrow airport and took the escalator to departures. He was almost there.

Jacqueline

The crime scene is cleared and sealed. A choreographed dance: the inner cordon first; followed by the outer cordon; the crime scene tape; the body bag; the interviews; the endless questions; door-to-door enquiries; phone records checked; computers confiscated; alibis confirmed. The police have created a timeline of her final day, and the coroner an indication of the circumstances surrounding her death.

Anna's naked body lies on a slab now. I wonder how she was dissected, what conclusions of violence they have drawn. I worry they do not have a blanket for her. I know it is not logical to worry if she is cold, but I still do. A life snuffed out. Her eyes were still open. I wonder what her last memory was, what her final thought was. I have no answers from Anna now.

Death feels very real and close now – too much so. Bleak. Brutal. Banal. Anna's death encompasses all the darkness of humanity. She was doomed from the moment of her employment. She was in an impossible situation, and I was the person who put her there.

The house is haunted with memories of Jacob and Anna. I immediately knew I could not stay there any longer. The children and I needed to relocate permanently. For now, though, we reside in a suite in The Four Seasons Hotel.

I had Jacob's mother, in the days that followed Anna's death, she was defiant: *Jacob would never be responsible for such a crime. It could never have been my son.* I wonder how far he'll have to go before she will see him for who he is. Her defence of him is distasteful. The last time I saw her I left her speaking to the police, whilst I gathered my things. I've informed the detectives where I am staying should they need me. The children ask questions of course. I do not know how to answer them, so I don't.

Anna's death seems incomprehensible to me. I knew my husband was capable of atrocities, but I had not understood the magnitude of his evil. Before I called the police I had found the CCTV footage. I did not watch it; I did not want to see. I deleted it without a second thought: one last act for my husband.

EPILOGUE

Stephanie

I found out of the birth of Daniel Matthew Abbey on a cold autumnal morning, the leaves had begun to lose their vibrant orange hues and instead were on the cusp of turning brown. The wind whipped through the streets, and everyone huddled under their coats and oversized scarfs. There was a dangerous chill in the air that morning and I had not been able to shake the heaviness of sleep.

I felt numb as I trudged the streets to work. It had been months since I had seen Matthew. We had avoided all contact since the evening we had dinner and he had told me the news of Annalise's pregnancy. I made my way to the coffee shop near chambers desperate to warm my hands and have a burst of caffeine before the onslaught of the day began.

I had my cinnamon latte in my hands, and I was exiting the café when I saw him. He was on the opposite side of the road. His long black coat billowing in the wind. He was on his mobile, a look of concentration on his face; a look I had seen so many times since our university days, a look I had not realised I missed so much. I was taken back by how handsome he was. I had forgotten.

I partially lifted my hand to wave, unsure how to communicate since our wordless admission that evening. He went to step towards me and hesitated as a van came into sight. I made to leave, dismissing him with another wave of my hand and a smile, but he called my name.

"Stephanie, please, please just wait. One moment."

I staggered forward then stopped, and I turned to see him crossing the road towards me.

"Stephanie..." he went to talk, to begin with the usual pleasantries that you do when you greet a friend, a "Hi how are you? What's news?", but I saw him stop. The recognition in his eyes that we had taken a step too far and we could no longer be casual with one another. He leaned towards me and held me in his arms, he smelt my hair, a moment too long for it to be a mere greeting rather than a hug of comfort.

"It's been a while," I said. I tried to smile.

"It has..." He looked down and shuffled his feet. "I had a boy, Steph. I had a little boy. I didn't know whether to ring, or email, or text but I wanted to tell you... I really did, I wanted to tell you."

"Oh wow, that is amazing, oh God, congratulations! That is fabulous, everything okay with the birth? My goodness, a dad, Matthew! When? When was he born? I mean I knew Annalise was due around now, but I just assumed she was still pregnant." I was babbling, my speech fast and uncontrolled.

"Last month, he's fine, so is Annalise, not much sleep but good, she's good..." he trailed off and looked at the ground.

"What's his name?"

"Daniel." He looked up at me, our eyes momentarily meeting. "His name is Daniel Matthew Abbey."

I blinked back tears suddenly, caught unawares by this

sudden surge of emotion, of realisation that we, whatever you could have called us, were well and truly over.

"I am sorry, Stephanie."

"Don't be silly, I'm pleased for you, I'm really pleased for you that's why I'm upset. I'm happy-sad. Congratulations, I mean you're a dad, that is amazing." I smiled this time, my eyes brimming over, but I managed a smile.

I suddenly became aware of the traffic of the people surrounding us, for a moment there it had seemed like we were the only two on the pavement; the universe suspended whilst we crossed paths. Matthew looked at his feet again, an awkward silence filled the space between us.

'Well, I better be– I better–"

I stopped him mid-sentence with a gentle hand on his arm. "Tell Daniel he is going to have a great dad, Matthew, maybe someday I'll meet him if our paths cross again, hey?"

"If our paths cross again?" He looked at me perplexed.

"This was never temporary, Matthew. I can't do it again, us, our friendship... not now."

He nodded. We both understood what I was saying.

"I'll give him a kiss from you, Steph. I'll tell him that one day you hope to meet him, and that one day his dad hopes to meet you again too."

He placed his hand over mine, and we stood for a moment. Stillness enveloped us as we silently said goodbye. I nodded, I could no longer talk, it was all too much. I turned on my heel, my hand over my mouth as I desperately tried to get away fast enough so he couldn't witness how much I now realised I had lost. The sound I emitted once I got around the corner was borne of love and pain, and loss and hope, and sadness and hurt, all rolled into one. It was only after I reached the office I realised I was not holding my coffee. I had lost it along the way.

A letter arrived on my desk in chambers two months after I

had bumped into Matthew in the street. I had not expected any further contact with him; I had not thought he would reach out to me. I had recognised his handwriting immediately when Audrey had handed over the envelope from the front desk that morning.

I sat with my morning latte and read what I did not know then would be the last communication I ever had from Matthew. He was to move away the following year to Canada, our communication severed. I would hear on the grapevine that he had two more children over the next five years, and I would think about him always, my forever what if. Occasionally, I would get his letter out of the drawer I kept it in, and I would sit silently and brew over his words. I often wondered if across the seas, we were thinking about one another at the same time or if he had been able to put me away, in a little compartment, all the memories from his old life.

Stephanie,

To miss someone whom you chose to miss is the hardest kind of longing, because ultimately it is only my own fault. Losing you was my choice. And regret is now forever my burden. The realisation too late, now in turn is too painful. You quite simply were meant to be mine, and I will forever be sorry that you were not and cannot be. We cannot rewrite history, we can only pave our future, and to do so we needn't waste time digging up the path that lies behind us, because it is a wasted exercise. We have already travelled forward; we need not and cannot go back. I hope in time, Stephanie, you can let us go, you can find the happiness that would wash over me in waves when I have sat beside you. I hope you can find that happiness again. I wish for you endless momentum moving forward. If I could, I would propel you towards love, to freedom from sadness, towards happiness. I will think of you always, Stephanie Beaumont, and when I do a smile will linger on my lips, and I'll remember all the good times. You

will always be dancing in my thoughts, the bright and beautiful
memory of you.
Look after yourself, Steph.
Goodbye, with love always,
Matthew x

Richard

He had returned to the law in the end, after a brief stint working jobs with no responsibility he'd discovered that he missed exercising his intellect. He was no longer a practising barrister. He'd become a lecturer in criminal evidence. As he stood before the students in his classes he tried so hard to instil a sense of justice, a moral compass. He often referred to his old life, he'd talk to the students of his time in London: his life before Cornwall.

Occasionally, he would tell them of his previous cases, he would talk them through the injustices of his career. It had taken him years to eliminate the guilt he'd acquired through numerous failed cases; the birth of his daughter had helped. He still thought of Molly Smith, he often wondered what happened to her.

His daughter bounded towards him, her blonde ringlets bouncing on her shoulders, her laughter consuming the beach. He grabbed her round her waist and spun her around until the sea blurred into the horizon, and they didn't know which way was up. They fell onto their backs on the sand, he could hear her still faintly giggling with glee. He turned to look at his lovely little girl and wondered how such beauty was possible.

She looked nothing like either of them. He and Malika had no idea how they'd created such an angelic looking child, so pale in complexion. Fatherhood had unfurled a primal protectiveness he had never known possible, the thought of any harm coming to his daughter, Savannah, unimaginable.

Savannah leapt to her feet, and she ran off towards the sea, beckoning him to chase her. He ran behind her, the wind whipped in their face, and he caught her as she reached the shoreline. He flung her in the air and cradled her in his arms as she came to land: safe from harm. She screeched with delight, "Again, Daddy, again."

Jacob

He'd slipped onto the last plane to Malaga that morning. Sadly, the flight was only EasyJet, so he didn't have his usual comforts. Spain wasn't planned, but it was the only flight available out of Heathrow at the time, and he couldn't risk waiting until later that day. He would have preferred to have left Europe, but fate had other ideas.

He knew he needed to contact the police: the longer he left it the worse it would appear, but he felt trapped. He did not know how to explain that it was merely sex gone wrong. He had not even thought she was dead. He'd read enough newspaper articles to understand there were other cases similar to his and Anna's. Consensual sexual violence was a viable defence now, or so it appeared in cases such as the wealthy businessman who had inflicted forty injuries on his partner, including internal trauma, a fractured eye socket and blunt force injuries to her head, before spraying her with bleach: he'd got away with manslaughter. Surely Jacob would be able to explain that something similar had occurred with him and Anna.

He had pictures of her on his phone to start with, pictures of her previously enjoying rough sex, he had her non-disclosure agreement where she had given her written consent to partake in S&M. He had evidence that Anna was a willing participant. Rough sex went wrong sometimes, that was the nature of the thrill. Maybe he had held her neck too long, maybe he had taken it a bit far. He couldn't really remember, the night had all been a bit of a blur until he came to.

He needed to get his story straight, he needed to recuperate before he headed home. He'd lie low in Spain for a while. He needed a break. He'd discarded his phone in the UK, and he knew better than to leave an electronic trace. The cash he'd taken from the household would suffice long enough. He'd found a small village: there wasn't much there, a grocery shop, a market on a Sunday and one small bar he was yet to frequent, but it'd do.

Jacqueline

The week before Anna's death I'd discovered the allegations in his workplace. I'd found out he'd paid to silence some of the girls in his office. I didn't know the details, but I knew one of them was a work experience girl – too young.

When I found Anna, she was barely conscious. I knew what I needed to do to stop him. It seemed rape was not enough of a crime to curtail my husband. I didn't think it through, of course if I had I'm sure I wouldn't have gone through with it. I needed to stop him, I just knew I needed to stop him.

It's not that I didn't value Anna, but sometimes you must make sacrifices. I could no longer live as I was. Maintaining this act was breaking me, and I needed Jacob to leave indefinitely.

Her breath was already shallow, I could see how much pain he'd inflicted on her. I could see how awfully he had treated her. She was broken, her throat was already covered in deep purple bruises and there was blood everywhere. Her hair was a wet matt of red. She was barely conscious, if at all.

I was putting her out of her misery, she was clearly suffering and in pain. Who was to say she would have survived anyway. I reached for the pillow. I stroked Anna's hair back off her face, she was frighteningly pretty, even lying here so tarnished. She moaned. I could not work out if she was attempting to form words. I told her everything was going to be okay, I told her to close her eyes.

I lifted the pillow very gently, and then before I could consider it any longer, I placed the pillow over her face. I held it there with mild force – she did not have much fight left in her. She flailed her legs momentarily and attempted to pull the pillow off her face. This almost broke my resolve, but she did not battle for long.

When her body was entirely limp, I lifted the pillow and placed it by the door, I would need to get rid of it. I rose to my feet, exited Anna's bedroom and took the stairs, the pillow under my arm. I told the children to remain watching the TV in the lounge with Brittany, whilst I burnt the pillow in the back garden. I returned inside when the evidence was destroyed, and I calmly rung the police.

It was far easier than I thought to feign hysterics, far easier to name my husband as the perpetrator of the entire crime, far easier to sacrifice Anna for my own personal gain than I'd ever imagined.

Molly

I had stayed in Spain. I could not leave. Whenever I had searched flights home to the UK, I'd had the uncontrollable urge to slam the laptop shut. In the end, there had been nothing left for me. London no longer felt like home.

I had moved out of the apartment Colin and my mum shared, and I had found an out-of-season long-term rental, which was cheap enough that I could cover the costs from my job waitressing. The bar I worked at was nothing special, but I did not want anything pressurised or glamorous. I liked being anonymous. Occasionally I helped decorate holiday homes to supplement my income, I had forgotten how much I enjoyed the pastime.

I hadn't intended to stay so long, but five years had crept by so quickly. I was fluent in Spanish now, my skin a light mocha and I'd allowed my wild blonde curls to grow back. There had been no men since, but I had friends again: Carlos and Antonio, the brothers who owned the bar, had taken me under their wings and I felt like their adopted little sister.

They did not know of my past in the UK: no one did. There were some stories I didn't want to share: Jacob was one of them. Some days I still think I see him. Of course, I don't. I have to remind myself I'm not in London. It is as if I feel his presence behind me. Some days I drown in the memory of him, of the court case, of my past – other days I tread water. Then there are some days that I break the surface, the sun shines down on my face, and I forget all about Jacob Walker-Kent and I am happy once again. He is just a fragment of my past.

THE END

ACKNOWLEDGEMENTS

This book was inspired by a criminal evidence lecturer who instilled in her teachings the lesson that law should be about justice, as opposed to winning. For the countless women who have had to endure any of the experiences discussed in this novel – sorry. I hope the horizon in the future is different in this area of law and our everyday lives when it comes to attitudes towards sexual assault and rape change.

Thank you to Betsy and Fred at Bloodhound Books for all their hard work and giving me the opportunity to be published. Thank you to my editor, Clare Law and to Tara Lyons, for all your help and hard work. Thank you to Shirley Khan for proofreading and to our publicity manager Maria.

Thank you to my partner, Matt, for all your support. Thank you to all my family and friends either side of the border, particularly Becky Shellard, Katy DeVall and my mother who all read the very early drafts of this book and encouraged me to keep going.

And, a big thank you to Kizzy Thomson, my agent, who was invaluable whilst trying to get the book published, with advice, suggestions and support.

Last but not least, thank you to all those that have taken the time to read this novel, I really appreciate it.

Lightning Source UK Ltd.
Milton Keynes UK
UKHW011217240321
380903UK00001B/171